Judgment In Time

Judgment In Time Series Book I

Judgment In Time

New People Publishing

Follow us on Facebook and Twitter to keep up with
Judgment In Time conversations and updates

Facebook: Search for Judgment In Time Series
Twitter: @JITSeries

Available in Hardcover, Paperback, and
eBook as ePub, Kindle, and Nook

Fiction: Action and Adventure, Political Intrigue, Alternative History, Romance, Mystery, Thriller, Historical Fiction, Military Fiction, Science Fiction, Naval Battles

Judgment In Time Series

Book I:	Judgment In Time
Book II:	Imagine A New World
Book III:	Another Fine Mess
Book IV:	Another Side of Armageddon
Book V:	Title Coming
Book VI:	Judgment of the Gods

New People Publishing
www.NewPeoplePublishing.com

Editor: Robert Allen Fisher
Cover Art and Full Page Illustrations: Jennifer Cole
Production Design and Illustrations: Tom Hultgren

IISBN-13: 978-0-9835020-7-4
Advance Edition: Trade Paperback

Printed in the United States of America by:
Lightning Source

10 9 8 7 6 5 4 3 2 1

About the Author

Kevin Klesert, a successful independent businessman, has experienced firsthand how small businesses all over the country carried a disproportionate amount of the burden to meet their legal obligations. The steady erosion of Main Street USA under mountains of onerous regulations, licenses, taxes, and fees from Federal, State, and Local Governments have all but destroyed their ability to succeed and turn a reasonable profit.

His intense study of historical trends brought to him the correlation between the downfall of dominant societies of the past and the current struggle to maintain the most noble and ambitious political experiment in human history, the United States of America. He discovered the seeds of ruin were planted within the very generation that launched the United States to world preeminence.

Kevin Klesert's desire to shed light on this dire situation through the means of a thrilling adventure has produced a story worthy of the fight against these negative forces. The ideas for the Judgment In Time Series percolated in his adventurous imagination while he raised his four children and ran an award-winning design and construction company. A 3rd generation native of Southern California, Kevin Klesert imbues his writing with his passion for history, adventure, and fantasy.

Table of Contents

Characters

Main Characters

Rear Admiral UH Sean Phillips – Commander, Enterprise Task Force

Captain Anthony Knox – Chief of Staff to Admiral Sean Phillips

Rear Admiral UH Retired Alicia Calhoun – Secretary of Defense

Captain Renée Aslan – Naval Attaché to Alicia Calhoun

Secondary Main Characters

Dr. William Safire, PhD – Comstock Technologies Chief Specter Engineer

Dr. Rebecca Cutler, PhD – Comstock Technologies Lead Specter Engineer

Dr. Forrest Phelps, PhD – Comstock Technologies Computer Specialist

Commander Carl Eddington – First Officer, USS Missouri

Commander Logan Barrish – First Officer, USS Enterprise

Lt. Commander Daniel Osaka – Information Warfare Officer,
    USS Missouri

Captain *Dash* Nelson – Air Wing Commander [CAG], USS Enterprise

Commander Michael *Thorny* Thornton – Task Force SEAL Commander

Lt. Commander Edwin T. Layton – Codebreaker

Lt. W. J. Jasper Holmes – Codebreaker

Support Characters

Chief Warrant Officer Mark Brunel – Chief Engineer, USS Missouri

Chief Warrant Officer Brad Sanders – Chief Engineer, USS Enterprise

Chief Warrant Officer Patrick Callahan – Chief Engineer, USS Decatur

Lt. Commander Harold Ramis – P-3 Orion reconnaissance pilot

Lt Franklin Morris – SEAL Squad Leader

Lt. Anatoly Ginsberg – Russian Language Interpreter

Ensign Gloria Layworth – Bridge Communications Officer, USS Missouri

Enterprise Task Force Captains and Their Ships

Captain Charles Folger – Commanding Officer, battleship USS Missouri

Captain Steven Brewster – Commanding Officer, carrier USS Enterprise

Captain Frederick Johnson – cruiser USS Chancellorsville

Captain Gordon Lincoln – cruiser USS Princeton

Commander Regis Goddard – destroyer USS John Paul Jones

Commander Steven Holmes – destroyer USS Decatur

Captain Mark Daily – attack submarine USS Seawolf

Captain Marlowe Turner – attack submarine USS Hampton

Commander Andy Gable – cargo ship USNS Amelia Earhart

Lt. Commander James Peck – fleet oiler USNS Laramie

Enterprise Task Force Formation

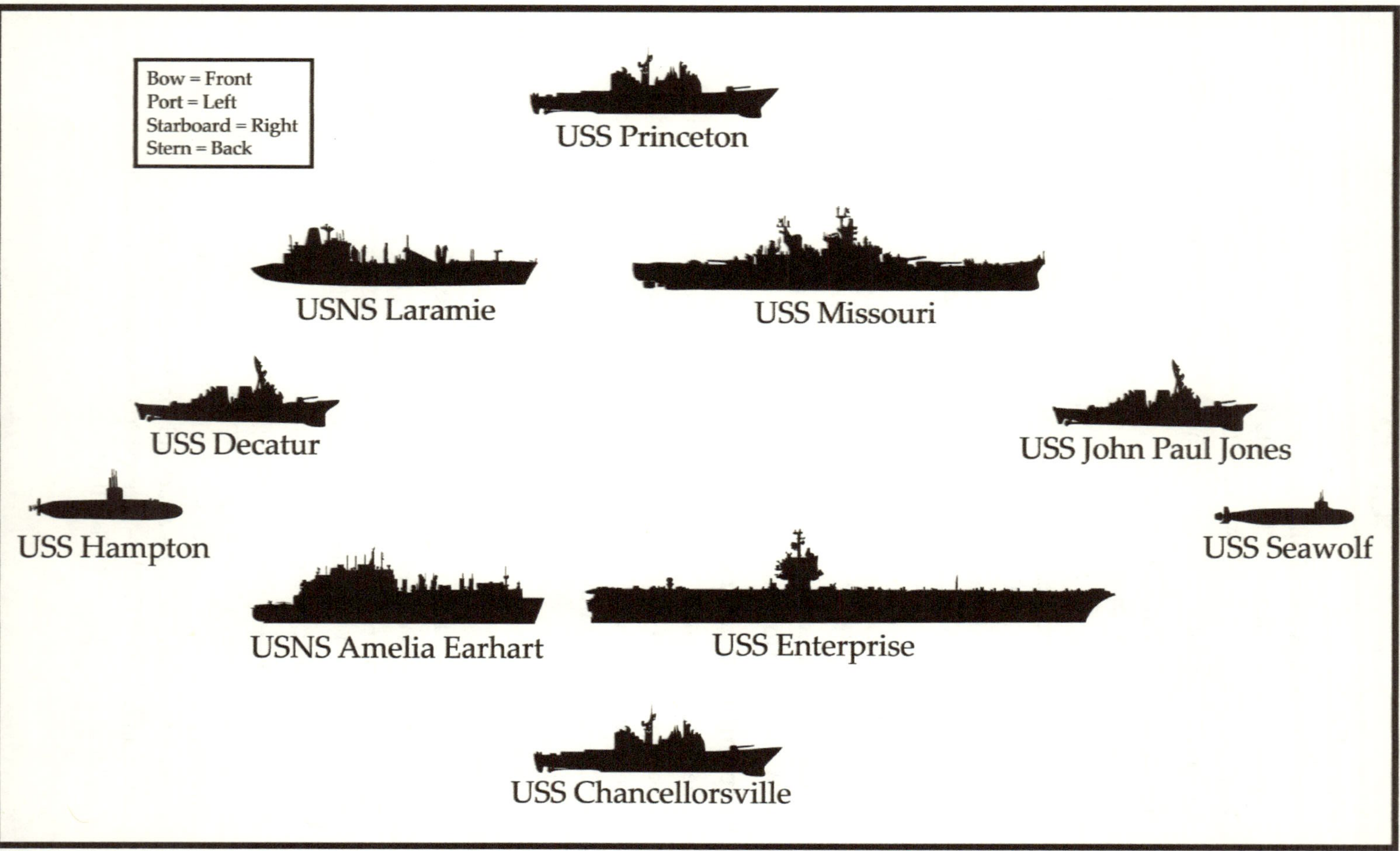

Chapter One

The Other Side of Light

Two F/A-18Es from the supercarrier USS Dwight D Eisenhower CVN-69, on station in the Persian Gulf during the Spring of 2010, turned north on their second pass over suspected smuggling routes along the Iran-Iraq border. Before they could complete the maneuver, beeps from their aircraft's search radar warned that Iranian ground radars had locked on them. "Looks like someone down below wants to play."

Considering this was a daily occurrence while patrolling so close to Iranian air space, neither pilot took the threat seriously, that is until, "Holy shit! They launched on us. I count two; I repeat two missiles headed our way."

The flight leader ordered his wingman, "Break right, launch counter measures!" The F/A-18s immediately broke formation and began juking wildly all over the sky, while ejecting chaff to avoid the missiles. The wingman, who broke right, managed to attract both missiles, and despite his best efforts, took a hit on his craft's left wing. Though the pilot and his weapons system operator ejected safely before the F/A-18 exploded, the wind unfortunately was not in their favor as they slowly drifted across the border into Iran.

With Rear Admiral Benson in emergency surgery in Kuwait, it fell upon his Chief of Staff Captain Anthony Knox sitting in the Eisenhower CIC [Combat Information Center] to rescue his pilots. Tony turned to the CIC Officer. "Get a message to Washington for permission to enter Iranian airspace."

"Yes Sir," the Officer replied.

After two minutes trying to locate someone to okay the rescue, he reported to Tony. "Sir, it is Sunday morning in DC, and the Secretaries of State and Defense are on the talk show circuit giving interviews. The only official available is Under Secretary of the Navy Fred Haynes. They are attempting to locate him now."

Tony had served as a Commander under him when Haynes was Captain of the Ticonderoga class Aegis guided missile cruiser USS Vincennes. "Great," Tony thought, "the only thing that asshole ever cares about is covering his ass." He knew Haynes would deny his request, so he closed his eyes for a moment to consider what other options he had.

Tony called out to the CIC Officer, "Launch the F/A-18s on ready alert, with the rest of the rescue package to follow immediately."

"Sir, you're not going to wait for orders?" The CIC Officer regretted his question as soon as he said it.

A clearly agitated Captain Knox turned and stared at the unfortunate officer until every member in the CIC felt the gathering storm. "The Iranians just shot down one of our planes, and you think I care whether some asshole in Washington will allow me to rescue my men? If there is a single person in this room who thinks we should wait, speak up so I can send you home to look for a new career. The United States Navy *never* leaves one of their own behind."

Ten minutes later, six F/A-18s had launched and now circled the Task Force. Tony was about to give the go ahead, when the Communications Officer spoke. "Under Secretary Haynes, Sir."

After Tony explained the tactical situation, he silently listened to Haynes response. "Yes Sir," was all Tony said as he cradled the phone. "Launch the rescue package."

"Thank God he agreed," the CIC Officer said with relief.

Without looking up, Tony retorted, "Who said he agreed?"

Thirty thousand feet over St. Louis, the luxurious C-37 Gulfstream carried only two passengers, one of whom had until recently worked directly with the President.

"You know I haven't talked to Tony in over a year. Even if I wanted to, your schedule has made it impossible for me to pursue a private life. Besides, he hasn't exactly broken down my door." The woman speaking was Captain Renée Aslan, a career officer in the United States Navy. Though she stood only five feet four inches, she possessed a physical presence an assailant would think twice about arousing. No one would mistake her appearance as beautiful, but this suited her personality. Whoever was lucky enough to have her in their life, better be able to deal with all she had to offer. "The only reason we are on our way to San Diego is *your* relationship with Admiral Phillips. So you don't have any room to mock me when both of us will be spending God knows how long on a naval exercise with *those* two men."

Secretary of Defense Rear Admiral UH Retired Alicia Calhoun teased her US Navy attaché. "Me thinks you protest too much, fair lady." Alicia tried to hide a smile at the thought of seeing Sean for the first time in over a year.

Striking in appearance, Alicia Calhoun drew a double take from both men and women the first time they met her. Although now in her mid-forties, she still carried the body of someone fifteen years younger. At five feet eight inches tall and 135 pounds, with piercing green eyes framed beautifully by her thick black shoulder length hair, she could have chosen modeling over a naval career. However, it only took a moment of conversation to discover her mental acuity matched her beauty.

Alicia has served the President as his Secretary of Defense since January of 2009. Within the first year, she realized the only difference between this president and his predecessors was the political machine that ran him.

The President kept her on as long as he did to supply the window dressing needed to keep the independents who still paid attention from rioting over Washington's control over every facet of life in America. Alicia's reasons for not leaving earlier were that if the few *true* patriots left in government quit, it would be an admission the dream of 1776 was dead. Besides, she still had some political capital as the daughter of a war hero.

Now with the President in the second year of his second term, his administration had marginalized her to the point her last face-to-face meeting with him was over three months ago. This trip was Alicia's last official function before her resignation became final. It wasn't a surprise she was on the way out; the surprise was that she had lasted five years.

Alicia continued to rib Renée. "You know the *only* reason I want to be there is to make sure Sean has political cover. Everyone in both the Pentagon and the White House picked him to be the fall guy if this exercise fails. Besides, there isn't any comparison between the two of us and your former relationship with Tony. Sean and I have never been more than the best of friends."

"Yes, Madam Secretary," Renée responded with feigned acquiescence. "And there's a Cadillac in the bottom of every Cracker Jack box."

On 14 October 2009, harbor tugs moved the magnificent USS Missouri BB-63 from Battleship Row in Pearl Harbor to the shipyard for what the Navy reported to the press to be a sand and paint to handle rust. Over the next six months, contractors secretly brought her engines, wiring, navigation, and communication systems up to modern standards in preparation for a revolutionary technological covert operation. In April 2010, even though her engines were available, the Navy towed her to San Diego Bay under the pretense the famous battlewagon would now split its time as a memorial between Hawaii and Naval Station San Diego.

One year later, the Missouri closed to the public for six months before the real work she was there for commenced. Over the next two years in plain sight, but out of mind, technicians covertly added another *upgrade*. Three months ago, after another humiliating tow over to the San Diego Naval Shipyard to install her above deck weapons, she finally steamed out under her own power for sea trials that led to a surprise recommissioning.

Today, January 22, 2014, bristling with Harpoon anti-ship missiles, Tomahawk cruise missiles, and her original 16-inch guns, the USS Missouri proudly waited at her berth on the north side of the San Diego Naval Station's amphibious pier, in plain view of the Hotel Coronado Veranda, where two naval officers in their starched white dress uniforms waited for their lunch.

The server was accustomed to naval officers, and at first glance, nothing stood out about these two. The one on the left was the slimmer built and four inches taller. Though you could see the fifty plus years in his face, it was obvious he still worked hard to keep away the ravages of time. Though the waitress didn't find him attractive, after a brief conversation while they ordered lunch, she could tell he took an honest interest in strangers. She also noticed that he consciously presented himself in the finest traditions of the Navy in the way he filled out his uniform. The two stars on his collar identified him as a Rear Admiral. If he were fifteen years younger, the twenty-five year old thought he would have been great husband material.

The officer on the other side of the table was the absolute counterpart in build. She thought general casting could put the two together in some buddy-adventure flick. Built low and wide, with a mass of thick black hair inherited from his Italian roots, you wanted this man next to you in a brawl. Contrary to the shoulder boards that identified him as a Captain, he looked like he would be more comfortable belowdecks. She imagined he would be a great booty call, but a whole lot of trouble to hold onto. As she left the table after delivering their meal, she wished her man had half the testosterone that oozed from him.

The shorter of the two officers looked over at the large battleship from another era. "That sight still overwhelms me. I can't believe you asked me to serve as your Chief of Staff on the last battleship in service. It still feels like a dream." Captain Anthony Knox lifted his iced tea to toast his friend and commanding officer, Admiral Sean Phillips. "Thanks for pulling my sorry ass back into the Navy. I was running out of excuses to give the old man."

Sean clicked his glass to Tony's and asked with a grin, "You mean your father couldn't understand why shredding thousands of dollars running a charter service for tourists off of Molokai instead of taking over the family business was the proper way for you to behave?"

Tony didn't see it that way. "Seriously, could you picture me dealing with the politics involved with selling search radars to the Department of Defense? After I went into the Navy to get away from him, it took my old man ten years to accept I wasn't coming back."

Without looking up from the piece of fish he was slicing, Sean asked his friend, "Yet, whose money have you been shredding since you lost your commission?"

"Ouch, that cut deep. I never said I didn't *enjoy* spending his money. After twenty years of sea duty, don't you think I deserved a little me time?"

Tony figured this would be a good time to change the subject. "All I know is I'm happy you were able to get me reinstated before her sea trials. I don't know how you and Charles [Captain Charles Folger, Commanding Officer, USS Missouri] managed to survive all of those Comstock geeks running all over the ship installing Specter. I'm sure I would have killed one or two of them."

Sean chuckled at the image. "The Mighty Mo is certainly not the same ship they towed into harbor four years ago."

This sent Tony off into reminiscing. "I remember falling in love with the idea of going to sea after reading about the Iowa class battleships in junior high school: the Iowa, New Jersey, Wisconsin, and Missouri. Built on a hull bearing 57,000 tons, at 888 feet long, 108 feet wide, and protected by 18 inches of armor plating, the Iowa class was the apex of battleship construction. I remember one class at Annapolis where I impressed the professor so much with my knowledge of the ships that he overlooked some of my other deficiencies and gave me a better grade than I deserved."

"So refresh my memory, Captain Knox," Sean said sarcastically. He like Tony could recite every fact about the Missouri and never tired of hearing them.

Tony raised his voice a little in response to the sarcasm. "Well, *Admiral* Phillips, the Missouri carries 9 Mark Seven 16-inch guns on 3 massive turrets, 2 forward and 1 aft, capable of firing 2900 pound armor piercing shells to a maximum range of 24 miles."

Sean fired right back. "Driven to speeds of 33 knots by 4 steam turbines putting out 212,000 horsepower, the Missouri was fast as well as powerful."

"Commissioned 11 June 1944, her first action was bombarding the beaches of Iwo Jima," Tony countered.

"She participated in the bombardment of Okinawa and was the first to attack the Japanese home islands since the Doolittle raid in 1942."

"And the Japanese surrender in September 1945 occurred right under her aft 16-inch guns."

After they bantered back and forth like two boys on the

playground, they laughed at their competitive nature.

Sean was silent for a moment before he recounted his feelings about the ships. "One of the most depressing naval pictures I've ever seen was of the mothballed Missouri and her sister ships the Iowa, Wisconsin, and New Jersey, tied up in a row after WWII. If it wasn't for the Korean War those beautiful battleships, the last of their kind, would have been broken up for scrap."

"Yeah," Tony agreed. "And after the Korean War, the Navy mothballed the Missouri again until President Reagan's massive military buildup in the 1980s.

"Correct me if I'm wrong, but wasn't one of her officers a young Lt. Commander by the name of Sean Phillips who served on her during the first Gulf War?"

"I was, and you never let me forget how envious you were while stuck on a destroyer at the time. As exciting as it was serving on her, it didn't make up for how depressing it was when she was decommissioned in March of 1992."

"Not as depressing as *my* decommissioning in 2010," Tony countered. "If I had to do it all over again, I still would have sent the rescue package into Iran. However, I guarantee you if Admiral Benson hadn't been in Kuwait suffering from appendicitis, he would have done the same thing and Washington wouldn't have dared to make such a stink about it."

"Even considering the boneheaded stunt you pulled decking Haynes after the Senate hearings, there wasn't any way I was taking on this mission without you."

Tony immediately tensed from the memory. "You know he had it coming. You along with everybody else wanted to punch him for years. I still get the occasional bottle of Scotch from some newly retired officer complimenting my actions."

"You said the key word – retired. The difference between our wanting to punch him and you actually doing it is *we* kept our commissions," Sean admonished.

Captain Knox leaned back in his seat and thought of the day following the Senate hearings. "Look, public opinion supported the action, and we did manage to return everybody in one piece."

"Yes, but then you had to let the media bait you into an interview outside the Senate chambers with Haynes standing there."

"Have you forgotten how I had to listen to him testify to the Senate committee for an hour about my history of defying civilian authority, and his accusation that I ordered the F/A-18s to fly close to the border with Iran to instigate an incident. I can't help it if he butted in with the same accusation during *my* press conference. I remember thinking I just didn't care anymore so I decked the son of a bitch."

"You broke his jaw in three places on national TV and he had to eat out of a straw for six weeks," Sean chimed in. "I play the video of it to soothe me when I catch some idiot politician lie in an interview about information I know to be false."

"All I know is, you probably used up every favor owed to you to get my commission back, and for that I can never properly thank you."

"Well Captain Knox, in that case you can get the check." Sean took a second to look at this watch. "By the way, I did have help getting your commission back." Sean then segued without waiting for a response. "We have a meeting at 1500 and we both have things to do beforehand."

"Wait a minute, Admiral Phillips. Who else do I owe a debt to and how much is it going to cost me?"

Sean only smiled as they headed out of the hotel.

Tony harped on the mystery all the way back to the ship to no avail.

"I can barely hear you over this line." The new XO [First Officer] Commander Carl Eddington was on the bridge comm trying to get a straight answer from the communications engineer regarding the high level of static on the internal comm lines. Commander Eddington calmly turned to his agitated Captain who looked like he wanted to rip somebody a new one. "Would it help Sir, if I went to the CIC [Combat Information Center] and pushed things along?"

"Permission granted. Also, find Chief Brunel [Chief Warrant Officer Mark Brunel – Chief Engineer, USS Missouri] and inform him to leave alone anything that isn't crucial to the safe operation of the ship or Specter until we are underway. Pearl should have handled these issues during the refit instead of dumping them on us."

Both men turned as an Ensign approached Captain Folger and saluted. Charles briskly returned the salute. "The Officer of the Deck wishes to inform the Captain of visitors asking permission to come aboard."

"Granted Ensign, and notify Captain Knox.

"Commander Eddington, let's go welcome our guests."

The Officer of the Watch snapped off a salute with, "Captain's off the bridge."

Two attractive women and a rumpled, gray-haired, middle-aged man stood waiting as Tony, Captain Folger, and Commander Eddington approached the gangplank.

Tony greeted them with a respectful salute. "It's good to see you again Secretary Calhoun," as he gave her a brief hug. The hug he gave the other woman lingered a little longer. "It's been too long, Captain Aslan." Reluctantly he extended his hand to the man. "You must be Senator Boyle. I look forward to your stay with us aboard the Missouri."

Tony stepped back to address the group. "Admiral Phillips sends his compliments but he is preparing the final details for his briefing at 1500; three o'clock for your benefit Senator Boyle. This is the Missouri Commanding Officer, Captain Charles Folger and his

First Officer, Commander Carl Eddington."

"Thank you for your hospitality, Captain Knox," Secretary of Defense Alicia Calhoun quickly added before the Senator could complain. "I can appreciate how busy Admiral Phillips must be getting his ships ready, but I must say I feel slighted he isn't here to greet us personally." With a wink, Alicia turned to look out on the bay.

"Admiral Phillips is only making sure of command and control protocols, so when we put to sea there won't be a need for extraneous communications Secretary Calhoun." Tony could see a slight smile on Captain Renée Aslan's face as she enjoyed his discomfort while he performed a political function for which he was clearly ill suited. Knowing Renée as he did, Tony shot her a withering look.

"If you could take your eyes off Captain Aslan for a moment, maybe we can get on with it." Senator Boyle was impatient with Tony's attention to the women, because he was the one usually getting his ass kissed by the military brass.

"As you wish Senator. Commander Eddington will escort you to your cabin."

Commander Carl Eddington motioned to a steward to take the Senator's luggage.

Tony felt sympathetic for Eddington as he watched him lead the agitated Senator away.

"Ladies, allow me to show you to the second best quarters on the Missouri." The remaining stewards picked up the women's luggage and followed. After the Senator was out of sight, Tony exclaimed, "God I hate politicians."

"Try to behave around the Senator," Alicia cautioned. "If we screw this up, Congress won't hesitate to take the Navy down to the lowest deployment levels since before World War II. Or more specifically, if you screw up, nobody short of God will be able to save your ass." The look she gave Tony confirmed she was the one with the connections Sean had referred to after lunch.

"Yeah, I got it. Don't mess up."

"Don't do it for me, do it for Sean," Alicia implored. "He has worked his ass off to get the Navy and Comstock's techies on the same page, but all the wrong people want to see him and this exercise fail. Why do you think the good Senator is here?"

"And I thought he was here because he heard we had entertainment set up for him in the men's head. Hell, I was even practicing my toe tap."

Alicia fought back a laugh as they arrived at Tony's cabin, now assigned to the women. "You know Tony, most people would consider me a politician these days," Alicia admonished playfully.

"With all due respect Alicia, you will always be Navy first to those of us who had the pleasure of serving with you. That and you chose someone with such incredible talent as Captain Renée Aslan as your Chief of Staff."

Alicia smiled as she entered the cabin. Renée stepped in, turned so only Tony could see her, and spoke in a low voice as she closed the door. "Who said you don't know how to kiss ass."

Five minutes later, Tony entered the Admirals Ready Room below the bridge. "Our guests are getting squared away in their cabins."

Focused on a stack of paperwork and without the need to look up, Sean asked, "How's she look?"

"She looks the same as the day I said goodbye to her in Monterey two years ago, beautiful as ever," Tony deadpanned.

Sean fired back without missing a beat. "I didn't know you and *Alicia* spent time in Monterey."

"Oh yeah, Alicia looks great too. I should have known she was the one who helped me with my commission. There's no way a political idiot like you could have pulled it off."

By prearrangement, Secretary of Defense Alicia Calhoun arrived at the meeting thirty minutes early. When she entered, Admiral Phillip's heart skipped a beat. He took a second to steady himself before he walked over to give her a hug. "It seems like every time we get together someone's trying to end my career. I'm glad you decided to come." He stepped back to look her over. "You look more beautiful every time I see you."

"Thank you for the compliment, Sean. I only wish it were true." She then returned the favor. "The additional gray I see in your hair looks good in a distinguished, Cary Grant sort of way."

Alicia then became serious. "I can tell you have mostly ignored my advice to stop rocking the boat. You haven't made any friends with the demands you've been making."

"What can I say; old habits are hard to break. Can I get you anything?" Sean asked graciously.

"A cup of coffee would be nice, thank you," Alicia answered, as she relaxed on the couch. "You've managed to get the attention of a few powerful members on the hill who didn't think there was any way in hell you'd meet their ridiculous schedule."

She took the coffee Sean handed her and continued as he sat down next to her. "You've done a great job keeping the lid on Specter. The political damage would be devastating if knowledge of its existence got out."

"Thanks for the unwarranted compliment, but the military has been good at keeping secrets like Specter for years."

"Give me a break Sean. Take some credit for what you have accomplished for a change," Alicia admonished.

Realizing their time was short, Alicia shifted to what she needed to tell Sean. "As you know, the President does not have the political will to stand up to the special interest groups bleeding our country dry. However, he has to create the illusion of fiscal responsibility after the second Bush administration squandered over a trillion dollars without the slightest oversight. Therefore, his plan is to mothball two carrier groups by the middle of this year."

Alicia paused for a moment, uncomfortable with what she needed to say next. "This will create the opportunity to force some senior officers into early retirement, and you know, as your command goes, so do you."

"I appreciate the heads up," Sean replied, pleased by her concern.

This was how Washington worked and he knew where he stood within the Navy's political hierarchy. At the time Admiral Hendricks offered him this command, he understood if Specter failed, it would be the end of his career in the Navy.

"What about you Alicia? I've heard through the grapevine you've lost your own battle with the White House."

"Your sources are correct," Alicia sighed. "In the beginning, the President at least paid lip service to how I wanted to reform the Department of Defense. However, after six months of having every plan I offered rejected, I realized what the President wanted was a skirt to impress his progressive voters. I thought my experience would help the military, but it turns out military experience ran contrary to political reality. Therefore, I tendered my resignation, effective immediately after this exercise ends.

"The public is not aware of Specter and the billions poured into it. The President will pull the plug on any further funding if you can't prove operational capability during this exercise. In effect, you're the fatted calf on the sacrificial altar if this proves to be a cluster fuck."

"I am well aware of what I signed on to. I was standing right next to Admiral Hendricks onboard the destroyer John Paul Jones when the Princeton disappeared along with its radar signature. He made sure I understood the political repercussions before I accepted this command."

"For your sake, I hope you do, or it will be an early retirement for you," Alicia warned.

"You speak volumes of wisdom, my raven haired beauty; with much warnings of failure do I take heed of your advice," Sean replied with a twinkle in his eye.

"Seriously however," Sean continued, "the potential of Specter's technology makes it urgent we get it operational and deployed as soon as possible before another city disappears under a mushroom cloud like the ones in Pakistan and India.

"As it stands now, it only takes one tactical nuclear weapon to sink an entire naval task force. We could park a task force anywhere in the world with impunity if Specter lives up to its potential. An enemy might think twice before they launch or sponsor such an attack if they are aware of the risk of a rapid retaliation from a formidable task force they can't locate.

"However, with this current batch of elitist political demagogues, I am not optimistic about holding off Armageddon for long." Then Sean's voice rose in anger at the absurdity of it all. "There are too many religious fanatics wanting the End of Days to occur in their lifetime and who now have the means to make it happen."

A knock on the door interrupted their conversation. "Enter," Sean responded with regret. He knew this meant his time to get reacquainted with Alicia was over, for now.

Tony walked in and saw the concern on Alicia's face but decided not to ask. "Admiral, Madam Secretary. The senior officers will be here in a few minutes. I checked with Dr. Safire, and despite being his usual pain in the ass, I made sure he will be here."

Sean stood up. "Thank you. Shall we get ready for our guests?"

Captain Steven Brewster, Commanding Officer of the Enterprise was the first of the senior staff to arrive. Built in 1961, the USS Enterprise CVN-65 would normally be the flagship at the center of the task force, but this mission put her in a secondary role. She displaced over 92,000 tons fully loaded, and housed eight Westinghouse nuclear reactors that powered her to a speed of 33 knots. The only aircraft carrier built of her class; she eluded the scrappers for this last deployment.

"So how does it feel to lose the Admiral's flag to the Missouri,

Steve?" Tony held a strong dislike for the man and enjoyed tormenting him. Brewster's excessive authoritarian style of command and his extreme wrath-of-God beliefs were in sharp contrast to Tony's live and let live attitude.

"I don't mind at all. As the Chief of Staff, you are stuck on this old rust bucket. It does, however, fit your inclination to develop battle tactics more suited to this dinosaur's era."

Tony stated in a dismissive manner, as if he was sending a child to bed without supper, "You know, that's the problem with you Steve. You never took the time to understand that those who forget the failures of the past are doomed to repeat them. But then again, I should thank your utter lack of imagination. It's what makes you so predictable, which is good if you're married and raising children, but an awful flaw when planning war game strategies. Though batting .000 against me, you would think naval command would have replaced you by now to give me a more worthy opponent."

Before an offended Brewster could respond to the insult, Commander Steven Holmes of the Arleigh Burke class destroyer USS Decatur DDG-73, who had arrived with Commander Regis Goddard of the Arleigh Burke class destroyer USS John Paul Jones DDG-53, stepped in to lighten the mood. "You all would be sitting ducks if it weren't for us covering your asses. Besides Steve, we can get to know all the squids serving onboard our ships. You're more like a mayor of a floating city than the Captain of a warship."

Captains Frederick Johnson and Lincoln Gordon of the Ticonderoga class Cruisers, USS Chancellorsville CG-62 and USS Princeton CG-59, had walked in during the exchange. "Yeah, yeah, without our Aegis systems you'd all be like the blind leading the blind," Captain Gordon prodded, as he jumped into the fray.

Sean cut the usual banter short by addressing Captain Brewster. "Steve I know you're not used to such a limited role for the Enterprise, but if we flew the usual reconnaissance missions, it would be counterproductive to validating Specter's stealth capabilities. The success of the exercise will still rest with your aircrews. Is your squadron of F-35s ready?"

"We've trained to your operational orders. With only six strike aircraft equipped with Specter, I cannot guarantee much of a punch when we are over target." Although they had gone over his role many times already, Brewster felt a need to bring it up once again.

"If we avoid detection, why not launch an all-out attack, instead of leaving eighty percent of the Enterprise's offensive capabilities as deadweight. They would be back on deck before any retaliation could be launched."

Tony gave Sean a look that said, "I told you he was an idiot."

Sean ignored this and repeated their objectives with sarcasm thrown in. "Maybe you should read the operations statement again, Steve. Once again, destroying command and control along with disrupting traffic in and out of San Francisco is our primary mission. Of equal importance is to limit civilian casualties. If we sent three times as many aircraft, how would that work out? Besides, filling the sky with aircraft not equipped with Specter would not exactly aid our ability to remain undetected, would it?

"Now without any further interruptions," Sean said this directly to Captain Brewster. "We will launch cruise missiles from the cruisers and destroyers in coordination with the F-35 bomb runs. If this exercise proves Specter's capability, I am sure the plan will be to build a series of smaller aircraft carriers. Think of twice as many carriers stationed undetected around the world able to respond quickly to threats at a third of the cost."

Alicia greeted Senator Boyle when he arrived and steered him toward Richard Mulligan, CEO of Comstock Technologies, and away from the *boys'* conversation.

Fortunately, her time with the politician and the autocrat mercifully ended when the Bridge Communications Officer, Ensign Gloria Layworth, entered the room to report. "The Vice President and Admiral Casey Hendricks [Commander Pacific Fleet] are on secure video feed and waiting."

"Thank you Ensign," Sean replied.

Thirty minutes earlier, Tony had entered the aft hangar to remind Dr. Safire of the meeting. The tension in the facility housing Specter's main computers hung in the air like an oncoming migraine. Dr. William Safire was in the middle of his imitation of the stereotypical mad scientist from a bad 1950s horror flick. At five feet four inches tall, with a head too big for his short stature, the sixty-three year old man looked more like a cartoon caricature than a scientist. However, contrary to the stereotype, he dressed meticulously.

He always viewed the people around him as mere obstacles to ridicule whenever possible. His sense of intellectual entitlement didn't leave any room for debate. As far as Dr. Safire was concerned, there was only his genius. Both the Navy and Comstock executives wanted to replace him long ago, but his second on the development team, Dr. Rebecca Cutler, had only recently proved herself every bit as capable of understanding Specter's technology as Safire.

Upon entering the hangar, Tony could see that it was business as usual for the team working under the demanding scientist.

"The technology I engineered and built is so far beyond anything ever created, and all you monkeys can do is sabotage every brilliant step forward I make." As a communicator, Dr. Safire was never short on hyperbole as this latest rant validated. "Not one of you belongs in the same room with me, let alone laying a finger on Specter's programming. I want to see the Admiral here right now!" he screamed at the nearest man in a naval uniform his bulging eyes could find.

One of the Comstock civilian engineers had enough of Safire's abuse. "You jackass! The communications systems interface worked just fine in the original configuration. You are the one who screwed it up. If you could stop finding problems where there aren't any, we could concentrate on the shielding issues in the microwave transmitters. Contract or not, I've had it with you and your ridiculous histrionics," he concluded, as he threw his lab coat to the ground in disgust and stormed out of the hanger.

Their naval counterparts, who didn't have the option of walking away, shared a quick glance. From their previous experiences with the doctor, they knew the storm had only begun.

"I see we're not all playing well together again Dr. Safire," Tony interjected.

"Unless you get me a better group of trained monkeys to assist me, there isn't any way we can be ready for at least another month!"

"Doctor, we leave port tomorrow, and these are the people you will ship out with. Why don't you take a break and let everyone do their jobs. But remember, the Admiral expects your appearance in his cabin at 3 PM."

Grumbling loudly and his arms waving in frustration, Dr. Safire briskly walked out of the hangar.

Tony walked over to Dr. Safire's young eccentric assistant, Dr. Rebecca Cutler. He was still trying to get used to this genius whose appearance embodied the 1960s. "Will Specter be ready and the comm lines operational by tomorrow morning?"

"We'll be able to split on time if you can stop Dr. Safire from interfering with our diagnostic testing. He keeps freaking out every time I ask when he will let us finish shielding the comm lines and bring the onboard equipment up to full power."

"He's gone, so why don't you see to it now?"

"Far out!" She hesitated for a moment, unsure if she should let Tony in on a little secret. "What the hell," she thought. "Comstock is cool with me certifying Specter when I'm satisfied. The problem is they didn't bother to inform Safire, so…"

"So, you want me to get in the middle of it?" Tony already was in the middle. Earlier, after agreeing with Tony that Dr. Safire's instability could put lives at risk, Sean had placed a call to the Comstock Technologies CEO.

Dr. Cutler put one hand on her hip and struck a teasing pose. "Only if you want to get your ships out of the harbor on time, Captain Tony."

This sucked Tony right in. "I think I can keep the good doctor out of your way. Would three hours be long enough?"

"Two would be fine."

Tony left the hangar happy the powers at Comstock finally gained some sanity, and replaced their monster child. Tony wondered if that could explain Safire's latest outburst. If he suspected his position with the company was threatened, it would escalate his already intolerable rage. "I wouldn't put it past that maniac to sabotage our mission," Tony worried as he headed to the bridge.

Sean noticed an important person was still absent from the staff meeting and whispered in Tony's ear. "Where's Safire?"

Tony shrugged his shoulders. "He was pissed off when I reminded him to be here, but I didn't think the egotistical bastard would miss a chance to strut in front of the Vice President."

"Get someone to track him…" Before Sean could finish his sentence, Dr. William Safire stormed into the room and glared at Tony.

With a nod from Sean, Ensign Layworth transferred the satellite feed.

"Good afternoon, Vice President Rushmore," Alicia welcomed.

Vice President Clayton Rushmore returned the greeting. "Good to see you Alicia. Are you ready to get your sea legs back?"

"Feels like I never left, Sir."

Sean entered the conversation. "Knowing how valuable your time is, if there are no objections, I'm sure everyone here knows each other, so I'll begin without the usual formalities."

The Other Side of Light

Before Sean could continue, Senator Boyle spoke up to assert his self-importance. "I would like to say something before we begin."

Without waiting for approval, he continued. "You would think with all the Navy has riding on Specter, you could have responded to my request to allow my Chief of Staff to monitor your progress. That way I could have briefed the Senate Appropriations Committee funding this black operation to calm their concerns before they discussed next year's budget.

"The President directed Secretary Calhoun to review all Department of Defense projects and report to me the programs we could cut to help balance the budget," the Senator continued. "She chose to ignore my repeated requests, at Admiral Phillips' insistence I am sure, fully aware I do not agree with the billions of dollars already spent on Specter. Hell, most of the scientific community I have spoken to assured me it is decades away from becoming operational."

Sean was smart enough not to respond to the Senator's remarks, but he did have his own perspective on the issues. Politicians like Senator Harvey Boyle cared little for long term strategic planning, especially if the money spent didn't allow them to bring home the pork for their own constituents. In Senator Boyle's case, this meant becoming one of the longest serving Senators in history. It also didn't matter that his lack of achievement kept him as one of the Senate's most obscure members.

Three decades after the folly of Vietnam, the United States military had become a force unrivaled in history. Unfortunately, it only took the mismanagement of the George W. Bush administration to wipe out most of those gains with two ill-conceived foreign wars and eight years of misspent appropriations.

After wasting a couple of trillion dollars, the efforts to recondition existing systems and re-equip US military forces to fight the wars of the 21st Century would tie up military budgets for at least the next decade.

Sean broke in before the Senator could continue. "I assure you Senator Boyle, there will be plenty of time later to voice your opinions. Now if you don't mind, I'd like Dr. Safire to say a few words about Specter's capabilities."

Tony thought Sean was courageous to let Dr. Safire address the group, but then taking calculated risks is what separated Sean from most others.

Dr. Safire rose and with bold strides, headed to the front of the conference table where a large LCD monitor on the wall displayed a Comstock Technologies logo over an image of a wraith.

"First off, I did not originally develop Specter for the Department of Defense. It has always been my goal to engineer the bending of light waves as a practical means to understand the relationship between time and space." Then, in a voice dripping with disgust, he bit the hand that fed him. "Unfortunately, in today's world the only way to advance science is to whore yourself to the only institution with the pockets deep enough to fund your work. The only way a scientist can receive the necessary funds from the government anymore is if you can prove that your technology can kill twice as many people as before."

Tony glanced at Sean and wondered how long he would allow the doctor to continue to ramble. Richard Mulligan looked ready to reach out and choke the man while everyone else squirmed uncomfortably in their chairs.

Sean finally interrupted. "Could you please stick to why we are here Doctor? We are all aware of your political opinions."

"Are you all also aware this is a big waste of my valuable time?"

Sean wasn't having any of it. "If that's the way you feel, I'll send for Dr. Cutler and have her take your place."

Before Sean could pick up the phone, Dr. Safire pressed the button on his remote. A split image of the cruiser USS Princeton appeared on the monitor, with views of both its port and starboard sides, as it steamed on an empty ocean. Then on the port view, the ship abruptly vanished, while on the starboard view, the ship serenely sailed on. The port view camera panned back and forth for 3 minutes until it showed the ship a half mile away and ninety degrees off its previous heading.

"As all of you are aware, not only did the ship disappear from visual sight, but all attempts to acquire it on radar also failed. In effect, the field powered by the electromagnetic generator created the same effect you see when light reflects off a drop of water. Though this simple concept applied to a ship has incredibly complicated technology behind it, this does not mean that I will stand behind the idiots you hired to install it."

The Vice President ignored his sarcasm. "How come our radar systems didn't pick up the energy created by this field?"

Like a teacher scolding an inattentive child, Dr. Safire fired back. "Anyone who owns a cell phone knows the range of its signal is limited to a short distance. Finding this signal on the vastness of the ocean would be like finding one proverbial needle in the middle of millions of haystacks."

Mr. Mulligan interjected. "That's why Comstock approached the Navy to develop Specter. If you knew where to look, it would be easier to track the energy signal. For example, if a car stuck in a Los Angeles traffic jam disappeared, you would have a smaller area to focus your search."

Sean broke in. "Moving on Dr. Safire, could you please explain how you designed Specter to cloak the task force?"

"With the Princeton already equipped on the port side, we equipped the Chancellorsville on the starboard side, the John Paul Jones forward, and the Decatur astern. We form them up in a simple box formation, with the Missouri in the middle to create overhead coverage, the most difficult to achieve. I needed to layer the waves from the high peak over the top of the ships, and then taper the waves sent out by the other ships along the outer edges. This allows for the overlapping coverage that ensures a complete cloak over the entire area."

"Excuse me Dr. Safire," the Vice President interrupted again. "Scientists I've conferred with are concerned about the possibility of radiation poisoning to the crews operating the ships. What assurances can you give me there isn't a risk of this happening?"

Before Safire could respond, Mr. Mulligan answered for him. "We have conducted hundreds of tests that prove the safety provided by the shielding built into the systems. You would get more exposure to radiation from a dentist's X-ray machine than Specter."

"Thank you, Richard." The Vice President sat back satisfied with the response.

Sean got up from his chair and approached the doctor. "I want to thank you Dr. Safire for taking the time to brief our guests." Before he could object, Sean put his hand on Safire's shoulder and guided him to the door into the waiting arms of Commander Carl Eddington.

As soon as the door closed behind them, Sean turned his attention to Mulligan. "So will Dr. Cutler have Specter's access codes connected to the bridge on time?"

"I still don't see why it was so damn important. However, to satisfy your concerns, I made it one of her top priorities."

"Why it is so *damn* important, *Sir*, is I don't trust Dr. Safire. This brings me to the other issue you have chosen to ignore. I meant it when I said these ships will not leave port until you remove Dr. Safire and put Dr. Cutler in charge of Specter's operation. You have yet to inform Dr. Safire. Why is that?"

Before Mulligan could reply, Vice President Rushmore rose to the CEOs defense. "Admiral Phillips, why do you feel it is necessary to insult Mr. Mulligan?"

"It's all right Clayton – excuse me – Mr. Vice President. Crazy or not, Dr. Safire hasn't done anything to allow Comstock to break his contract. Legally I can't remove him."

Sean turned to Tony. "Captain Knox, you were in the room when this came up last November. Can you please refresh Mr. Mulligan's memory?"

"It would be my pleasure. My recollection of the moment you refer to was, and I quote, 'I'll put it another way, Mr. Mulligan, we won't leave port until I have complete control over all personnel while at sea.' Then you hesitated for a moment and threatened to do something drastic, like resign your commission."

Not accustomed to such cavalier treatment, the Vice President snapped. "Admiral Hendricks. Are you going to allow this insubordination to continue?"

Admiral Hendricks knew he should suppress his urge to add to the lack of respect for the Vice President, but couldn't resist. "I'm equally disappointed with Admiral Phillips lack of decorum Sir, and if given the order I will replace him. Of course, you realize it will take weeks to bring a new Commander up to speed, and the other elements of the exercise will have scattered to their next deployments. By then Comstock will have missed their deadline to deliver Specter to the Navy."

"All right, I get it." All Mulligan could see was billions of dollars swirling down the drain, and more importantly the bad press. "As long as Dr. Safire is still allowed to remain aboard, I can work the details out with the lawyers. I'll meet with Dr. Safire and Dr. Cutler before I leave."

"Thank you, Mr. Mulligan," Sean politely acknowledged. "Now we can proceed?"

The Vice President wasn't ready to let it go, and foolishly added his own warning. "I will end your career after this exercise because of your boorish behavior. But then again, I shouldn't be surprised you have so little respect to civilian authority under the current DOD administration."

His threat, and the not so subtle insult to Secretary Calhoun, went too far. Sean walked over to the video conference camera, and with his face inches from it, smiled. "You don't have to worry,

Clayton, after this exercise is over, I'll be long gone."

Alicia quietly listened throughout the tense exchange, impressed with how Sean decided to end his naval career, death by political suicide. "What the hell," she thought, as she interrupted the fun. "Excuse me, gentlemen. Let's cut through the bullshit and finish this little dog and pony show. *Clayton*, everyone here knows you are a pompous asshole, and I know you are the one mostly responsible for spreading the rumor all over the beltway that I am a lesbian. I'm sure Dick Cheney is proud of the way you've taken up his mantle in the character assassination for political gain department."

The veins in the Vice President's neck were visibly throbbing, and he was about to explode, while Tony and the rest of the senior staff of the task force enjoyed their good fortune to witness this venting of three decades of frustration with inept bureaucrats. Though he would have enjoyed letting them continue, Tony knew it was time to take control of the meeting. "This isn't getting us where we all want to go, which is getting these ships out to sea. Why don't I go ahead and lay out how we're going to execute our mission."

When no one objected, he took his place in front of the group. The screen displayed the west coast of the United States with a symbol that represented their current location in the San Diego Harbor. As he began, the symbol moved west out to sea.

"After we assemble the task force outside the harbor, we'll head due west to a distance 50 miles off shore. After we engage Specter, we will change course to north by northwest. At a point 2 miles off Santa Barbara, we will set a course toward San Francisco. Based on previous experiences, the opposition's reconnaissance efforts will focus further out to sea. They will not expect us to operate with so little sea room.

"Our first target will be a simulated attack on San Francisco, followed up by the destruction of the CVN Ronald Reagan Task Force deployed out of Bremerton, Washington to defend against us. The next target, if we are successful, will be the defenses around the Hawaiian Islands and a simulated attack on Pearl. Our meteorologist is tracking a major storm coming down from the Aleutians that should be over San Francisco when we arrive. Are there any questions?"

After a moment of silence, Admiral Casey Hendricks spoke up. "I don't have any questions for you, Captain Knox. I do need to inform you all of a change in the scope of this exercise. After I briefed the President, he ordered me to expand the scope to include elements of the combined Pacific 3rd and 7th Fleets. He expressed his concerns regarding Russia's escalating naval presence in South American waters and their troops again massing on the Ukrainian border. He wants to expand this exercise to gauge their response. The President is also deploying the Atlantic 6th Fleet, putting all major elements of the United States Navy at sea in a show of force.

"After meeting with Central Command, and taking our commitments in Iraq and Afghanistan into consideration, the expanded planning calls for all other forces in the Pacific to have their alert status upgraded to be ready to deploy on a moment's notice. Because of our deteriorating relations with Russia, the President may need to end this exercise early. I am flying out to the USS Blue Ridge to take overall command of the Pacific portion of the exercises. The President has decided this is a good time to flex a little US Navy muscle.

"Joining me on the Blue Ridge to direct the forces opposing you, will be Admiral Connor Haskell in command of the 3rd Fleet and Admiral Alberto Delgado commanding the 7th Fleet. They already briefed Secretary Calhoun on their likely responses, some of which are already underway. Good luck Admiral Phillips and make sure we get Secretary Calhoun and Senator Boyle back in one piece."

After a few curt goodbyes to the Vice President on the monitor and Mr. Mulligan, Tony pulled a flask out of his pocket and handed it to Sean. "I want to know what you've done with my buddy Sean, because the Sean I know would never have bitch slapped one of his civilian bosses. And that was very unladylike behavior on your behalf Secretary Calhoun."

Alicia grabbed the flask from Sean and took a good pull from it. "As unlikely as it is to agree with anything Tony says, on this I have to. What got into you?"

Sean shrugged his shoulders. "If they didn't want to give me complete command control, they should have chosen someone else. Besides, it was time someone shut the ignorant jerk's mouth."

"Which ignorant jerk?" Tony asked mockingly. "Anyway, who cares? So if this is to be our last hurrah, I say let's make it something special."

"Okay, enough of that," Sean cautioned. "Let's get down to business. By the sound of Admiral Hendricks's orders, Washington is going to deploy the 6th Fleet to confront the Russians in South America. Do you think it could come to trading missiles with them?"

Alicia took another swig from the flask. "I don't see the President with many diplomatic options with the President of Venezuela climbing in bed with the Russians, especially after his blatant support of the overthrow of the Columbian government. It's the domino effect of the Cold War all over again, except without any of the same restraints on pushing the nuclear button. I sure wouldn't mind being invisible under Specter's cloak if that happens."

With this ominous turn of events, the pace in the harbor quickened to get the ships loaded with the additional stores they would need for the possible emergency deployment to South American waters.

Tony arrived in the CIC [Combat Information Center] and found it filled with small groups of technicians in animated conversation. He fixed his attention on Lt. Commander Daniel Osaka [Information Warfare Officer] who was in a heated conversation with the eclectic Dr. Rebecca Cutler. Like everyone else onboard, Tony looked forward to seeing what crazy 60s outfit she would wear on any given day. Today it was psychedelic swirls, splashed all over a chiffon mini dress, with matching accessories, and knee-high laced black leather boots – all accented by her gorgeous red hair. The effect was stunning.

Tony tried to shake off the image and focus on why he was there. "Osaka, the Admiral needs to know if you have control of our comm lines yet, and if not, do I need to tell him we won't be ready to sail. This ship can't move if we can't communicate."

Osaka responded. "Dr. Cutler and I were running diagnostics when she noticed a constant power surge that might be responsible for the static." He directed his gaze at Dr. Cutler who took her cue.

"Someone piggybacked an extra circuit onto the comm lines. At first it looked like it accessed ship communications, but the problem appears to be a redundant circuit that doesn't lead anywhere. Daniel and I are going back to the hangar where we think the problem occurred. We should have it cut out of the system and your comm lines cleaned up and operational in an hour, as promised."

"Thank you Dr. Cutler. Osaka, I'd like a word with you." Tony led him out of the room where he continued. "If someone did try to access our comm lines, find out who it was, but keep it quiet."

"Yes Sir."

Two hours later Sean was in the Admirals Ready Room with Alicia. "I wish it wasn't necessary to invite the Senator to dinner."

"I don't like him either, but he'd only think we have something to hide if we didn't."

"Do me a favor and focus his attention on anything but the exercise." Sean glanced at his watch. "I wonder what's keeping Tony and Renée."

"Renée told me Tony wanted to take her aft to show her Specter's operating systems. The way they looked at each other, you'd think there's something going on between them." Alicia's smile gave away her knowledge of their unfinished business.

"You mean to tell me you don't know their history?" Sean answered, tongue in cheek.

A knock on the door announced Tony and Renée's tardy arrival. Before either of them could say a word, Sean poked fun at Tony. "It seems after Tony's early retirement, he flew out to California and spent the weekend in Monterrey with a certain destroyer Captain." Tony and Renée looked at each other and pretended to back out the door.

"You don't want me to share my personal life with you ever again, do you Sean," Tony responded with mock pain. "Besides, if you two weren't my superiors, I'd have a thing or two to share about your twenty-year dance."

Another knock announced Senator Boyle's arrival. Dinner went off without a hitch because Alicia was able to keep Senator Boyle occupied by listening to his sophomoric tales about his Senate colleagues. Sean broke up the diner party at 1930 hours to make sure everyone got enough rest before their early morning departure.

The task force put to sea an hour before the USS Missouri BB-63 slipped her moors at exactly 0400. Admiral Sean Phillips stared out on the bay while alone in his quarters below the bridge. His mood matched the gray of the fog surrounding the Missouri. This exercise would likely finish his naval career, and the fear of its failure recalled unpleasant memories of his youth.

Raised the youngest of four children by a single working mother, Sean spent his early life making the most out of limited opportunities. Throughout a childhood of poverty and without the advantages his peers enjoyed as their birthright, he built his world around a love of books. From the moment his second grade teacher read aloud Charlotte's Webb, he became hooked on the magic they offered.

Sean devoured the books in his school and public libraries, and in the process learned how to research any subject that aroused his curiosity. This led him to his passion, the sea. It began when he pulled a book from the shelf with a picture of a clipper ship, The Sea Witch, its acres of canvas stretched to the ripping point as the ship tore through a stormy sea. In the early years of his friendship with Tony, they had both lamented they were born two hundred years too late.

While in junior high school, Sean became enthralled with the adventures of John Paul Jones, the father of the United States Navy. He would imagine himself as Captain Jones on the quarterdeck of the Bonhomme Richard when he forced the superior British frigate Serapis to surrender while his own ship sunk under his feet.

This exploit, along with his raids against coastal English villages, was a major embarrassment to the mighty British Navy. Like his childhood hero, there wasn't much Sean couldn't overcome by the sheer force of his will. However, his refusal to allow political considerations to affect his naval responsibilities kept him from achieving the recognition he deserved.

This image of fierce determination in the face of overwhelming odds, led Sean to other great leaders such as Thomas Jefferson, Abraham Lincoln, Winston Churchill, and the warrior, General George Patten, all who thrived under crisis. Also at an early age, Sean understood the adage: great leaders came out of great events. These early life experiences helped him gain a perspective on how he could get the best out of those around him by understanding what motivated them. Little did Sean know how severely this ability would soon be tested.

When the Missouri cleared the breakwater and reached the open ocean, the tugboats cast off their lines and the ship shook violently as the turbines brought her to life. As she surged forward, a smile broke through Sean's dark mood.

The task force was complete five miles west of the San Diego coast when they made contact with the two nuclear attack submarines that would complete the task force, the USS Seawolf SSN-21 and the USS Hampton SSN-767.

They continued to sail west for another forty miles, five miles short of where operation JTFEX-14-1 [Joint Task Force Exercise], code named Missile Slayer, would begin.

On the bridge of the Missouri with Sean, Alicia, Renée, Captain Folger, and Commander Eddington, Tony waited for news from the CIC about the overflight of the SIGINT satellite, Intruder. This was one of the nation's spy satellites in a geosynchronous orbit that could track their movements. These satellites relayed information to the CICs on the other warships engaged in the exercise, which also included the command ship Blue Ridge. Lt. Commander Osaka was responsible for satellite intelligence, which included the positions of civilian international overflights that their opponents could access.

Tony was on the bridge comm to Osaka in the CIC as they closed in on the fifty-mile mark. "We're on target Osaka, can you confirm yet?"

"We're still a couple minutes away Captain. I'm checking final confirmation on a French commercial satellite they re-positioned a couple of weeks ago."

This was not what Tony wanted to hear. "You were the one who told me we only have a three-minute window to maneuver unobserved, which we are now about to enter. It will be disappointing if we will have to sail in a circle for another day because of some French satellite."

"Give him another…" was all Sean got out before Osaka reported.

"All clear Captain. You're good to go."

"Got it! Thank you Commander," a relieved Tony acknowledged.

Sean immediately entered his access code into the bridge console. "Dr. Cutler, you are cleared to engage Specter."

⊰⊱

The day before in the aft hangar, Mr. Mulligan, before leaving the ship, had informed Dr. Safire he would be taking a back seat to Dr. Cutler. This of course set him off into a violent rage. When Mulligan further informed him that he would not receive the new security codes and that only the Admiral could release access to the console, did he do something those who witnessed his previous reactions to such a bombshell hadn't expected.

He immediately calmed down and a strange smile replaced his usual rage. "I will cooperate, but know this. If something happens because you chose to put an amateur in charge, you have only yourselves to blame." With great deliberation, he calmly took off his lab coat and started to leave the hangar.

Dr. Cutler looked over at him and tried to muster up some sympathy she definitely didn't feel. "I'm sorry this happened, but things haven't changed that much. It's still your baby, and all the honors will be yours to enjoy when we validate its potential."

Without looking at her and with all the spite he could muster, he fired back as he stalked out of the hangar. "I don't need your sympathy!"

Mulligan shook his head. "That went about as well as could be expected. Make us proud, Dr. Cutler."

"I'll do my best, Mr. Mulligan, Sir."

⸻◈⸻

"Well if anyone has anything to say now would be the time." Dr. Cutler's finger hovered over the command key.

When everyone looked around at each other as if to ask, "Like what?" She shook her head in disappointment. "Here we are about to make history and no one has something profound to say to mark the moment?"

One of the young techs across the room yelled out, "What else did you expect from a room full of scientists." Everyone around Rebecca nodded their heads in agreement. "We're not exactly wired for that," he added when he saw Rebecca's expression change to WTF.

Shaking her head in defeat, she unceremoniously pushed the key and launched Specter. "When we get back you people are going to have to get a life."

It didn't escape Dr. Cutler's attention that Dr. Safire had kept separate from the rest, as if uninterested in his own creations success. All kidding aside, she would have to watch his every move. "Would you please help me monitor Specter's operational parameters Dr. Safire?"

Without a word, he came over and sat down next to her.

At first, the sound of a low bass hum filled the hangar, followed by the sound of a rumbling distant storm as it spun up to speed. Two minutes later, the machinery settled into the rhythmic sound of water rushing over a fall. The sound even penetrated the 12 inches of shielding used to protect the crew from the magnetic energy field produced by the generator. After both she and Dr. Safire checked the figures sent from the other six generators, Dr. Cutler contacted the bridge. "All systems are within their operating parameters and signal strengths confirm integration at the required 360 degrees out to one mile."

As far as the personnel onboard the ships could see, nothing changed. The view throughout the fleet continued to be of eight ships cruising in tight formation under clear skies with visibility out to twenty miles.

Tony looked over to Sean, who gave a nod of approval. "Change course to 085 degrees north by 7 degrees west." He relayed the order to the rest of the task force to make the sweeping ninety degree turn to the north, which they did in flawless unison.

"Ensign Layworth," Sean ordered, "contact Captain Nelson. [Captain *Dash* Nelson, Air Wing Commander [CAG], USS Enterprise]."

"I have Captain Nelson Sir." Sean took the phone from the Ensign. "You're cleared to launch Captain."

The plan called for a Specter equipped F-35 Lightning to orbit outside the umbrella over the fleet to ensure their stealth, make sure the modified transmitter aboard the F-35 could reacquire the fleet, and test the communication links.

From the bridge on the Missouri, they watched the F-35 catapult off the Enterprise and then suddenly disappear as Captain Nelson engaged Specter.

Alicia, who witnessed Specter's abilities for the first time, commented on the ramifications of the plane's disappearance. "This could be considered the end of deterrence as we know it. How do you fight what you can't see?"

Sean was more interested in whether the plane was lost to the radar systems. "Tony, see if we are still tracking."

Tony reported after a few moments. "Not only did the F-35 disappear off radar, the infrared signal dropped to almost nothing at two miles, and we completely lost contact at three miles." Tony turned on the bridge overhead speakers so everyone could monitor the F-35's communications.

"My locator beacon is turned off," *Dash* reported. "I am not receiving any radar signatures of the task force, and I don't have a visual on the fleet. All I see is an empty ocean. I am switching on the locator beacon. I have acquired a radar lock on the Enterprise." *Dash* sent only quick radio transmission bursts, and used only his passive radar to limit the risk of exposure.

With their binoculars fixed on the Enterprise, they searched the empty sky for the F-35. Within seconds, the jet appeared when the pilot disengaged Specter a mile in front of the carrier on final approach.

"This is going to take some time to get used to, watching fighters popping in and out like that," Tony observed.

After he gave everyone a moment to soak in the implications, Sean broke the mood. "It's time to announce to the crew what this mission is about." With only Admiral Hendricks aware of their capabilities, he could only imagined what the reaction among the other top rank brass onboard the USS Blue Ridge might be.

❦

"Looks like you boys have a problem," Admiral Hendricks deadpanned.

"There is certainly more to this exercise than we were read into," Vice Admiral Delgado complained. After a moment to get over his frustration, he barked an order to his Chief of Staff. "Get on the horn with Admiral Van Holland on the Reagan [Nimitz class nuclear-powered supercarrier USS Ronald Reagan CVN-76] and confirm he received the same data we did. Order him to position his task force 55 miles west of San Francisco if he confirms."

Delgado turned to Vice Admiral Haskel as his Chief of Staff rushed to carry out his orders. "Deploy the attack submarines out of Pearl to cover the approaches to the islands. Let's hope this capability of theirs can only block long distance transmissions." He said this mostly to himself. "Oh, and get every Orion and F/A-18 reconnaissance aircraft available on the west coast and Hawaii up and flying until they locate the Enterprise."

Delgado impressed Admiral Hendricks with his rapid shift from disbelief to action. The true mettle of a Commander in war is the ability to absorb a catastrophic setback and still find a way to succeed. Unfortunately for them, Admiral Hendricks understood that with the apparent success of Specter, they were playing against a loaded deck.

❦

Onboard the Missouri, Dr. Safire monitored Specter while Dr. Cutler monitored him. When Mr. Mulligan gave Rebecca authority over the project, he instructed her to spy on the doctor's interaction with Specter. This order made her feel more like an over educated babysitter rather than the accomplished scientist she was. She desperately needed a break from the crazy scientist so she could get some of her own work done. "With everything running smoothly, why don't you split and grab a nap or get something to eat?"

Without looking up, he shunned her offer. "I'm fine right here, and if I wanted something to eat, I'll have one of these primates bring it.

"You'd be at least some use to me if you were monitoring operations onboard one of the other ships than wasting both our times spying on me. I'm sure everyone believes I might screw with their toy ships. Little men with little minds."

He continued to speak under his breath, so Rebecca could barely hear what came next. "They think I'll allow them to treat me this way, as if I don't matter. Without me there wouldn't be any Specter."

Rather than risk another outburst, she let it drop. "Well I'm hungry, so hang loose and I'll catch you in an hour." Rebecca got up, and stretched before throwing a smile at Dr. Forrest Phelps, who would monitor Safire's actions until she returned.

Recruited straight out of MIT to work on the Specter project, for the first two years Rebecca did not have to deal with Dr. Safire. Even if she had, her enthusiasm for the cutting-edge technology would have ensured she stuck it out in spite of his abuse. Though Dr. Safire would never give her any credit for her part in how fast the project accelerated after she arrived, she knew by the size of her paycheck where she stood. Rebecca did feel angry about how he could squash all the excitement and joy projects of this magnitude could give the people who participated in them.

After Rebecca left, Dr. Safire returned to the dark thoughts that had escalated since Sean rudely removed him from the briefing the day before. Unknown to anyone, he had previously installed a back door into Specter's operating system, and as he had planned, the idiots found the circuit that created the static in the comm lines. The doctor knew they lacked the imagination to find the real reason for it being there. He only wished he had more time to add other gremlins to frustrate and misdirect the primates.

No one knew how far Dr. Safire's mind had progressed into the realm of paranoid schizophrenia brought about by years of self-imposed isolation. It didn't help his development that his parents never tired of making excuses for the boorish behavior he showed at an early age. They believed his lack of assimilation into society was the fault of those who were jealous of his obvious genius.

Though Mr. Mulligan promised the Navy he would replace him with someone more stable for the exercise without bothering to inform Safire, what he didn't know was Safire already knew. Two months earlier, he had hacked into Mulligan's emails and found out. Ever since then, his rage built up to the point that all he could think of was executing his revenge.

Later that day as the task force cruised unseen up the coast, they could see storm clouds on the northwest horizon. Shipping traffic is light in January because of the heavy storms common to the region this time of year, and that was one of the factors for scheduling the exercise now. Weather reports showed the center of the low front had moved down from Washington, and now centered over Portland, Oregon. It was looking like the Enterprise Task Force would arrive off San Francisco at roughly the same time as the storm, just as the meteorologists had predicted.

As they entered the leading edge of the storm, an oil tanker outbound from Alaska passed unaware of the naval task force to the west by a mere mile and a half.

By the next morning, the storm packed a powerful punch with wind gusts of fifty-five knots and a steady rain that reduced visibility to half a mile. Onboard the Missouri, the quiet disciplined manner in which the crew carried out their duties belayed the anticipation of the coming war games most felt.

The next day, the task force had closed to within fifty miles southwest of San Francisco. Sean scanned the storm tossed seas with his binoculars from the bridge. "Tony, call over to the Enterprise and confirm they're ready."

"Aye Aye Admiral. This is the only time I miss being on a carrier. There is nothing like the ballet of flight operations." Tony noticed Sean barely listened to what he said. "Of course after they're through, they ride elephants around in the hangar."

That got Sean's attention. "I'm sorry, what did you say?"

"Never mind. You seem to be somewhere else this morning. What's up?"

"I can't shake the feeling Dr. Safire might do something to screw up the exercise."

"Stop worrying about the crazy fool. I'm already one step ahead of you. Last night I stationed additional Marines in the hangar."

Sean didn't want to take any chances. "Get Dr. Cutler on the phone."

"Dr. Cutler, please," Tony asked the Marine who picked up the phone. The Marine informed Tony that Dr. Phelps was the only one available.

Unfortunately, Rebecca had not yet arrived to spell Dr. Phelps, who had the unfortunate duty to spend the night listening to the mad scientist's tirades.

"Put him on."

"This is Dr. Phelps."

"Is Dr. Safire still being a pain in the ass?"

Dr. Phelps looked over at Dr. Safire, who appeared disinterested in who was on the phone. "To tell you the truth, I'd rather have spent the night listening to the sound of fingernails on a chalkboard. The man is one of the most spiteful individuals I have ever had to endure. He did not let up on us all night. Outside of that, he mostly spent his time monitoring power outputs from one ship to the other on his computer.

Based on what I observed, he only directly accessed the Princeton's system. When I questioned what he was doing, he screamed that it was none of my business. The only time he was out of my sight was when he went to the men's room. While he was gone, I checked, and found nothing suspicious. The only thing of note to report was that the power from the Princeton's generator had dropped close to the bottom of its operating parameters."

While Dr. Phelps delivered his report, Dr. Rebecca Cutler arrived and took off her rain soaked parka. Everyone stared at her except Dr. Safire, who Dr. Phelps thought must be gay. The dress she wore would have looked right at home on the set of a Sean Connery, James Bond movie. The splashes of bright colors, strategically placed over her chest and down from her stomach to her thighs, left the men in the hangar breathless. She accented this with bright red boots that laced all the way up to her knees and set it all off with multiple colored ribbons to tress her hair in various bunches and lengths.

"Dr. Cutler has arrived Captain. Would you like to speak to her?"

Tony could tell from Forrest's voice how Rebecca's appearance had affected his men, yet again. "Put her on and get your mind back on Dr. Safire, if you can."

"I can't say I'm sorry I don't have your military discipline Captain. Hold on, I'll get her."

"How's it hanging, Tony?" Rebecca asked, obviously well rested.

"I can tell from Dr. Phelps' reaction you are determined to keep my crew from focusing on their duties."

"I put on something a little different today, considering the momentous occasion. You wouldn't want me to remember the day dressed up in something old and frumpy would you?"

"Please keep yourself wrapped up when you're outside the hangar. We launch the attack in forty-five minutes, and I need my crew's attention on their duties." As Tony checked his watch, he noticed Sean's impatience and quickly wrapped it up. "I want you to act as liaison between Dr. Safire and the bridge during the attack so I'll know I'm receiving the information I need."

Rebecca turned serious in turn. "I'll make sure there won't be any problems from our end."

With that taken care of, it was time to turn the group into the wind in preparation to launch the strike package. Forty minutes later, the task force was in position as the storm continued to increase in violence.

"Light 'em up, Captain." With this order from Sean, the simulated destruction of San Francisco's infrastructure began. Sean and Tony left the bridge to meet their guests, who were waiting for them in the CIC to monitor the results.

Twenty-five miles offshore at 0800 hours, six F-35s launched from the deck of the Enterprise, formed up, engaged Specter, and headed toward their targets. It only took a few minutes to reach the bay where they split into two groups of three. The first group headed to the Golden Gate Bridge.

Onboard the Blue Ridge, a flash message from the Missouri notified Admiral Hendricks the attack was underway. He rushed to the CIC to find Admirals Delgado and Haskel in a state of disbelief. Reports had confirmed the simulated destruction of the Golden Gate Bridge and the Oakland-Alameda Bridge, followed by news that confirmed further attacks on the San Francisco airport, communication centers, and municipal buildings. For added effect, Tony had targeted the symbol of San Francisco's elite, the hotels on Knob Hill.

With a sly smile, Admiral Hendricks assured the powerless Admirals. "Don't feel bad, gentlemen. You never had a chance to begin with, so none of this will be a blot on your records."

Like Sean and Alicia, the Admiral realized that after this exercise ended, so would his career in the Navy. That he survived twenty years trying to keep up with the rapid evolution of technology to reach such a lofty command level did not fool him into the belief he could adjust to the changes Specter would bring. "Oh well," he thought, "I had a nice ride."

"As soon as the Enterprise recovers her planes, let's move the fleet to deep waters so we can have more room to maneuver when we find and engage the Reagan task force." After he listened to the unchallenged success of the attacks, Sean became subdued, because like Hendricks he understood the implications of their success.

The CIC Officer reported to Sean, "Sir, the meteorology informs that the center of the storm is approaching from the northwest and should be over us within the next hour."

Not seen, but felt by the ship's violent motion in the cramped space of the CIC, the storm was an ominous presence over the task force. The sea sent twenty-foot waves over the bows of the screening ships, while the skies overhead delivered jagged shafts of bright lightning, followed by the rumblings of thunder that vibrated through the sailors unlucky enough to be on watch outside.

"I'm headed back to the bridge." Tony's first concern was the safety of the task force, and he needed to be on the bridge for the surface action he knew would come.

The weather made Sean nervous. When he had previously questioned what emergency measures were in place if Specter malfunctioned, Dr. Safire gruffly assured him the system's surge protectors would shut down Specter before the magnetic generators overloaded.

In the CIC, Alicia continued to babysit Senator Boyle. After an hour of listening to him talk out of the side of his mouth, she had enough. "But then again, there wasn't any way you could lose. As chairman of the appropriations committee, if it failed you could slash the Navy budget and give it to the Air Force, but now as Specter's sponsor, you can take credit for its success." Alicia noticed the Senator looked a little green from the swaying motion of the ship.

"Specter's success will only confirm what I said earlier about the need for smaller surface forces, crewed by a tenth of the sailors this ship requires. Also, we already have plans to use this… technology throughout… the military." Senator Boyle had trouble focusing his thoughts as he fought to keep down his breakfast.

"It sounds like you want to intensify the chaos in a world already on the verge of destruction," Alicia retorted. She knew through her own experiences how hard it was to regain international diplomatic trust after the disastrous George W. Bush administration. "Our diplomatic efforts would totally collapse if we unilaterally decided to equip our military with Specter. There isn't any way I'll recommend the expansion of this program until the State Department has a chance to brief our allies." It made Alicia livid the President had kept these plans secret from her.

"I'm sure your replacement at Defense doesn't share your view Madam Secretary. The only reason you are here is he wanted you out of the way while he conferred with your replacement about the new direction he wants to take the DOD."

"There it is," Alicia thought.

She looked at Sean, who only shrugged his shoulders as if to say, "How could I know if you didn't?"

The Senator gleefully gave away the rest of the administration's plan to use Specter for offensive operations. This was madness. Historical fact validated that when the United States political policies took a first strike mentality, the nation suffered expensive and long drawn out defeats.

Rather than debate this with the seasick Senator, Alicia changed the subject. "I think it would be a good idea if we helped you to your cabin before you throw up all over some very expensive equipment."

Sean made a call for a Corpsman [an enlisted medical specialist] who arrived minutes later and helped the Senator to his cabin. He only got a few steps out the door, when his stomach got the better of him.

With the Senator gone, Alicia was free to express her anger. She was horrified to think her government wanted to ratchet up military pressure in a world that was already coming apart at the seams. "Specter should only be deployed if it can become part of the political bargaining process to reduce nuclear proliferation. If the administration tries to use Specter to launch tactical strikes against regional threats, the United States will only have England and Israel left as allies."

Sean agreed with her assessment. "The neocons control the agenda, and the President has decided to escalate the military option in order to take the nation's mind off the failed economy. The Senator was right when he said you were no longer a player after you tendered your resignation. I felt all along it was a mistake for you to walk away from your Congressional seat."

"I knew what I was getting into," she replied, still angry. "The President promised to expand the diplomatic process with the hope that the public would start to pay attention. I figured it was worth a shot."

Sean admired her optimism, and though he knew she had taken a hit to her ego, he also knew Alicia would bounce back quickly. "That's okay, when we return they'll hand us both a gold watch, and someone else can worry about saving the world."

With nothing left to add and losing his own battle with the violent motion of the ship, Sean prepared to leave. "I need to get some air." He nodded for Alicia to follow him outside the CIC. After Sean closed the door behind them, he asked her for a favor. "Would you mind keeping the Senator out of my hair when he recovers? I need to head to the bridge."

"That depends on how long. I can't guarantee I won't have him tossed overboard if I have to babysit him for the entire exercise."

He gave her a quick kiss on the cheek. "I owe you."

When Sean arrived on the bridge, Tony reported. "Alpha Whiskey

[Air Warfare Command assigned to the cruisers on twelve hour shifts controls all task force offensive and defensive capabilities] on the Chancellorsville has picked up multiple contacts approaching from the southwest that will close on our position within five minutes. They have ordered the Hampton and Seawolf forward. With the weather worsening we should launch now."

Sean took a long look at the storm that raged outside. "Stand down the F-35s. This is only an exercise, and I don't want to risk the loss of any aircraft in this weather. It's time we used our other assets. Turn the task force to the southwest."

Sean would do it the old-fashioned way and eliminate the Reagan task force in a surface action. The offensive missile and torpedo weapons systems on the destroyers, cruisers, attack submarines, and of course, the Mighty Mo were more than enough to do the job.

In the hangar of the Missouri, Dr. Safire maintained his focus while the rest of the Specter team monitored the systems as they tried to ignore their queasiness from the violent motion of the ship. Dr. Phelps unfortunately lost his battle with the rocking motion and rushed to the bathroom already occupied by a technician violently letting go. Taking advantage of their misery, Dr. Safire opened a file on his computer and began to type.

In the CICs of the screening warships, weapons officers were itching to go active with their search radars to target the Reagan Task Force. Out in front of the Enterprise Task Force, the crews of the Specter equipped Seawolf and Hampton, impervious to the fifty-foot swells, were all business readying their weapons systems.

Onboard the Seawolf, Captain Mark Daily ordered his boat to silent running. The next five minutes felt like an hour, then the news all submariners lived for arrived. "Captain, submerged contact bearing 015 degrees north, five thousand yards off our bow. Estimate speed at fifteen knots on a course straight at us." The sonar operator quickly added, "It's the Virginia, Sir." [USS Virginia attack submarine with the Reagan Task Force]

The control room came alive as Captain Daily calmly gave his orders. "Get a firing solution on the Virginia and keep alert for any signs of the North Carolina."

At three thousand yards, with the Virginia's position plotted and programmed into the Mark-48 torpedoes, Captain Daily ordered the simulated attack. "Fire one, fire two." The crew waited as the computers tracked the torpedoes.

Over on the Virginia, Captain Tomlin, who spent the last two days chasing ghosts, was shocked when his radar operator came to life in a rush of excitement. "Torpedo, locked on, bearing 170 degrees southeast, at 2800 yards. Twenty seconds till impact."

"Emergency dive to 300 feet, change course to 030 degrees south, and release chaff." Captain Tomlin knew it was too late to avoid his fate, but discipline demanded he make every effort to avoid the simulated destruction of his boat. "Contact the Reagan and send them our position."

"Captain, I haven't been able to establish a contact anywhere near where the torpedo appeared," the sonar operator reported.

Eighteen seconds later the Virginia disappeared from the exercise, two seconds off the radar operator's estimate. Three minutes later, Captain Marlow Turner aboard the Hampton repeated this action against the Virginia class attack submarine USS North Carolina.

Aboard the Reagan, the destruction of both the Virginia and the North Carolina came across the computer screens that monitored the exercise. Unlike Admiral Phillips, who refused to launch aircraft in the storm, the already embarrassed Rear Admiral Van Holland's frustration grew even greater when the F/A-18Fs he had launched couldn't find any trace of the Enterprise Task Force.

"Set a course to the Virginia's last reported position. Have all ships launch chaff on one minute intervals." Out of options, the Admiral blindly charged toward his attackers hoping to get a visual before all was lost.

After notification of the Reagan's course change, Sean ordered an increase in speed to close the distance and ordered his attack submarines to rejoin the task force.

Fifteen minutes later, Tony received confirmation from the Chancellorsville that the Reagan task force was dead ahead. With a nod from Sean, he gave the order. "Launch the attack." Immediately, every warship in the group went active with their search radars long enough to acquire their targets and launch their Harpoon II anti-ship missiles. As soon as the missiles locked on their targets, they quickly shut down their active radars to avoid detection.

The radar screens of the Reagan Task Force lit up with incoming missiles, which elicited disbelief among the frantic operators about how they came out of nowhere without any time to respond. One by one, the ships of the Reagan Task Force, with over 8500 officers and sailors, disappeared from the computers on the command ship Blue Ridge.

On the bridge of the Missouri, Tony remembered the devastation a single demonstration Harpoon missile created on a decommissioned cruiser in a naval exercise he had witnessed. "This isn't warfare, it's murder. You know the politicians will have to justify Specter's expense by using it to excess in the name of national security."

"Let's face it Tony, the days of mano a mano on the battlefield are long gone," commented Captain Renée Aslan, who along with Secretary Alicia Calhoun had joined them on the bridge. "The white knight was laid to rest decades ago."

"The exercise is a success, and we have proven Specter is

viable." Sean looked at his watch to see 1145. "It's time to give our condolences to Admiral Van Holland. And Tony, no gloating," Sean commanded. "Afterward, I want to congratulate Dr. Safire on Specter's flawless success."

In the hangar, while almost everyone present enjoyed the celebration of their overwhelming success, a green Dr. Phelps congratulated Dr. Cutler and added, "Thank you for bringing me up to speed on Specter so I could be a part of this historic event."

"You're welcome Forrest." Rebecca glanced over at Dr. Safire and noticed a crazed look on his face while he pounded furiously on his keyboard. She started to walk over to him, but before she could take a step, the electromagnetic generator began to surge dramatically.

This got the attention of everyone in the hangar as they all turned to see Dr. Safire behaving like the Dr. Strangelove character, hysterically laughing as he waved his computer keyboard over his head.

"What the hell are you doing?" Rebecca shouted above the now screaming generator, while engineers and technicians rushed to shut it down before it blew out the ship's electrical grid.

"It's too late for you to do anything to stop it. I created it, and now I've destroyed it to keep it out of all your foolish hands." He smashed the keyboard to the floor before two of the Marines could tackle him.

On the bridge of the Missouri, with everyone else seeing to their tasks, Renée was the only one who noticed the appearance of a green mist that was slowly growing brighter as it worked its way up the hulls of the surrounding ships. She turned to face Sean, as she pointed out the window. "Will you please explain to me what that is all about?"

In the time it took Sean to look out, the green mist had risen over the top rail of the Missouri. Between bright flashes of lightning, they watched the cloaking shield expand up into the powerful storm. Before Sean could react, the bridge lights doubled their illumination and electrical circuits overloaded. Seconds later, the sky lit up in a blinding green flash. When their eyesight recovered, they were on calm seas, dead in the water.

Chapter Two

Moving Again

The Lockheed P-3 Orion land based turboprop reconnaissance plane had flown in and out of severe thundercloud formations since takeoff four hours earlier. The pilot was not pleased with the view twenty miles ahead. In front of the Orion was a formation of clouds that towered into the stratosphere like a vision of Thor, the Norse god of thunder, and discharged lightning as if thrown about by the angry god. The sheer size and power of this light show gave off a sense of both awe and beauty, mixed with the pilot's awareness that to go around it would take them miles off their search pattern.

"Looks like we've got to extend our mission," he announced to the groans of all aboard the cramped Orion, as he banked sharply to the west to avoid the center of the storm.

When ordered to engage in this exercise, the pilot and his crew were two days away from a well-deserved leave. After hours of fruitless search, the usually even-keeled Lt. Commander believed the Enterprise Task Force was by now hundreds of miles away and headed to Hawaii. In addition to this frustration, the girlfriend he hadn't seen in three months had arrived in San Francisco yesterday. Not being there to meet her probably meant the end of that relationship.

"Commander, I've received confirmation the Virginia has been lost," the radio operator reported.

"Jesus, what else could go wrong?" he muttered under his breath. Then he calmly asked, "You have a fix on their last known location?"

"Radar still hasn't picked up any sign of the Enterprise Task Force, but I have the Reagan Task Force ten miles south of their last contact with the Virginia on a northeast course. You are not going to like the order Admiral Van Holland just sent. He wants us to drop down to get a visual on the Reagan."

The radio operator took a moment to stare out a small window in front of him. "In this weather we'll have to be right on top of them."

"That doesn't make any sense. Why would we need to see the Reagan? Did he bother to mention why?"

"All the Admiral said, was to report back when we get a visual on the Reagan."

Frustrated with this news, he pulled tight the straps that secured him in his seat. "Great," he thought. "A task force that defies detection, the loss of an attack submarine without explanation, and now an Admiral who isn't making any sense, how could the situation possibly get any worse?"

"Buckle up tight, boys, we are going in," he warned as he swung the four-engine plane back to their original course, and dropped the nose.

"I've got another flash message, Commander. The Reagan reports they are under attack. Wait a minute."

"Wait a minute for what? What did they say?"

"They are gone, Commander. All communications with the entire Reagan Task Force have stopped."

"What the hell is going on? This can't be. You don't lose an entire task force in seconds."

"Everything checks out boss. I can't explain it, but we've lost all contact. Hold on. I've got something coming in from the Blue Ridge." Moments later, the radioman reported. "I have received confirmation from the Blue Ridge. The entire Reagan Task Force is lost to enemy action."

"Did they say how?"

"Not a clue boss, just that the entire Reagan Task Force has been destroyed."

Contrary to his earlier thought, the situation was about to get much worse. Baffled and confused, the pilot was about to return to base when an intense green mist bathed the cockpit. He turned away from the source of the electrical fireworks and clenched his eyes tightly against the searing light. When the explosion of light subsided, it took a moment before his sight cleared. What he saw when they did clear freaked both him and his copilot out. They were now flying under calm sunny skies, directly above the elusive Enterprise Task Force. In shock, the two pilots looked at each other for verification of the impossible.

"What in the hell is going on!" the Lt. Commander screamed, as he fought to keep from losing control to the mother of all hallucinations. "Are you seeing the same thing I am?"

"I hope what you see is the Enterprise Task Force." The copilot looked again before he continued. "I don't know how or why we didn't pick them up on radar, but there they are, and it looks like they are slowing."

"Commander, we've lost all our satellite uplinks, and the navigation equipment is nonresponsive." The radio operator's frustration about his gear's failure made him more angry than confused. "I'll be damned if I can explain it. The coast of California should be directly to the east of us, but it's not there."

This news, along with the surreal event they had witnessed, further unnerved the pilot of the Orion. It took a moment for him to regain control before he responded. "See if you can contact the

Enterprise and find out if they know what the hell is going on."

⊰⊱

"What happened?" Tony fought to focus his mind in an attempt to understand how it was they were now on calm seas in daylight. Stunned by the suddenness of the change in their environment, he stared out from the bridge as the Missouri, with her turbines dead, gradually lost speed. After a moment of silence, everyone except Sean, filled the vacuum with a stream of conversation as each struggled to give voice to what their eyes now witnessed.

Tony shouted above the noise to address Sean. "Toto, I have a feeling we're not in Kansas anymore. Either we died and went to Navy heaven, or you have some 'splaining to do, Lucy."

Sean didn't respond to Tony's nervous chatter. He scanned the ocean as he replayed the events that led up to this strange development. There wasn't any plausible explanation, so he took a few moments to collect his thoughts.

The Enterprise Commanding Officer, Captain Charles Folger, immediately went into action. "Ensign Layworth, do we have intra-ship communications?"

After repeated attempts to reach any of the ship's departments, she shook her head. "No good, Sir."

"Helmsman, grab the sextant and plot our position."

"Aye Aye Captain." The helmsman found the rarely used sextant, and stepped outside.

Sean regained his composure and decided what should come first. "Captain Knox, head aft and ask Dr. Cutler if she has any idea about what happened."

"Aye Aye Admiral," Tony acknowledged.

Captain Folger ordered his XO, "Commander Eddington, go to Sickbay to find out if we have suffered any casualties."

"Aye Aye Captain."

Sean stepped outside with a pair of binoculars and scanned the seas around the task force. After a 360-degree sweep didn't further his understanding of their situation, he called out to Captain Folger. "Charles, it appears all our ships have lost power. I don't see the Reagan, and she was only five miles away. Where did she go? None of this is making any sense at all."

It was then Sean heard a plane and trained his binoculars skyward. "There is an Orion above us. Ensign Layworth, see if you can contact them."

"All communications are down Sir." Gloria grabbed a signal lamp from one of the cabinets, and left the bridge to stand outside with Sean. "I'm going to see if I can make contact." As she began to flash in Morse code, the Orion executed a banking turn and circled the Missouri.

The copilot spied the flashing light and jotted down the message. "They want to know if we know what happened, or where we are."

"I'm going to drop down," the pilot responded. "Grab the signal lamp and let them know all our communications and satellite navigation gear are down."

Gloria watched as the plane made its next pass and read the response.

Alicia and Renée came out in time to hear the crew of the Orion was as mystified as they were. "We could be hundreds of miles from God knows where, without any place for the Orion to put down," Alicia worried.

Sean agreed. "Ensign, ask them what their fuel status is."

After the Orion reported they could stay in the air for another four hours, Sean ordered the pilot, "Have them fly due east to get a fix on their location."

After Gloria sent the message, Sean noticed Captain Aslan seemed unsure about what she should do. "If Secretary Calhoun doesn't mind, would you go down to the engine room to find out how long it's going to take to get power back? Report your findings to Captain Folger."

"Go ahead Renée," Alicia approved.

Renée saluted the Admiral and stepped across the bridge to report to Captain Folger. "Along the way I'll station some sailors to relay my report to you."

"Thank you, Captain," Charles acknowledged. "While you're at it, pass on to the crew to remain at battle stations."

"Got it. On my way."

Alicia turned to Sean. "What can I do?"

"I think both of us should sit tight." Sean wanted to be sure that they were not in any danger before he let Alicia out of his sight.

When Sean and Alicia stepped back inside the bridge, she was having trouble relating to the abstract nature of their situation. "Any thoughts about what happened?"

"Give me a little time to work on it. First, we have to make sure we are still where we are supposed to be, because there certainly isn't a logical explanation for what happened. How can a raging storm and a carrier task force disappear right in front of us, and what did the green mist have to do with it? Either we're all in the middle of some crazy dream, or the little that we know about quantum theory is all wrong."

Then Sean lowered his voice so only Alicia could hear. "If that were the case, I'd sure like to know how my mind came up with this crazy reality. If it were my dream, I would be on an exotic beach, a Mai-Tai in one hand, and your hand in the other. Oh – and there wouldn't be a Navy uniform around for miles, if you know what I mean."

Sean's offhand remark brought a slight smile to Alicia's face. "If this isn't a dream…" Alicia pinched herself. "Nope, that hurt, not a dream." She then got serious. "So, it's not a dream and the system we are testing bends light waves. Hmm. Do you think Dr. Safire had something to do with it?"

Moving Again

"Whatever Safire's role was, do you really believe he has discovered a way to manipulate the reality of seven thousand people at once?" Sean answered. "I went over Specter's surge protection systems with Dr. Cutler before we left port, and the breakers separating Specter from the ship's power grid should have triggered. If he was responsible, he had to have found a way to disable them."

"What do you think happened to the Reagan?" Alicia added. "I don't know about anyone else, but David Copperfield's act has nothing on the disappearance of an entire carrier task force."

Sean pictured a giant curtain thrown back to reveal an open ocean where the Reagan should be, and laughed at the absurdity. Despite the monumental insanity of the moment, Alicia's Copperfield comment and Sean's laughter broke the tension on the bridge.

When Tony returned he reported to Sean. "Dr. Cutler informed me that Dr. Safire had what the ship's doctor diagnosed as a psychotic break. He entered commands into Specter when we completed our attack on the Reagan, and the generators spiked immediately afterward."

"What's the damage?" Sean asked. "And has anybody figured out how he managed to alter Specter's program without any of the technogeeks finding out about it?"

Before Tony could answer, a sailor from the messenger chain reported to Captain Folger. "Sir, Captain Aslan reports the Electrician Mates will have power to the bridge shortly along with inter-ship communications."

"Thank you Seaman."

Sean turned his attention back to Tony. "Continue Captain."

However, before Tony could say a word, the Seawolf broke the surface two hundred yards off the Missouri's bow. Moments later personnel appeared on the submarine's conning tower and signaled the Missouri.

After she exchanged signals with the Seawolf, Ensign Layworth reported to Sean and Tony. "The Seawolf is completely unaffected. Captain Daily reported nothing unusual, until he lost contact with us."

"Thank you, Ensign," Sean acknowledged as he refocused on Tony, who continued his report.

"Dr. Cutler said Specter shut down before it suffered any major damage, and she is working with the engineers to figure out what Dr. Safire did. She also said to tell you to not attempt to restart Specter yet."

At that moment, the bridge power came back on. Captain Folger immediately picked up the phone and contacted the engine room. The Missouri's Chief Engineer Mark Brunel answered.

"Mark, how long before you can get my ship moving?" Charles demanded.

"I've got Electrician Mates scrambling through the ship's schematics repairing burned wiring and replacing blown breakers. It will be an hour before we are underway. As it stands, we managed to get the generators to deliver power to the missile launchers, bridge, and CIC figuring these areas would be your first priority."

"You figured right Chief. Make our ship-wide intercom system your next priority. I need to talk to the crew as soon as possible. Keep me informed if anything changes. Put Captain Aslan on."

"Yes Sir," the Chief acknowledged. "Here is Captain Aslan."

"Captain Folger, everybody belowdecks have the same questions. What happened and where are we?" Renée reported. "The crew is at battle stations and awaiting orders. You know anything yet?"

"No, we are still clueless. Your next priority is to check on the Damage Control parties, and see if you can find my wayward XO. Thank you Captain Aslan, and Captain Knox wants a word." With so little information to go on, Captain Folger wanted to make sure all of the Missouri was still where it should be.

Tony took the phone from Charles. "Captain Aslan, when you

are finished, please join us on the bridge."

"Yes *Sir*, Captain Knox, *Sir*," Renée acknowledged with a tease.

"That's *Chief of Staff* Captain Knox."

Ensign Layworth reported to Sean. "Admiral, all ships report they lost their satellite feeds. Their diagnostic tests ruled out their systems as the problem. It's like the satellites aren't where they are supposed to be."

"Thank you, Ensign."

The helmsman returned to the bridge after he had sighted their position and was not sure how to report what he found. "Admiral, either I've forgotten how to read a sextant, or we are approximately 2200 miles south-southwest of our former position. Sir, I checked the ship's charts, and that would put us 1200 miles southeast of Hawaii."

"Take another reading to be sure," Sean ordered.

"Yes Sir."

Tony then asked Sean, "What's the condition of the rest of the group?"

"The Princeton and Chancellorsville report conditions similar to ours, and they'll be able to get underway within the hour, with another day needed to sort out the electrical damages. The Enterprise reactors did scram without damage, but it will take longer to bring them back on line. The good news is the reactors shut down early enough to protect most of the electrical circuits on the Enterprise from the overload. They are better off than we are and should have their reactors operational within a couple of hours."

Sean suddenly remembered a forgotten asset. "Ensign Layworth, contact the CIC and get a report from the Orion."

"Aye Aye Admiral."

"Tony, call Captain Turner, and have him surface the Hampton as a safety precaution."

Tony spent the next five minutes talking to the Hampton's Captain, and then filled Sean in. "They had the same experience as the Seawolf. All satellite uplinks are unresponsive and attempts to communicate outside the group have failed as well. I ordered him to conduct a thorough sweep of the area before he surfaces."

"Good idea."

Ensign Layworth waited until they were finished. "Sir, the CIC reports the Orion hasn't located any ships in the area or sight of land. I have the Orion on the line and the pilot sounds unnerved."

"I can't say I blame him." Sean took the phone from the Ensign. "This is Admiral Phillips. Who am I talking to?"

"Lt. Commander Harold Ramis, Sir. It's good to hear from you. Have you figured out what is going on?"

"The only thing we know for sure is we are over a thousand miles from land, and you need to head back toward us."

"No offense Sir, but what are your plans when we return? There isn't any way to set this plane down on the deck of the Enterprise."

"Looks like your crew is going to have to strap on their parachutes and jump near my ships. Are you up to executing a water landing Commander Ramis?"

While Sean talked to the Orion, Tony took the opportunity to locate Lt. Commander Daniel Osaka. "Go to the CIC to see if you can get the damn communications gear to make contact with the Blue Ridge. Report back to me every half hour even if you have nothing new to add."

Tony turned to the helmsman, who could only shrug his shoulders. "I don't have an explanation Captain, but we are definitely not off the coast of San Francisco anymore."

"What have you found out Admiral?" Tony was curious about the Orion.

"They are in the dark as much as we are. While we are waiting to recover the Orion's crew, have all the ship Captains, including the supply ships, report with damage assessments. I also want them to conduct a head count to ensure we still have all our sailors onboard.

You do the same here."

"Will do."

In the aft hangar, Dr. Rebecca Cutler headed a table of civilian and US Navy engineers and technicians who poured over Specter's computer program trying to find the back door Dr. Safire had planted. Other technicians worked to bypass burned out circuits. Fortunately, Rebecca managed to crash the computers during the melee with Dr. Safire before the overload fried them.

Over the next twenty minutes, she tracked the command signal back to a secondary maintenance program that interfaced with the surge protectors. It wasn't long until she high-fived the nearest technician. "Dig this. I found hidden in the ship's communications software commands sent to the surge protectors to ignore power spikes. This explains the problems three days ago with all the static."

Rebecca felt stupid for not checking the program when they found the extra circuit to nowhere. This mistake of omission made her more determined to find out if there were any other surprises hidden in the software.

Lt. Commander Daniel Osaka arrived in the CIC and tried to restore contact with the outside world. For all the communication gear at their disposal, the silence shook the nerves of the sailors in the room. They were used to their integration into a world of instant communication with the click of a mouse. Osaka could see they were confused by this disconnect and didn't know how to think beyond their usual digital reality.

Now forty, Osaka grew up on the cusp of this technological revolution. Throughout his fifteen years of service to the Navy, he witnessed how automation had replaced sailors to minimize the cost of operations. Osaka's own interests lay in codes, the encryption formulas, and the abstract thought it took to break them down. However, what gave him the greatest joy was the study of the history of cryptology in warfare, and Daniel was a library on its evolution.

When on shore leave, he sat in mind-numbing seminars, while his shipmates indulged in the usual variety of carnal conquests. It became only natural for him to become an Information Warfare Officer. The way he trained his mind opened up a world few could understand, but this left Daniel lacking rudimentary social skills. His Asian heritage wasn't any help in this stereotype, and he did nothing to try to change this view. This actually gave him the privacy necessary to focus in his abstract world. The integration necessary to connect Specter into the Missouri's communications was this type of abstract application. With these lessons in mind, he switched gears and went old school.

"Stop your attempts to re-establish the communication links and focus your efforts on short band signals."

This order prompted a few confused looks from those in the room. After a moment of fumbling around, they began to check the signal bands normally associated with amateur Ham operators. A few minutes later, one of the radio operators motioned him over and handed Daniel his headset. "Sir, I'm picking up a conversation on the Single Side Band."

Osaka put on the headset, and after he listened for a moment to nothing but static, he heard pieces of a conversation. "ucky to be in unshine its rain erable right ow wish I as in awaii with you ow. Looks like you were ight Harry they might be utting us down soon than I thoug."

Osaka handed the headset back to the operator. "According to the signal strength, they are either transmitting from a ship, or out of Hawaii. See if you can tune the signal in better?"

After the radio operator spent a few minutes adjusting the settings with the help of two other operators who began to warm to the task, he motioned Osaka over while he scribbled furiously on a pad. Osaka looked over his shoulder and began to read the unbelievable content.

"…already outlawed civilian short band in Europe because of that idiot Hitler. Now, it looks like it won't be long before they shut us down as well. According to what I read in the QST Magazine, they are saying the right to operate for all ARRL members [American Radio Relay League] could be suspended at any time – over."

Lt. Commander Osaka's first reaction to what he read was to assume these two were part of a re-enactment group. However, as he listened he got an idea. "Break into their conversation and ask them why the government would shut them down."

The radioman gave it some thought for a moment, and then he keyed his mike. "This is Seaman Steve Langley. I don't mean to cut into your conversation, but I heard you say the government might shut us down. Do you know why? And where are you transmitting from – over?" With a shrug in Osaka's direction, he waited for a response along with the curious sailors who looked on.

"This is Paulo, transmitting from *The Big Island*, and I am reading you loud and clear. What do you mean you don't know why? Have you been in a cave the last three years and not heard most of the world is at war? By the way, from the looks of your signal strength and direction, you are broadcasting somewhere in the middle of the Pacific Ocean. Are you on a merchant ship Seaman Steve Langley – over?"

Osaka thought for a moment before he formulated a reply. "Tell him you're on a private yacht in route to Maui while on a one month leave from the Navy, and you are new to operating on this band."

He sent this out and quickly added, "Listening in to guys like you helps break up the monotony of the long trip. Hell, I don't even know what day it is – over."

They all waited, hoping the day was still 24 January 2014.

The other half of the conversation broke in. "This is Reginald Freely broadcasting out of Santa Barbara. I used to be in the

Merchant Marines. I know what boredom is, and if it will help get us back to our conversation, it is 2 PM Pacific Standard Time on December 3, 1941 and we are under a clear sky on a beautiful day – over."

Now the final piece of solid ground fell away from all those present in the CIC. As it turned out, theirs was not the only radio in the task force to find out the fantastic had now become the new reality.

Back on the bridge of the Missouri, Tony was in contact with Lt. Commander Ramis as the Orion circled the task force. "How's your crew holding up?"

"I've got to tell you Sir, none of us are happy. I have parachutes on the crew, but the flight engineer thinks it would be safer if I ditched with everybody still onboard. He thinks the plane will float long after everyone gets off, and I'm inclined to agree with him, Sir."

Tony thought about it for a moment and then asked Sean, "Do you think it's riskier to have an inexperienced crew jump from a plane at two hundred fifty miles an hour than to ditch?"

Sean didn't hesitate. "The pilot knows his crew, let him decide."

"It's your call Commander. If you believe you can bring your plane down safely, give me ten minutes to put the rescue helos in the air. Wait until you hear from me before you ditch. Go ahead and dump your fuel."

Tony contacted the Enterprise and ordered its rescue Seahawks [Sikorsky MH-60S Seahawk multimission helicopter] into the air. Ten minutes later, they watched on the bridge as the Orion began its shallow dive a quarter of a mile off the Missouri's port bow. It slowly glided a hundred feet above the water with the plane perfectly level and in good shape.

As it closed on the water at one hundred and ten miles an hour, the nose of the plane came up, and to everyone's horror, the tail caught a small wave that forced the Orion to pitch over and brought the starboard wing into the water first. Before they could speak a word, the plane began to cartwheel end over end. The starboard wing folded at the root, which sent the props tearing into the fuselage. Seconds later, it was all over, with only flaming wreckage scattered in the water to mark the disaster.

The two Seahawks swooped in, and after they surveyed the wreckage, two divers dropped into the water. The divers hauled two survivors into the helicopter and returned to the Enterprise, while the other stayed on station for another fifteen minutes before it returned empty.

Without a moment to allow the shock of the tragedy to sink in, Sean made contact with Brewster to find out the status of the two survivors. The news came back quickly. "They've got one in critical condition, and another who lost an arm, but they think he'll survive. The crew of the John Paul Jones pulled five bodies from the water, including Lt. Commander Ramis."

Osaka arrived on the bridge and waited for Sean to finish.

"What have you got Commander?"

"Admiral, I know it's a bad time to bring this up, but I have confirmed today's date."

"The mere fact you're bringing up the date Commander, already tells me you're about to make our day worse than it already is."

All the nervous Lt. Commander could manage to spit out was, "3 December 1941."

Sean was silent for a moment, and then shook his head. "Commander, if you're still alive fifty years from now, I hope you remember how you felt when you informed your Admiral his command went down the rabbit hole to arrive in the middle of the Pacific four days before Pearl Harbor."

"Yes Sir, thousands of miles from where we should be."

"I got it."

Ensign Layworth broke in. "Admiral, I have Captain Frederick

Johnson on the cruiser Chancellorsville."

Sean motioned for Osaka to wait, before he took the call from Johnson. "Admiral, we picked up short wave communications between the British Admiralty and the battleship Repulse in the Indian Ocean. Apparently we are in 1941."

"Yes Captain, that appears to be the case. Continue to hold Alpha Whiskey until further notice."

"Yes Sir"

Sean turned to Tony who was just getting off the phone. "Status?"

"All the other ships are underway again, except the Enterprise. Captain Brewster reported it will be another half hour until they are squared away, leaving us the only ship still dead in the water."

"Have all the ship Captains report to my ready room at 1600. I'd like a report from the ship's doctor about Dr. Safire's condition, so make sure you tell him his attendance will be required."

As Sean said this, they felt the rumblings of the ship's turbines as they came back to life, which prompted Captain Folger to call down to engineering.

Before he acted on Sean's orders, Tony asked Alicia, "So Secretary of Defense Calhoun, do you have an opinion about what we should do under these circumstances?"

Alicia had kept her own council over the last hour and a half and her response was short and to the point. "Find a way to get back."

Tony laughed sarcastically. "To do that, don't we first need to figure out how we got here?"

Alicia rolled her eyes. "You're right smart ass, so instead of sarcasm, why don't you do something useful, like, oh I don't know, carry out your Admiral's orders?"

Sean agreed. "After you set up the meeting, go find out if Dr. Cutler needs anything from us. I'm going to wait here until our radar systems are tracking again." Sean would not take any chances until he knew more about the world they had entered and if there were any immediate threats to the safety of his ships and crew.

Moving Again

With intra-ship communications fully restored, Captain Folger finally received a complete report on the Missouri's condition. "All stations have reported in Admiral, with all hands accounted for. Engineering has power to most of the ship's systems, and the mess crew is delivering food and water to the sailors at battle stations." Then to Tony who was heading out he added, "Find my missing XO!"

"I've got my radio if anything happens while I'm gone."

As he left the bridge, Tony realized that regardless of the absurdity of their situation, he was as excited as a little kid. He hadn't felt this alive in years. "What's that say about my life?" he wondered.

Minutes later, he reached the aft hangar and cornered Dr. Cutler. "Can you get Specter up and running again, or not?"

"Who do you think I am, Lex Luthor? I just got power back," Rebecca scolded as she pushed him aside. "The sooner you leave me alone, the sooner I can find out if the mad doctor murdered his own creation."

"Sorry if I seem to be a little rushed for answers Doctor, but we need to figure out what happened." Tony decided to take a different tact. "Look if there is some great power that turned our world upside down, I'd like to know before flying saucers show up and start riddling us with laser beams."

"Sounds like a scene out of War of the Worlds. I love that movie, especially the part where…"

Tony interrupted. "Whoa, slow down. This is important. I need us to prepare for anything Doctor, and if we do run into a threat, without Specter we have one less tool to defend the task force with, so please tell me if you've learned *anything*."

Rebecca stopped and smiled. "As you wish, Captain Anthony Knox, Sir. As soon as we locate and remove any and all of the traps Dr. Safire programmed into the operating system, I can run a series of diagnostic programs to make sure Specter is clean, but that will take a while."

"You may not get the chance to be so thorough. Call me when you're ready to run your test."

As Tony turned to leave, Rebecca had to add, "Scuttlebutt down here says Specter dropped us into the Bermuda Triangle. What's your take Captain?" She didn't give Tony a chance to answer. "On the other hand, maybe aliens picked us up and moved us into the past for their sick entertainment. Did we rip the fabric of time and space, and hurl into an alternate bizarro world, where good is bad and we'll have to prove ourselves worthy to some higher power before we can return to our own dimension?"

Rebecca closed her eyes, clicked her shoes together three times, and slowly opened her eyes. "Anything change?"

"Nice try Doctor. However, I think we need the lion, scarecrow, and tin man here for that to work." Her little performance helped to lighten Tony's mood. "You're going to be fun to have around." Then Tony thought to himself, "Under the circumstances, we could all use Rebecca's off-center perspective."

Tony remembered one last thing. "Dr. Cutler, we're going to have a staff meeting in the Admirals Ready Room at 1600 hours and the Admiral wants you there. I would love to stay here and explore all of the possible absurdities with you, but I have to inform the Senior Staff and the ship's doctor of the meeting." Tony turned to walk away again, but had another thought. "And Rebecca, while you're there it would be wise if you kept your more extreme theories to yourself."

"I already do. You'd really be freaked out if you knew some of the other possibilities rattling around in my brain."

"Heaven help us."

Tony arrived back on the bridge at the same time the Yeoman Sean sent to get Senator Boyle reported. "Sir, the Senator isn't in his room, or anywhere else I could think to look. No one, including the Corpsman who treated him, saw him leave his cabin."

"He's probably in the head puking his guts out." Tony grabbed the mike to the ship's intercom. "Attention Senator Boyle, please report to the bridge. If anyone has seen Senator Boyle, contact the bridge." Tony imagined the prick fell overboard during the storm, and though the thought pleased him, unfortunately, he was responsible for his safety.

Sean turned to Alicia. "I want you and Renée to accompany Tony and me on an inspection of the crew before the other Captains arrive." Sean wanted to let the crew know they were in control and not in any immediate danger, a tall order considering how little they knew.

Sean turned to Commander Eddington who had finally surfaced. "Report."

"Sickbay has tended to twenty-seven sailors who had severe burns from the electrical overload discharges. Dr. Safire's tirades in Sickbay added to the confusion. It took some time to convince members of the crew that we have everything under control."

"Thank you, Commander. Let's hope that we don't make a liar out of you. Go greet the ship Captains when they arrive and show them to my ready room."

With nothing else to plan for now, the four left the bridge to inspect the crew.

As they toured the 70-year-old battleship, Sean could see in the faces of the sailors he came upon that they expected him to return them safely home. He could also feel the fear beneath the bravado and knew there would be little room for error in the decisions he and his senior officers made. He resolved that whatever befell the task force, he would not sugar coat the truth. They had heard enough lies in their young lives already.

Sean stopped for a moment when the reality hit him that their chain of command no longer existed. While no one could challenge his command of the group, there was the complication of his civilian boss, Secretary of Defense Alicia Calhoun. There could be confusion about who should be in overall command of the task force. With this in mind, he pulled her aside.

"I think we should have a talk before we meet with the senior staff.

"Excuse us Tony, Alicia and I are going to my cabin. You two finish inspecting the crew. Make sure you're back in time for the meeting at 1600."

When Sean and Alicia left, Tony and Renée looked at each other.

"So who are you betting winds up on top?" Renée joked.

"As much as I respect Alicia, there's no way Sean allows anyone to interfere with his command while at sea, especially under such extreme conditions."

"She is his civilian boss. What's the matter? Are you afraid of a woman giving you orders?" Renée teased, though she knew Tony only cared about whether the person who gave the commands was capable.

When Sean was alone with Alicia, he asked in a conciliatory voice, "How do you want to handle the command situation?"

She smiled at the smoothness of his deferential question. After years of knowing Sean, she had already prepared her response. "It's obvious we're in literally uncharted waters, and I can't think of any person better than you to guide us through. Therefore, if you don't mind, I'll be your silent partner while we're at sea. However, if we have entered either a parallel universe or just as miraculously traveled back in time, when we meet with civilian authorities, I assume political command, agreed?"

The leap Alicia made in her interpretation of their situation impressed Sean. "Agreed. However, if Specter was responsible, we should be able to duplicate the conditions, and we won't need to worry about command issues. Then again, if some mystical force whisked us through a portal in time, I realize it might be impossible to replicate that. There may be too many variables and not enough data. We may not have any control over whether or not we remain stuck in this nightmare."

"You're telling me. The thought of living out my life in an era where women were expected to be baby-making machines doesn't exactly excite me."

Sean couldn't resist. "You forget you hold more power under your command than this era in its entirety. You might become the voice for radical change!"

Sean figured if they were stuck here, thank God he had Alicia with him. Regardless of how much time they had spent apart, their connection had grown strong over the years. They were a perfect fit and complimented each other on every level. Their partnership set them up to share responsibility over the now isolated seven thousand plus members of the task force as patriarch and matriarch. This combined with their unresolved sexual undercurrents, could be construed as proof, that if God was responsible for their situation, It had a very strange sense of humor.

A message from Captain Brewster interrupted them. He requested postponement of his arrival on the Missouri until his ship was underway, which Sean granted. He needed the Enterprise to be able to launch her aircraft and begin an air search of the surrounding seas as soon as possible. Although they were over a thousand miles away from land, having the center of his task force dead in the water would make any Admiral nervous.

Tony arrived with Renée five minutes before the meeting, to find the rest of the senior staff already seated in conversation with Sean.

"Good morning. Did I miss out on the donuts?" Tony quipped.

Captain Mark Daily of the attack submarine Seawolf tossed Tony a Danish. "I wouldn't want to see the master planner going hungry. We were giving the Admiral a rundown on how our crews are holding up."

"The consensus among the ship Captains," Sean added, "is the sailors need to be busy within the normal routine of shipboard life rather than have time on their hands to worry about what happened to them. This won't last long if we don't redirect their energy. The loss of the Orion crew so soon after our displacement has surely added to their trauma."

Captain Jonson of the Chancellorsville handed Sean a report. "Here are the intercepts we picked up confirming what we already knew."

Commander Regis Goddard of the destroyer John Paul Jones and Captain Gordon Lincoln of the cruiser Princeton added their findings and the meeting began in earnest.

"There hasn't been any commercial air traffic on the ship's radar or any sign there is a network of satellites in orbit. For that matter, we haven't picked up shipping anywhere near our current location to support normalcy." Sean put the papers down and motioned to the ship's doctor. "Any hope of getting anything coherent out of Dr. Safire?"

"I'm not a psychiatrist, Admiral, but based on what I see, I'd say he doesn't have any comprehension of his surroundings or what he did. I believe he had a complete psychotic breakdown."

"Thank you for your efforts. Keep me informed if there are any changes.

"Dr. Cutler, please bring us up to date on Specter's status."

"Do you want me to stand, or is it all right if I stay in my seat? I don't mind either way, whichever is groovy with you." Rebecca was not used to the attention coming from a roomful of uniformed warriors while wearing her pleated miniskirt, accented with knee-high boots. Fortunately, she had the common sense to wear her lab coat over what the men could only guess was underneath.

"Whatever makes you comfortable Dr. Cutler."

"Out of sight. Okay, what I can tell you so far is Safire accessed a secondary program to disable the surge protectors. We managed a shutdown before we fried Specter's circuits, but I still do not have any idea what else the little maniac has buried in the software. He designed it, and with so many assistants working on the project over the years, it will be impossible for me to know exactly where to look."

"Are you saying we will not have the use of Specter's cover?"

"No, I am saying when I turn it back on, I can't be sure there aren't any other surprises lurking in the programming that will come leaping out like the Joker to create more mayhem. However, if we monitor the systems 24/7, I'm pretty sure we'll be able to isolate these without any further damage to your ships."

"Thank you Dr. Cutler."

Sean stood up and addressed everyone in a calm voice. "We have to come up with a logical reason why we are no longer where or when we should be. I might have a few ideas, but I want to hear from all of you first."

"If we are to work with the theory we traveled back along our own time line, then a paradox comes to mind. If I were to run into my father, would I still be born, and if I'm never born how can I be here in the first place?" Captain Daily began, obviously thinking along classic modern theories about the Quantum Physics of traveling back in time. "There is also the theory that if you added matter to an existing dimension, it could act as antimatter and cancel the whole dimension out of existence. Seeing as we're still here, my vote says we are no longer in our own dimension."

Captain Marlowe Turner of the attack submarine Hampton added to the discussion. "There's the theory of multiple dimensions, where we could still be occupying the same space and time, and we somehow opened a door to another parallel universe or parallel reality. However, I'm not sure if that theory is compatible with our case, because wouldn't the time line be the same, instead of running behind the one we came out of?"

Regardless of Tony's warning, Rebecca couldn't help herself. "I'm partial to the idea there are visitors from some far-off galaxy, who recognized the trouble our world is in. Maybe they decided to give us a do over and plopped us here to see if we could fix the future."

For all her brilliance, it was obvious she had an imagination to match. "There is scientific research that postulates you could time travel through wormholes and they might exist right here on earth. I read a book that hypothesized this is what takes place in the Bermuda Triangle, which would go a long way to explain all the mysterious disappearances."

Sean smiled at Rebecca's enthusiasm, but needed to get back on track. "Considering there isn't any evidence to confirm a definitive reason for our situation, for now let's assume Dr. Safire set off a series of events that created a bridge from our dimension to this one. If this is correct, there shouldn't be any adverse effects created by our presence or from our taking action now that we are a part of it. On the other hand, if we went back along our own timeline, then there could be serious repercussions if we interact with it. Adding to the mystery is the disappearance of Senator Boyle. Did he fall overboard during the storm while seasick, or did he stay in 2014?

"The bottom line is we are sitting 1200 miles southeast of Pearl Harbor, 4 days before the Japanese attack. We swore an oath to protect the United States against such aggression, and considering our current reality, I propose to do just that." Sean gauged the expressions of the staff, as they absorbed the import of this bold plan. From the looks of their reactions, he knew they could be convinced.

Tony remained quiet. He knew from experience, there were many who thought his relationship with Sean was too cozy.

However, Lt. Commander James Peck, Captain of the fleet oiler USNS Laramie, was willing. "Considering our choices are limited, and we can't sit here in the middle of the ocean rusting, what about contacting Pearl to establish chain of command with the Pacific Fleet?"

"The problem with your idea Jim is no one from this generation understands the power we can project, or how to direct it. The Enterprise alone has both tactical and strategic nuclear weapons capable of leveling cities. Do you want these in the hands of people without the knowledge of their seventy year history?" Sean wouldn't turn control of his ships over to anyone from outside the group until he understood exactly what they were dealing with.

"So who do we answer to?" This question came from Commander Andy Gable, Captain of the cargo ship USNS Amelia Earhart. "We can't roam the world's oceans until we run out of fuel and supplies. We are going to need to be resupplied from somewhere."

Tony quickly forgot about staying on the sidelines. "I for one would much rather figure out if we could get back to our own time, than plan for actions in this era. However, since we can't just sit still, why not set a course for Hawaii? Hell, it's two days away, and by then maybe we'll find out it's as simple as clicking our heels three times, returning home, and spending the rest of our lives denying this ever happened."

"I'm not comfortable playing God. Who's to say if we interfere with the past, there might not be a future at all? In some twisted way we might be the harbingers of the apocalypse set out in the Book of Revelations." No one was surprised this note of doom came from Captain Frederick Johnson of the cruiser Chancellorsville, who, though not as fanatical as Captain Brewster, possessed a streak of that good old time religion.

Captain Folger warmed to the absurdities bantered about, as the group enjoyed the metaphysical aspects of their situation. "Who's to say God's hand isn't in this? If you follow that thought, in his wisdom we might be his choice as the best chance for the salvation of humanity. If you think about it Fred, isn't everything in his hands to begin with, including our being here? If I understand the tenets of your faith correctly, all this has to be in your God's plan."

"Enough. None of this is getting us anywhere." Once again, Sean had to get everyone to focus. "We don't have time for this. If I don't give our crews something to go on, it won't be long before discipline breaks down."

Sean's experience in the Navy taught him senior officers had to have the confidence of their sailors. In their current uncharted waters, he couldn't show the slightest indecision. They had deployed only two days ago with mostly raw sailors, so this didn't give Sean much time to find a way to minimize the shocking reality that they may be separated from their families forever.

Sean took control. "We will need an attack plan as soon as possible Tony. Get together with Commander Peck and compute maximum range with the fuel we have on hand. I want the cruisers and destroyers topped off on the 5th, starting at 1200.

"Andy, supply the ship Captains with anything they will need in case we do go into combat."

Tony was thinking armament. "The bottom line is once we fire a weapon, there won't be any replacements, except for the 16-inch and 5-inch guns of the Missouri. We can minimize the use of our missiles by planning around the 16-inch shells of this ship, in combination with the cast iron bombs on the Enterprise. Add Specter's protection and we can combine the old with the new to conserve our missiles."

"That makes sense," Sean acknowledged.

Sean wanted to make sure the senior staff got a crash refresher course on the war in the Pacific before they planned any further. "I think we should access as much historical data as possible about the Japanese attack on Pearl Harbor, including the exact time and location of their launch. The fleet's computers should provide us with most of what we need. I also think we should gather any useful historical information from the personal computers of the crew. We can use the servers on the Enterprise to compile the information."

Sean thought of the perfect candidate he should delegate this to. "Secretary Calhoun, would you mind if I sent Captain Aslan over to the Enterprise to coordinate this job?"

"I'm sure she would be of more use to the fleet than me under the circumstances," Alicia agreed. "I'm not much use aboard the Missouri either, so why don't I go over to the Enterprise and brush up on the civilian and command personnel on the American side of the conflict. That way when we establish contact, we're talking to the right people."

"If you don't mind, I think it would be better if you to remained here. Under these queer conditions, I'd prefer you stayed close. I could use your council over the coming days." Sean's mind began to consider the consequences of their plan if they had truly traveled back along the same timeline. Besides, he was comfortable having her around.

"You're right, but I need a place to work."

Sean turned to Rebecca. "Is it possible to set up a workstation here for Secretary Calhoun Dr. Cutler?"

"No problem. I'll send a technician from aft to set it up. Do you guys want videoconferencing to go with it?"

"Whatever you think we will need. However, I need you to get Specter operational as *your* priority."

Tony was none too happy to lose Renée's company so soon after reconnecting, but rank has its privileges. However, he quickly let it go when he thought about Osaka's fascination with cryptology. "I think it would be a good idea if you sent Commander Osaka with her. His off duty hobby deals with the history of the codebreakers and the formulas they used."

Sean shook his head in approval. "Whatever you need Tony."

He then noticed Dr. Rebecca Cutler looked worried. "You have a concern?"

"Yes I do. Has anyone considered a different course of action other than an attack on the Japanese fleet?"

This killed all conversation in the room as everyone turned and waited for her to explain.

"Wouldn't it be more humane if we appeared in front of their fleet, and launched a missile at one of their destroyers and then disappeared? We have enough firepower to scare the hell out of them. It should freak them out enough to turn away.

I for one would rather no one dies. I mean what if we don't have to kill thousands of Japanese sailors if we don't have to."

Alicia held her arm out to stop Sean. "That would work in a perfect world Dr. Cutler. However, we are now dealing with a world absorbed with nationalistic fanaticism. In Germany, Russia, Italy, and Japan, all the people who would listen to our attempts at moderation are either already dead, forced into concentration camps, or gulags.

"At this point in history, Japan had already invaded China, and the United States stood by while Hitler conquered all of Western Europe. They were so emboldened by our apathy that after Japan attacked Pearl Harbor, they demanded the United States cede control of all Asian waters to them.

"In Europe, Hitler's response to United States peace overtures was to mock Roosevelt publicly in front of his Reich staff as too weak to challenge Germany. The American President had his hands tied by a country of isolationists determined not to become involved in another European war so soon after bailing them out in WWI.

"The world of 1941 was not a place for dialogue. Joseph Stalin, Adolf Hitler, Benito Mussolini, and Hideki Tojo were leaders who looked only to expand their power by force of arms, and it did not matter to them how many died to achieve their goals.

"After years of appeasement, the Axis powers believed the United States lacked the will to counter their aggression. In 1941, the United States military strength was that of a third world country, so the sudden appearance of one superior force wouldn't change a thing." After she finished, Alicia motioned for Sean to continue.

Moving Again

Sean wanted to wrap things up. "Assure your crews all efforts are being made to figure out how to return home. I'm heading over to the Enterprise to set Renée and Osaka up with Captain Brewster. If you don't have any more questions, let's get to work." The tone of Sean's voice made it clear there wouldn't be any further questions, and the Captains returned to their ships.

Tony walked with Sean to the Seahawk helicopter that would take them over to the Enterprise. "Are you sure Osaka needs Renée's help?"

Sean responded with laughter at his friend's disappointment. "Maybe the next time you're on a beach alone with her, you'll say something to make her believe she means more to you than a weekend."

"You're a cruel man Admiral Sean Phillips, and may I add, at least I remember that weekend on the beach."

Tony snapped to attention and saluted, smiling at the dour expression his jab left on Sean's face. "Admiral."

The Seahawk took only minutes to reach the still stationary aircraft carrier. Anxious over his ship's vulnerability, Captain Brewster stood waiting as Sean stepped onto the flight deck. After he briefed the Admiral about the condition of the Enterprise, they headed to the Admirals Quarters high up on the carrier's island. When they got there, Sean relayed what Captain Brewster missed in the staff meeting.

"No offense Admiral, but we don't have the right to affect history by taking military action."

Sean expected this reaction. "Steve, short of having the intellect of a Stephen Hawking to provide us council, our options are limited. Would you have us sink the group with all hands onboard? Because barring this, our mere presence changes the future."

"Admiral, it's not the timeline examples I'm worried about. If you believe in God's plan as I do, you would see our situation does not fit. This leads me to believe our meddling could be the work of something more sinister." There it was. In Captain Steven Brewster's narrow born-again mind, their situation was the work of the Devil.

"I won't get into a theological debate about the pros and cons of whether God or the Devil or a leprechaun guarding his hoard of gold at the end of a rainbow had a hand in sending over two hundred thousand tons of mass and seven thousand people from one time and place to another. My responsibilities lie with the men and women who have to struggle with *this* reality. Sitting in the middle of the Pacific Ocean pondering God's role in it is certainly not an option. When we are able to launch reconnaissance flights, I will base our role in any future actions on what they find. In the meantime, Captain Aslan and Commander Osaka will be attached to your ship to research the best ways to use this group."

The Admirals Ready Room phone rang. Sean answered it, and then handed the phone to Captain Brewster. "It's for you."

After he listened for a minute, Brewster acknowledged and hung up. "They've got the reactors operational Admiral. We can be underway again in half an hour."

"Good. As soon as you become operational, Alpha Whiskey will launch four Specter cloaked F-35s to and a CAP [Combat Air Patrol] of two F/A-18s to screen the task force within the cleared area.

"I'm going to stay onboard the Big E until we have reconnaissance confirm we are clear of contacts at for at least a two hundred mile perimeter. Until we can get visual contact to confirm radio intercepts, we are only dealing with conjecture anyway.

"I will address the group about my intentions as soon as there is confirmation as to where we are. Go ahead and return to the bridge Captain and inform Captain Knox when you will be getting underway."

"Yes, Admiral."

After Captain Brewster left, Sean thought of the opportunity they might have to change the disastrous results of the last seven plus decades, if in fact they were stuck having to relive it. The Constitutional interpretations by the United States Supreme Court over the last seventy years had not been healthy for the Republic. From the impact of religious fundamentalism that quashed individual liberties, to the absolute corruption of the Federal Government, individual freedoms had become a distant memory in America society.

Sean had dreamed many times of the ways he could change the course of the dystopia they had lived under for too long. "What the hell, I might wake up any minute, so I might as well enjoy dreaming of a better world."

Sean picked up the phone and called the CIC. "Have the task force stand down from battle stations, but keep everyone on ready alert."

Dr. Rebecca Cutler returned to the hangar on the Missouri in time to find Dr. Phelps had finished with the diagnostic tests on Specter's program. "How's it hanging Forrest? Have you found anything?"

"Following your suggestions I found and removed several anomalies, though I can't see how any of them rose to the level to create what happened."

As she reviewed the mountain of printouts in front of her, Rebecca smiled. "I appreciate your abilities, but I can see we still have a lot to do."

For the next two hours, they ran further tests and when they finished, she still wasn't convinced. "Forrest, my Spidy senses are tingling, which tells me there is still venom buried deep in this programming."

"I don't see how you hope to make enough headway without the supercomputer at Comstock to help. There is too much coding. Heck, to go over the interface between the ships alone will take weeks."

After spending most of her time with dinosaurs like Dr. Safire who were clueless who the Black Rebel Motorcycle Club is, Forrest's youth was a breath of fresh air. For what he lacked in charm and good looks, he more than made up with his knowledge of obscure references he threw out at random times, like now.

"You know if we arrived on Jupiter in time and space instead of here, its atmosphere would have crushed us to paste, and we wouldn't be worried about anything right now."

Rebecca totally missed Phelps last comments. She was stuck on his opinion that it would take weeks. "Forrest, you're brilliant. I can say with almost total certainty that Dr. Safire's ego wouldn't allow him to put in a program he couldn't personally control. I have to call Captain Tony."

After Tony listened to her, though he still had concerns he agreed with the assessment. "Removing Dr. Safire's access ensures he can't affect Specter's operation, but does nothing to convince me Specter itself didn't send us here. Honestly Dr. Cutler, does Specter have any properties that can rearrange reality?"

"Nope. Not one that I'm aware of, and if I'm not aware of one, neither is any other scientist on this planet. Yet on the other hand, it is cutting edge technology and might be capable of bending more than light waves."

Tony knew he was going to regret it, but had to ask, "And what does that mean?"

"Think about it Tony, the universe is almost 14 billion years old, yet we only got out of our caves 10,000 years ago. We are just now beginning to consider the idea there may be thousands of other dimensions besides our own in the galaxy. Now think about an alien civilization that has been around for let's say 1 million years would know. Science has already determined that intergalactic space travel is impractical considering the vast distances..."

In what was quickly becoming a habit, Tony interrupted her.

"Rebecca, please."

"It's possible Specter opened a door to one of these dimensions."

"Thank you. I'll inform the Admiral, and thank you and your staff for the quick response. The Enterprise is about to get underway, and I'm sure the first thing the Admiral will want to do is reactivate Specter. I'll call you after I get confirmation."

"I will rotate monitoring Specter with Dr. Phelps and only Dr. Phelps. So please make sure we are left alone if you want me to guarantee Specter won't be sending us off to somewhere like Jupiter." Rebecca winked at Forrest as she said this.

"No problem. I've posted Marines here and around the electromagnetic generators on the other ships, but you need to inform me before you let anyone else near Specter's operating console. That's all for now, and thanks again."

As he put the phone down, Tony thought about what Sean's ultimate objective would be when the task force returned to full operational capability. The need to plan tactical operations against 1940s technology had its own set of issues. The one he worried the most about was the intractable reality there wouldn't be any way to replenish their 21st Century weapons systems. They would need the support of the United States Government to stay at sea, and how Sean and Alicia planned to make this happen should add many complications to their adventure. One thing for sure, they would have to deal with the fears and suspicions their presence would evoke.

With this on his mind, Tony sat down to plan how to destroy the six Japanese carriers under the command of Vice Admiral Chuichi Nagumo. After six hours, he decided to take a break, and headed to the Admirals Ready Room to visit Alicia to see what progress she had made.

When he arrived, she was so busy working on a list of questions for Renée to research that she didn't look up. "Come in Tony."

Tony waited until she looked up before he spoke. "The Enterprise will be underway in the next ten minutes, and they'll be launching the F-35s and F/A-18s. I know that in the meeting Sean sounded pretty serious about setting a course to Pearl, but do you really believe he intends to engage the Japanese?"

"I talked to him a few minutes ago. He is asking some esoteric questions a millennium's worth of theologians and philosophers couldn't come up with acceptable answers to. We on the other hand have less than three days to justify to over seven thousand sailors that we have picked the right ones."

Tony chuckled. "All I know is I certainly don't have the balls to make such a monumental decision."

Just then, the phone rang. "Do you mind?"

"Go ahead Tony."

"This is Captain Knox. —Yes I'll relay the news to the Secretary." Tony hung up the phone. "The Enterprise is underway, the CAP is up, and Sean has ordered the task force on a course northwest. Hawaii it is. It looks like the time for worrying about the what-ifs has come to an end."

"Amen to that," Alicia added.

"I better get back to the bridge."

"Cheer up Tony. It could be much worse."

"Like how?"

Alicia laughed. "We could have been sent into a future where someone like Donald Trump became president."

"Now you're just being silly."

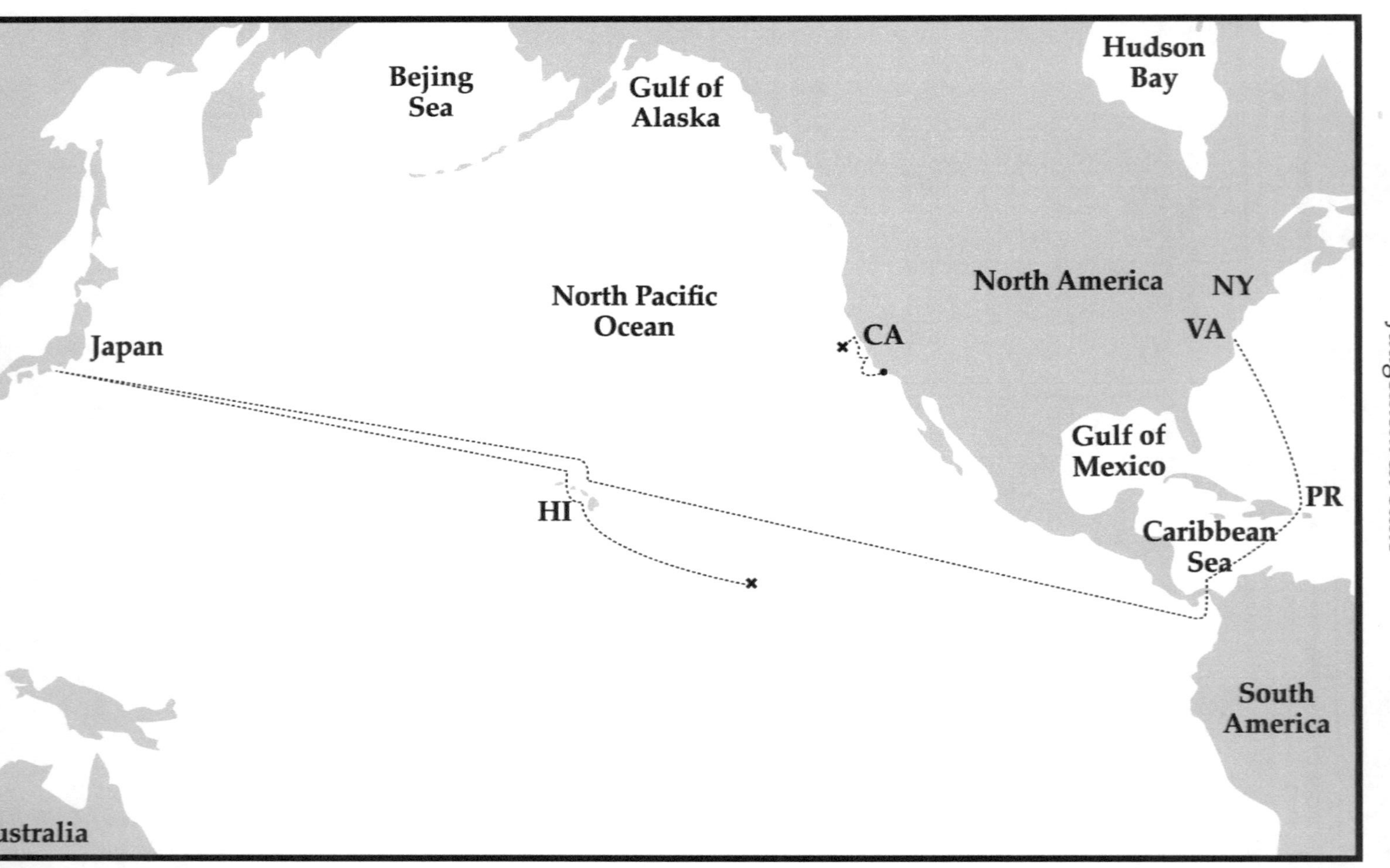

Hudson Bay
Bejing Sea
Gulf of Alaska
North America
NY
VA
North Pacific Ocean
CA
Japan
Gulf of Mexico
PR
Caribbean Sea
HI
South America
Australia

Chapter Three

The Voice

Armed with a fresh cup of scalding coffee, Sean watched the first F-35 Lightning catapult off the deck of the carrier. As it made a 180 degree turn to the southeast he smiled, satisfied they could finally use their full capabilities. Captain Brewster stood alongside him, and always with the wrong thing to say, asked, "Didn't you used to date Secretary Calhoun?"

"No Captain. The Secretary and I have never been a couple. We shared assignments at the Pentagon, where I discovered she possessed one of the sharpest minds I have ever known." Sean paused, turned, and with his face only inches from Brewster's, stiffly demanded, "And why is my personal relationship with Secretary Calhoun of any interest to you?"

Brewster almost tripped trying to back away. "Nothing personal meant by it Sir. But under the circumstances, don't you think having a civilian in charge might be asking too much?"

"Is it because she's a civilian, or is your concern she's a woman and one of my best friends. You seem to forget, Captain, that Alicia Calhoun is a retired Rear Admiral who served twenty-one years in this Navy with distinction, and then became one of the most powerful political women in the country."

"I haven't forgotten Admiral. The reason I bring it up is her lack of combat experience while she served those twenty-one years. You know as well as I do that she spent most of her command years posted to the diplomatic corps, and has only limited blue water experience."

Sean thought to himself, "How did this guy ever get command of a carrier?" He then remembered Brewster's family connections to the former administration. Those ties enabled Captain Brewster to skip over more deserving officers more than once during his undistinguished career. The idea that you rewarded friends and family with the spoils of victory were part of the political process since the days Phoenician warships ruled the Aegean Seas.

As if being a mediocre Commander wasn't bad enough, his moral certitude that he was an instrument of God's will made him a pain in the ass to deal with. This fit into the era's swing to political control by the fundamentalist right, represented most notably by the wingnuts of the Tea Party who claimed anyone to the left of David Duke was a Socialist out to rape your daughters. When Sean found out Brewster was the Captain of the Enterprise, he spoke with a friend at the Pentagon who told him that because of Brewster's lackluster performance evaluations and his political and religious extremism, his retirement would coincide with the decommissioning of the Enterprise.

Figuring nothing he said mattered anyway; Sean decided to speak frankly. "I'll be honest with you Steve. I don't like the way you pressure those under your command to mirror your fire and brimstone fanaticism. I have noticed you flavor all of your personnel assessments based on whether or not those under you share those views. I also don't want a Captain under my command who delivers sermons from the bridge. That ends now. Though you have every right to your beliefs, they belong in the ship's chapel, not on the bridge."

"I see nothing wrong with using my moral compass to assess those under my command. In case you haven't noticed Admiral, there is real evil in this world."

"That's just your excuse, Steve. I think the loss of man's dominance over the fairer sex threatens you, and you long for the day when women were barefoot and pregnant in the kitchen and rape meant she really wanted it. You made this clear early in your career when the female Lieutenant under your command filed sexual harassment charges after you pinned her down. If this had happened in today's Navy, you would have spent the rest of your career in the brig, not in command of a carrier. However, because of your connections you were never charged, while the Lieutenant was forced out of the Navy."

"Seeing as we're laying the cards on the table Admiral, is it your intention to use the power of our task force to secularize the world? Could it be you resent the fact your secular views haven't exactly advanced your career?"

Sean answered with disdain. "Because I believe ideologues like you shouldn't be allowed to strong arm an entire society into your medieval moralities, means it would be hypocritical of me to use the same methods to convince anyone you're wrong. I prefer to stick with facts to make my case. Such as when a woman makes it clear she is not interested in me, I don't take that as license to ruin her life."

"At least I have the certainty of my salvation," was all Brewster offered in rebuttal.

"Well, I'm happy for you Steve." Sean would have preferred to finish with this thought, "And if you're in such a hurry for salvation, why don't you jump overboard and leave the rest of us alone."

In reality, he was through wasting his time talking to an empty head. As irritated as he was by the conversation, it did give Sean pause to consider the fate of the task force if something should happen to Alicia, Tony, Captain Mark Daily, and him with Captain

Brewster next in the chain of command.

"If you can spare him, I'd like Commander Barrish to accompany me on an inspection of the ship's crew." Sean realized he better find out if Brewster's XO shared the same stunted view of the world.

"It's your prerogative if you want him to accompany you Admiral. I'll make the announcement to the ship's personnel to stand ready for inspection."

"That won't be necessary Steve. I need to get a feel for how the crew is holding up. Let me know as soon as the F-35s report."

With Commander Logan Barrish by his side, Sean exited the bridge. Sean remained quiet as they worked their way through the belowdecks maze on the Enterprise. Years removed from carrier duty, even a seasoned veteran such as Sean could experience trouble orienting belowdecks, where sometimes the quickest way to go up involved the need to go down. Coded messages on the bulkheads showed deck and ship orientation that once memorized were the roadways and alleys of this floating city of five thousand.

They made their way through, sailors struck crisp salutes, each dying to ask the Admiral what he knew. However, their discipline kept them quiet, except for one seasoned sailor who understood their current situation might allow for a breach of protocol.

"Admiral, I know I'm out of line, but the boys and I were wondering if you've been able to figure out what happened, and if you're going to be able to get us back home."

Commander Barrish read the name on the sailor's uniform. "You are out of line, Seaman Lupoli."

Sean decided to answer the sailor. "That's all right Commander. Where are you from sailor? Sounds like New Jersey to me."

"I was raised in Hoboken, New Jersey to be exact Sir. So what gives? I don't mind telling you I'm not scared of much, but I sure am getting a little, let's just say, *concerned* about what's going to happen to us."

"All I can tell you for now, Seaman Lupoli, is everyone is working hard to find a way to get us back home. In the meantime, perform your duties as if yours or your shipmate's lives depended on it. Under these bizarre conditions, I have the added responsibility to keep all of the sailors of this task force informed. All I ask in return from you is to trust the orders you are given. Now carry on." With Commander Logan Barrish in tow, he continued toward the CIC.

"Sorry to countermand your order Commander, but if you pick your spots well, it never hurts to give your crew assurances. Especially now, if it helps to take away some of their fear of the unknown. This ship will soon have a thousand versions of what I said to Seaman Lupoli. Hopefully the terms, trust, duty, and standing with your shipmate is what sticks."

"Yes Sir. But you should know Captain Brewster runs a tight ship and he doesn't appreciate sailors who talk out of rank," the Commander added reluctantly.

"In other words, Captain Brewster doesn't understand that without the support of the lower decks, this massive warship couldn't leave port. As a commander you need to respect the talents every sailor has to offer."

"Yes Sir," Commander Barrish acknowledged.

When they entered the CIC, the CIC Officer reported to Sean. "Alpha Whiskey reports one of the cloaked F-35s has spotted a contact two hundred twenty miles southwest of our position."

"Put the F-35 pilot on the overhead."

"Aye Aye Admiral"

The excited pilot's voice exploded over the speakers. "She's a cargo carrier riding low in the water, making roughly ten knots, and looks to be 2,000 to 3,000 tons. This ship looks like they built it a hundred years ago. She's got loading cranes fore and aft without a capacity to carry containers. I'm passing her stern now. The name on the stern is Lake Glaucus, and she's flagged with the Stars and Stripes."

The conversation level in the CIC rose in excitement with the news, forcing Commander Barrish to bring order. "Quiet down and focus on your jobs." His command quickly silenced the room.

Sean knew the Lake Glaucus was not from 2014, simply because there were few commercial ships still flagged under United States registry.

This was quickly confirmed when Renée checked the historical database and reported. "Sir, the Lake Glaucus was built in the Duluth Superior shipyards in 1918 for use in World War One, and later sold into commercial service. According to the registry, she was renamed the Norlindo in February 1942 and served in the Atlantic until her sinking by the U-507 on May 4, 1942. The U-boat fired a single torpedo causing the 2,700 ton ship to sink stern first in three minutes, leaving no survivors."

"Thank you Captain Aslan," Sean acknowledged before returning to the CIC Officer.

"Have Alpha Whiskey expand the search radius to two hundred and fifty miles, and then get me Captain Knox on the Missouri."

"Aye Aye Admiral."

After he filled Tony in on the contact with the Lake Glaucus, Sean figured now would be a good time to put into action some changes that he felt were necessary. "I'm transferring to the Enterprise, and as my Chief of Staff you're coming with me, along with Captain Folger."

"You want Charles to take command of the Enterprise?" Tony asked.

"I can't command the battle group as effectively from the Missouri, and I need my most experienced carrier Captain in command of the ship. I will transfer Captain Brewster to the Missouri."

"Have you told him this? Because if you did, I'm sorry I wasn't there to hear his reaction" Tony was thrilled with Brewster's demotion.

Sean ignored Tony's question. "Inform Commander Eddington

and be ready within the next hour. I also want Alicia to come over with you, so get going."

He then addressed the CIC Officer. "Order Captain Brewster to the Admirals Ready Room and have two Marines there as well."

"Aye Aye Admiral."

When Brewster arrived he found Sean seated at the conference table with the two Marines standing behind him.

Sean knew there wouldn't be any way to assuage Brewster's ego, so he didn't bother to sugarcoat the news. "I'm transferring my flag to the Enterprise, and because of the uncertain nature of our circumstances, I've ordered Captain Charles Folger to assume command of the Enterprise. You will take command of the Missouri for the immediate future, with Commander Carl Eddington remaining on the Missouri as your XO."

"I'm sorry Admiral, but you don't have the authority to make that decision. Besides the uncertainty of our situation, as you call it, is exactly why you should not. Captain Folger hasn't been in command of a carrier for over two years, and he knows nothing of my crew."

"Be that as it may Steve, but Captain Folger and I have served together for years, and I already know how he'll react in an emergency. Based on what I have witnessed of your style of command, I don't have the same confidence in you. We don't have the luxury of waiting to see how you will measure up. You have your orders, but if you feel I lack the authority, Secretary of Defense Alicia Calhoun, who I am sure you agree does, will be aboard within the next hour. Feel free to bring up your objection with her."

"Knowing your relationship with Secretary Calhoun, I'll pass. But I will say you're making a big mistake, and when we return to San Diego, I'll make sure you pay for this slight."

"Believe me Captain, if we do find a way to return, you might want to be more concerned about yourself, because I'm sure our government will make every one of our lives miserable.

Sean was through with this conversation. "Listen Steve, our reality right now is difficult enough without trying to explain the facts of life to you, so do us all a favor and get your ass over to the Missouri before I decide to strip you of all command. Try to remember the oath you swore as an officer in the United States Navy."

Without any recourse and seeing the looks on the faces of the two Marines, Captain Brewster stormed off without waiting for Sean to dismiss him.

Sean took a few minutes to get the bad taste out of his mouth before he called Tony. "Brewster didn't take the news well, and with the major elements of Specter's operating system aboard the Missouri, I want you to inform Commander Eddington to report to you anytime Brewster goes near it. Also, remind Dr. Cutler she is fully in charge of Specter and will report directly to me, not Brewster. Further, order the Master-at-Arms to back Dr. Cutler fully and to ignore any orders not coming from you or me."

"You think he's pissed off enough to sabotage his only way to get back home? It seems counterproductive if his plan is to see you court-martialed." Tony thought for a moment and joked, "Under our current situation he'd have to wait another seventy-five years for time to catch up to do so."

"It would be shortsighted of me to believe a high ranking member of my command with radical religious views couldn't be a threat," Sean stated. "After Safire's breakdown, I don't want to find out at the wrong time Brewster would put his personal agenda ahead of the safety of the task force."

An hour and a half later Alicia, Tony, and Captain Folger boarded the Enterprise. After a small ceremony on deck where command of the Enterprise transferred to Captain Charles Folger, Brewster boarded a Seahawk for the ride to his new command. Commander

Barrish accompanied Tony, Charles, and Sean to the ship's bridge, while Alicia went to join Renée and Commander Osaka in the CIC.

When they reached the bridge, Sean addressed Commander Logan Barrish. "Bring Captain Folger up to speed on the ship's operational status."

"Yes Sir."

This suited Charles fine, as it would give him time to meet with his senior staff. He needed them to know what he expected of them while serving under his command. After he listened for a while to the communications between the carrier and the reconnaissance flights, he began to feel at home on the bridge of the 100,000-ton floating airfield.

"Captain Knox, see to the transfer of the Admiral's Staff to the Enterprise and make sure I'm not interrupted for the next two hours. I am headed to the Admirals Quarters to get some rest before I figure out what I want to say when I address the sailors about our situation."

"Aye Aye Admiral," Tony acknowledged.

The next morning 4 December 1941, from the Admirals Ready Room on the Enterprise, Sean called Rebecca on the Missouri. "Have you figured out how long before you can safely reactivate Specter?"

"I don't know about you Admiral, but I'm a little worried. If we do, who's to say we won't wind up in the Jurassic period fighting off Pterodactyls?"

Her answer wasn't what Sean wanted to hear. "I understand your scientific mind doesn't want to let go that Specter was somehow involved in our misfortune without understanding how, but I need to get my ships out of sight."

Rebecca thought about it for a moment. "I don't know why I didn't think about it before. I'm *sooo* stupid. Because the Princeton's operating system is isolated, the answer is obvious. I'm so stupid for not…"

Sean didn't have time for this. "Dr. Cutler, could you please skip to the part where you explain what you want to do?"

"I'm sorry Admiral, I get carried away sometimes. Anyway, because the Princeton's Specter system is autonomous I can use it as a guinea pig. This way if anything goes wrong, they would be the only ones who go God knows where. If you don't mind taking the chance, I could get her revved up lickety-split. If after half an hour they're still around, and there aren't any complications, we can re-engage the rest of Specter's systems and cross our fingers."

"I'll have Captain Knox inform Captain Lincoln so you can coordinate with him. How long before you can be ready?"

"As I said, lickety-split."

"Dr. Cutler?"

"I can talk to my people on the Princeton, and we'll be up and running in thirty minutes."

"*Thank you.*" Sean realized he would have to better prepare for his conversations with Rebecca before the next time they talked. He chuckled as he thought, "Central casting couldn't have picked a better person for her role in our drama."

Rebecca was true to her word as half an hour later Specter was operational on the Princeton. Tony had ordered the Decatur to take up a position a mile and a half off her port side to confirm she was once again invisible visually and to radar. Over the next half hour, Rebecca reported only minor issues that were well within operating parameters.

Satisfied and with the Decatur back on station, Sean gave Rebecca permission to proceed. "Engage Specter throughout the rest of the fleet."

"You got it Big Daddy."

With Rebecca still on the phone, Sean turned his attention to Alicia who had just arrived. "You look like hell. Didn't you get any sleep last night?"

"Not really. Renée and I got so caught up in reviewing records pertaining to 1941 Pacific shipping traffic that we lost track of time," Alicia answered as she plopped down on the couch.

"Well, we are about to see if the Mad Hatter's ride is going to start up again."

After a few anxious minutes, with everything seemingly still in the same place and time, Sean asked Rebecca, "Well?"

"Right on. Everything is cool. No temporal anomalies to report as of yet, *Sir*."

Though relieved, Sean knew that in the greater scheme of things this didn't bring them any closer to understanding what happened. "Call me every half hour with an update."

"Even if there's nothing wrong?" Rebecca clarified.

"Even if there's nothing wrong. Thank you, Dr. Cutler."

After Sean hung up the phone, Alicia observed, "She certainly is one strange bird. Do you think she can stay focused enough to manage Specter?"

"Considering she fits the slang for bird, yes, she is a strange bird," Sean chuckled. "On your other concern, from what I've seen so far, she knows almost as much about how Specter works as Dr. Safire. She'll be fine. It's the crew of the Missouri I worry about with her in those skimpy 60s outfits she is determined to wear."

"Thank God there isn't a sun deck to be found," Alicia added, tongue in cheek.

"Ah, memories from the good old days." Sean walked over to the table, picked up some papers, and handed them to her. "Take a look at this."

She spent the next few minutes reading the draft of the speech he wanted to give to the task force. "Sounds like what we agreed to do. Have you shown this to Tony yet?"

"No I haven't, but that's a good idea." Sean agreed as he picked up the phone.

Ten minutes later Tony arrived. After he read it, he smiled. "I like it. This will help focus the crew."

"I want to speak directly to as many of the Enterprise crew as possible when I address the fleet at 1800 hours, so tell Captain Folger to have them assembled on the hangar deck. We can radio what I say to the rest of the task force."

"I'll get it set up." Tony then voiced a concern. "I also think it would be prudent to have the Marines ready to intercede if any of the crew rebel against what you propose. I don't think there will be a general uprising, but I want to make sure those wound as tight as Captain Brewster are kept on a short leash."

At 1800 hours, accompanied by Tony and Alicia, Sean made his way down the stairs to the cavernous hangar.

"Attention," roared out over the loudspeakers bringing the sailors as one to attention as he walked down the aisle. When he reached the podium, he he looked out on the over two thousand expectant members of the Enterprise crew.

"At ease. I'll be brief and get right to the point. It would only be speculation on my part if I tried to explain how we passed through time and space to get here. Therefore, I will not address what I can't yet explain.

"What I can tell you is shortwave radio communications have confirmed that the date today is 4 December 1941, seventy-three years in our past. Further, sextant readings show we are now twelve hundred miles southeast of the Hawaiian Islands. I would like to think every officer and sailor under my command understands the significance of 7 December 1941.

"I cannot tell you if we will ever return to our family and friends. I don't know if we have traveled in time, entered another dimension, or little green men from Planet X put us here to rob us of all our bodily fluids."

This got a laugh out of the older sailors who got the Dr. Strangelove reference. "What I do know is this task force is operational and crewed by the best-trained sailors in the world. I also know that our sworn duty to protect and defend the United States of America demands we take action against the Japanese fleet on its way to attack Pearl Harbor.

"What I ask of you right now, is to do the impossible. I need you to put home, friends, and family aside as if you were on a normal six-month deployment to a battle zone. We are currently on course to a position that is two hundred miles northwest of Pearl, and will arrive there on the evening of 6 December 1941. On the morning of the 7th, we will engage and destroy the Japanese carrier force led by Vice Admiral Nagumo before they can launch their attack.

"As of this moment, we are now operating under wartime conditions, and there will be little room for leniency for those who are derelict in their duties. Under these extraordinary conditions, half measures will get the sailor standing next to you killed.

"I don't know what the fallout will be when we take this action, but I do know we can't sit on the sidelines while American sailors and soldiers die in a battle we know is about to take place. When we engage in this conflict, we will change the course of history and give the world an opportunity for something better.

"After we successfully engage Nagumo's fleet, I will meet with Secretary of Defense Calhoun and my senior staff to discuss our next course of action. After we work out a sound strategic plan, I will keep you informed. The one thing you can count on is you will always receive only the truth from me, even under the worst of circumstances. That is all."

As Sean, Tony, and Alicia briskly left the hangar, the sailors rose to their feet at attention. As they climbed back up the stairs, they heard a few scattered cheers. By the time they reached the hatch, the cheers had risen to a crescendo, which caused Sean to smile.

Tony was the first to speak. "I've got to hand it to you Sean. It sounds like you bought us some time."

"Yes, very well done." Alicia thought the message set the perfect tone.

Sean's smile turned serious as his mind quickly shifted to implementation. "Tony, I want the senior staff in my ready room at 0900 tomorrow morning. This gives you the rest of tonight to finish your plan to attack Nagumo's task force. Keep it as simple as possible and leave out anything that might bring conflict within the senior staff. I want bulletproof, simple consensus, and the minimum of debate."

"Got it." Tony replied.

Then he decided would be a good time to cheer his buddy up. "By the way, Captain Folger has discovered something of interest in the short time he has been in command of the Enterprise. No one gives a rat's ass about Brewster, and are clearly relieved he is no longer in command. Of course, the same will be said about Charles when they see how difficult he is going to make their lives in a totally different way." He stated this with the knowing smile of one who was used to driving *his* crews to perfection.

Alicia noticed the lines around Sean's eyes. "I think this might be a good time for *all of us* to get some bunk time before you worry about tactical plans."

Sean was too tired to object. After the insanity of the last two days, and the efforts it took to hold his task force together, all the energy seemed to leave Sean's body at once. The effect of the hour of rest he got before writing his speech drained completely from his body. "Yes ma'am. I will as soon as I grab a quick bite and hear what the reactions from the other ships are."

"Renée and I have put together a list of Nagumo's warships for you Tony, including their position when they launched their attack on Pearl," Alicia offered. "We are still working to get the positions of the Japanese submarines stationed in Hawaiian waters, so you'll have the three-dimensional picture. You can use these *after* you wake up."

Tony was impressed with the amount of information the women

had put together in such a short time. A simplified attack plan was what the Admiral wanted, simple he would get. Tony had already factored in the use of weapons from 1940s technology they could replace once they established communication with civilian control. From there all he had to do was calculate the symmetry of movements that would dictate where he positioned the task force during the battle, and how close he dared to bring his ships to the Japanese.

The rest of the evening passed without incident, the noisy launches and retrievals of planes the only disruptions. Throughout the task force, weary officers and enlisted personnel came crashing down from the adrenaline rush the events over the last two days had brought about.

Sean had only slept for two hours when at 0500 the ring of the intercom next to his bed roused Sean from a deep sleep. The strange images in his dream of half-naked natives in over-sized outrigger canoes firing cannons bled from his memory as he reached for the phone. It was the CIC. "What is it?"

"I have Captain Daily for you as you ordered."

"Thank you and patch him through."

Captain Mark Daily on the Seawolf come on the line. "Good morning Admiral."

"Mark, I want you to set course to locate and then shadow the Japanese fleet. I trust you will manage to keep yourself out of trouble."

Captain Daily laughed at the thought of calling the kettle black. "Just make sure nothing happens to you while I'm gone. I would sure hate to have the rest of the task force arrive to find out I would now be the one in charge of this mess."

"Second in command, first to be able deny having anything to do with it when things turn upside down." Sean always enjoyed having Mark under his command.

"If we deploy within the next hour and travel submerged at flank speed, we would make contact late tomorrow evening."

Sean should have known Daily would have already calculated their position in relationship to the Japanese. "Thank you Captain. Inform Alpha Whiskey when you deploy."

When he finished, Sean had the CIC patch him through to Captain Lincoln on the Princeton, which held Alpha Whiskey duty at this hour. "Gordon, I'm going to grab some more shut-eye and Captain Knox isn't to be disturbed. If anything happens, no matter how unimportant it may seem to you, wake me up."

"Aye Aye Admiral."

Without anything else to see to that might threaten his command, it only took five minutes for Sean to fall back into a sound asleep. In the ensuing dream, this time he stood alone in the middle of a large woodland clearing with the feeling he was the only one left on the planet.

"That is because you are." Sean didn't recognize the voice, but strongly believed what it said.

❖

After Rebecca brought Dr. Phelps up to speed on Specter's operating status, she to finally felt confident enough to go get some sleep. After an hour of tossing and turning, she finally drifted off into her own troubled dream. She found herself in a world of black and white images of people silently walking through a dirty urban center she did not recognize. The smell of raw gasoline fumes from the old cars that jammed the streets overwhelmed her senses. Her panic increased as she discovered the black and white images of people maneuvered to block her escape. It was then she noticed they all carried strange objects. One man in a lab coat pushed a slide rule in her face, another held a rotary dial phone, and a smiling woman held a layered cake. The final straw that made her sit up in bed screaming was an IBM punch card machine spitting out hundreds of cards in all directions like a Disney cartoon. "Holy shit! I can't stay here. I don't want to have babies, I hate bras, and I'll be damned if I'll walk behind any man!"

Rebecca got up and paced the small cabin to clear her mind. Frustrated, she yelled out, "I'm stuck in a world where you could take all the computer power of the 1940s and download it onto a 1 GB USB stick. I'm going to spend the rest of my life reliving all of the same scientific breakthroughs over and over again. Where's the fun in that?"

She was startled out of her tirade by a loud knock, followed by a concerned voice. "Are you all right ma'am?"

Rebecca rushed to open the door, forgetting she wore only a sheer pink nightie styled after a picture she found in an old Playboy. The result on the young concerned Marine's face humored her enough to stand there and let him soak it all in. "Okay, that's enough. I'm fine, just pissed off."

"Thank you, I mean I'm glad there isn't anyone in your room… I'm sorry I didn't mean to suggest there was someone…"

"That's all right, I know what you mean. Thank you and good night," as she closed the door on the flustered Marine.

Throughout the fleet that night of the 4th, there were many strange dreams. Tony was the exception, and after three hours of sleep, he was busy planning the best way to minimize their resources, while still making sure it guaranteed the Japanese fleet's destruction. After another three hours, he was in need of a break, so he decided to take a walk around the supercarrier. When he arrived on the hangar deck, he wandered over to a member of a plane crew buried in one of the service hatches of an F/A-18F flown earlier that day.

"So how are you holding up?"

"How the hell do you think I'm holding up?" the sailor

sarcastically responded as he bumped his head getting out of the opening. Surprised when he found out who had asked the question, he presented an awkward salute and stammered, "I'm sorry, Sir."

"At ease sailor. I can't say my response would have been any different. It's been a rough two days on all of us."

The sailor took a moment, and then with a look as if to say *what the hell*, ploughed ahead. "No offense Captain, but I was just getting used to our old screwed up world. Now I've got to learn how to live like my grandfather did? No thanks."

Tony smiled and put his hand on the young man's shoulder. "Maybe something put us here to bring about a world where we could change all of that."

"Sir, the scuttlebutt going around from those who have served with you say if anyone can get us out of this mess it'd be you. The lifers have been getting everyone fired up about what you and the Admiral are trying to do, and they have kept the sailors who gripe in line."

"Let those who believe in carrying out their duty know I appreciate their efforts, and I'll try not to disappoint them. I'll let you get back to your work. Good night."

"Good night, Sir."

Tony found this to be the general attitude throughout the ship, and it re-established his sense of responsibility to live up to their confidence in him. As he walked on the flight deck, deep in thought about his plans to attack the Japanese carriers, Tony visualized the affect one 2000 pound bomb would have if it hit close to where he now stood and there were fully armed and fueled aircraft bunched together ready to launch. It would tear the ship apart in seconds.

His thoughts then turned to what would follow the destruction of the Japanese fleet, and the world discovered they were from the future. There would be a giant red bull's-eye painted all over the task force. Then again, as soon as the first bomb struck one of the Japanese carriers, and the future changed, they might cease to exist.

Tony's doubts did not last long, because in his mind blinked out of existence might be better than the reality they left behind.

With the disparity in technology, he knew the destruction of the Japanese task force would not be a problem. However, the political reaction to their presence made him uneasy. There was a real chance that instead of appreciation for their intervention, fear would provoke a violent response. A worried thought came into his mind. "What if our only option for survival meant turning our weapons on those we had saved?"

Early the same morning, Dr. Phelps reported to Rebecca when she returned to the hangar at 0300. "All the systems are operating well within safety limits with the only glitch from the John Paul Jones at 1:15 AM. Turns out one of the engineers spilled her coffee on the control panel. The backup kicked in, and there was only a temporary loss of power to the coils. After cleanup, she rebooted the computer without any further problems."

It was then Forrest took a close look at Rebecca. "Whose funeral are you dressed for? Or better yet, how is it you came to even pack it?" Rebecca was dressed from head to toe in a garish black mourning dress that would have fit the numerous funerals of America's assassinated leaders from the sixties, topped off with a pillbox hat complete with lace veil.

"I'm taking a day to mourn my lost future," Rebecca stated with an edge of rebellion. "By the way Forrest, we're now on Navy time, so that would be 0115 hours, and I brought the outfit along in case Specter blew up in our face. Ironic isn't it?"

Without anything he could say in response, Forrest left with a simple, "Call me if you find anything I missed."

"Thanks for the update. I'll call you if I need you." For the rest of the day Rebecca worked on Specter's coding. She intuitively knew there were other back doors designed into the program, and when she couldn't find any, she became irritable as system after system checked out.

She didn't realize how much time had passed until Forrest returned to the hangar and offered her a fresh cup of coffee 8 hours later.

"Have you had any luck?"

"I've searched everywhere to find where Dr. Strangelove could have planted contrary coding and came up dry." Frustrated by the thought she wasn't up to the challenge, Rebecca worried that she wouldn't be able to control any future disruptions to Specter. "I want to run a simulation with Specter offline, similar to the environment that triggered our leap through time. However, I shouldn't do it so close to the Hawaiian Islands."

With nothing to add, Dr. Phelps tried instead to cheer her up. "On the bright side, based on historical data the weather conditions will remain clear for the foreseeable future. For once there is a one hundred percent chance the weather predictions will come true."

"That's just great Forrest. We don't have a clue what Specter will do next, and you have to bring up perfect weather in an era where women are required by law to put a tent over their bodies. I might as well sew a burqa together."

"Uh oh, time for me to keep my mouth shut," Forrest thought as he hunkered down at his keyboard, eyes fixed on his monitor.

"To top it all off, the mere thought of strapping on the armor that passed as undergarments in the 1940s, is enough to make me want to tear someone's eyes out. Don't even get me started on how they treated women as possessions, rather than equals. The highest compliment given to women from this primitive era was *Rosie the Riveter*."

Dr. Phelps decided to change gears. "Show me where you left off, and I'll continue to look with a fresh set of eyes. You are dead on your feet, and frankly, I don't think you are at your best right now."

"At my worst I can still outthink three of you." Rebecca took a second to think about how bad that sounded. "I'm sorry Forrest. You are only trying to help, and I shouldn't take my frustration out on you. It won't happen again. I haven't eaten anything in the last 24 hours and I get bitchy when I'm hungry."

"That's okay. I've done nothing but eat everything in sight. It's always my fallback position when I'm freaked out. Take a break and get out of here Rebecca."

This brought a brief smile to her face. After she brought Forrest up to date on her progress, she made her way to the galley to get something to eat.

<hr>

In the CIC at 0100 hours on the morning of 5 December 1941, unlike everyone else, Lt. Commander Osaka felt like he was in a wonderful dream. Without many friends or family and surrounded with the clutter of his notes, he was in a world he spent most of his life dreaming about. He frantically uploaded encryption codes he had gathered over the last ten years to the historical database on the Enterprise servers. This included biographies of the major encryption officers involved in the conflict.

Considering the importance these codes represented, Osaka was excited they would be able to read Japanese communications in real time. For him, sleep tonight was irrelevant. When he finished his work, he would be able to put into operation a plan to disrupt the Japanese chain of command. Yes – Lt. Commander Daniel Osaka was born for this, and he was determined to make the most of the opportunity.

Then from out of his research, as an image materialized, he feverishly began to formulate a plan.

That same morning at 0500, Sean was on the bridge of the Enterprise with Tony and Captain Folger. "We should make contact with United States naval forces patrolling these waters today, or tomorrow at the latest. Do you have a Seahawk on ready alert in the off chance we make contact with Japanese submarines in the area?"

"Yes nervous Nellie. What kind of a Chief of Staff would I be if I didn't?" Tony quipped, before he hit Sean with a barrage of questions.

"Are you planning to stay out of contact with the American Navy until after we attack the Japanese fleet, or do you want to let Admiral Kimmel in on it first? What's the plan if we run into an American patrol? Do you intend to ignore the contact and sail around them?"

Sean took a step back. "I can tell you pulled an all-nighter. You might want to ease up on the Java."

"Sorry, I'm past tired. But those questions keep rattling around in my head."

"For now, let's one issue at a time. If we informed CINCPACFLT [Commander-in-Chief, U.S. Pacific Fleet] of our existence and that the Japanese plan to attack Pearl, it will only complicate matters. With the condition of the U.S. Navy at this time, they would be annihilated if they came out to meet the threat.

"Since Alicia transferred over from the Missouri, she has been working nonstop with Renée in the CIC researching naval archives. Once computer workstations were set up for them they moved to the Admirals Ready Room. I'm heading there to see how they are doing."

"How about I go with you?"

Sean shook his head. "You need some sleep. I'll take what you've got so far, and add their info, and if I need you, I'll wake you up.

"That goes for you too Charles. Get your XO up here to relieve you."

"Aye Aye Admiral."

Sean waited until after both men left and Barrish took command before he headed to the door.

"Admiral is off the bridge."

When he returned to his ready room, Sean found Alicia and Renée on the floor pouring over printouts in animated discussion about their meaning.

Renée rose up to salute, but he motioned to her to continue. "What have you two come up with since our last briefing?"

"Thank you Admiral" Renée answered. "You would be amazed at how much information the sailors contributed about the attack on Pearl. It seems like every aspect is covered based on their individual interests. Pooling all of this with the ship's archives, we were able to put together a comprehensive picture of the operation that included the Japanese advance and the day-to-day positions of their submarines. This gave us a complete picture of the major threats to our projected course.

"I didn't realize the Japanese stationed so many of their submarines around Pearl before the attack. So far, I've been able to plot fifteen in Hawaiian waters on the 7th. Based on the records, we only have to worry about these three, I-9, I-15, and I-17, since their patrol areas cross our course. Therefore, I don't see any major surprises, as long as we can remain cloaked. Besides, it isn't as if we won't hear them coming long before they can make contact even if Specter wasn't operating."

Renée showed Sean the positions on the computer of the Japanese submarine infiltration in the days before the attack that covered all of the avenues into the Harbor. The image displayed on the screen showed the current position of the Japanese Carrier force 800 miles northwest of Pearl Harbor, with the Enterprise Task Force eight hundred miles to the southeast.

Sean looked at his watch, and saw it was 0530. "Thank you Renée. You both have been up since, oh – the morning of 24 January 2014. Renée, I want you to grab a couple of hours of sleep before the staff meeting. It looks like you should do the same Alicia. I had your bags sent here. And don't worry; I'll wake you both at 0800."

Without objection, Renée left for her quarters as Alicia plodded wearily into the bedroom and plopped onto the bed.

Sean spent the next hour with an overlay of their data on Tony's preliminary battle plan. When satisfied he had committed it to memory, he contacted the CIC and not surprisingly found Tony had ignored his order. "So what did you do after you left the bridge? Hide behind the door until I left?"

"Nope. Headed straight for the CIC. I can get plenty of sleep when they send us to Rip Van Winkle land. You need me?"

Sean knew better than force Tony into something he didn't want. It would be easier to get a two year old to eat broccoli. "Might as well come to my Ready Room and read me in to what reconnaissance has come up with."

Ten minutes later Tony arrived. Sean poured himself a fresh cup of coffee and settled into his chair. When Tony went to pour himself one, Sean stopped him. "You don't get one, and after the staff meeting I'm ordering you to your cabin. What you do there is entirely up to you. However, while I have you here I might as well get your opinion on some thoughts I have."

Tony ignored him and poured a cup. "You want me alert in the meeting, so let it go. Oh and do you really want me to be honest about what I think?"

"Shut up and take a seat." Sean bent over and picked up his note pad. "Let's say that we were put here for a reason, and let's pretend that reason is to change the destructive path humanity is on."

Honesty it was. "Might as well say a pod of Dolphins figured out time travel and thought it would be a kick of the flipper to watch us believe such crap, but go on."

Think about an idea that with a little practical planning, might be able to replace the imperialism and nativism of the past three thousand years with a more live and let live concept. Instead of two superpowers fighting a forty-five year Cold War, maybe they could work together to build a multinational space agency that would cost billions less than the Cold War did."

"Let me get this straight. You think that just because some kind of freak of nature dropped us somewhere we don't belong, it is suddenly our responsibility to save the world from itself? Take a breath brother." Tony never was one to stomach anything that could remotely be construed as hubris, especially if it would involve his participation.

Sean tossed the papers onto the conference table. "You may not like what I am proposing, but what do think the United States government, and by government I mean all those who feed at the trough of the industrial military establishment, would do if they got ahold of our ships?"

"The same thing ours did. Use it to intimidate the rest of the world to get what they want, and of course make a couple of thousand zillionaires in the process. Don't get me wrong, I would love to stick it to the fat cats and their political toaddies, but people are people regardless of the year we occupy. Basques will continue to hate the Spanish, Sunnis will murder Shiites, and no one will ever get along with the North Koreans."

"All right so what is it that you think we should do?" Sean decided now would be a good time to change drinks and headed over to the liquor cabinet.

"I don't know. You and Alicia are the idea people, so whatever you decide is what I will back you on."

Sean had a hard time suppressing the urge to laugh.

Alicia joined the conversation while he regained his composure. "We can do all of that and bring alternative energy decades early so the need to exploit the Middle East never occurs. If the world's demand for their oil reserves doesn't materialize, then the region would be a geopolitical backwater without significance."

Tony smiled as he dissected the angles. "You mean limit an oil industry that dictates government policy based on the population's addiction, which allows them to manipulate prices with impunity?"

"Then there is the question of whether or not the UN should have created a nation for European refugees in the middle of the Arab world," Sean added as he grabbed the Jack Daniels Single Barrel.

Alicia didn't like the sound of that. "You sure you want to go there Sean? Are you questioning whether the State of Israel should exist? We start going down that road and we'll lose the support of half the sailors serving on our ships."

"I know. I keep coming back to the possibility that without Stalin and the ulcer of the Middle East after WWII, the world would hold the possibility of a future with unlimited potential."

Tony questioned the thought of trying to turn all of humanity 180 degrees on a dime. "I don't know Sean. Seems to me you are trying to buck millenniums of history. If we do take down this batch of egomaniacs, their replacements are already waiting in the wings to take their place. Add the religious fanatics, industrial despots, and simply too many people on the planet, and our plan to change all of this is what?"

"All of that aside, don't you think it would be better to try, than just accept the inevitable?" Sean asked, still holding the bottle.

"You know I agree with everything you said. However, before you do anything, you better come up with something that allows the Steve Brewsters of our merry band of sailors to feel their vision of God's good book is a part of it, or we'll have our own version of a holy war onboard our ships," Tony warned before he continued.

"As far as I can see, it really doesn't matter one way or another what we do. At best, we give the world a temporary respite from the madness and that might have to be good enough. Hell, or for all we know Japanese naval units from the 22nd Century might be waiting for us when we get to Pearl." Tony could always find the cynical side of things.

"Let it go," Sean pleaded.

Renée breathed a sigh of relief when a knock on the door interrupted them. Tony opened it to find Lt. Commander Osaka carrying a stack of printouts.

"Good morning Admiral, Madam Secretary, Captains. I was wondering if you have some time for me to share an idea I've been working on."

"As long as it doesn't have anything to do with speculation about our dilemma," Sean answered, thankful for the diversion. "It would be nice to hear something solid, but you have to make it quick Commander. The senior staff will be here within the hour."

"A few minutes are all I need Admiral. I spent the last fourteen hours correlating my files and detailing encryptions from the Japanese, German, Russian, and American intelligence units of this era. I entered them all into the ship's encryption database and informed the CIC Officer and the other Information Warfare Officers so that now we can read their radio traffic real time. I also made a list of the codebreakers who currently work at Pearl thinking they should be the first to be contacted." Daniel rattled this off while he still stood at attention.

This idea switched Sean's mind into a different gear. "At ease Commander and take a seat. What made you think your list of codebreakers holds the key to contact 7th Fleet?"

"I don't mean to be presumptuous by offering up my opinion Sir, but I think if you allowed me to contact either Lt. Commander Edwin Layton or Lt. Jasper Holmes, we might be able to convince them who we are. These men are part of the group who broke the Japanese code, and are two of the top scientists in the region. If we can make anyone understand our capabilities, it would be them."

Tony had a simple question. "If we're going to contact Pearl, wouldn't the obvious person be Admiral Kimmel? Because he would be the first person either one of your guys would contact the second you convince them of who we are."

"Captain Knox is right Commander. You would need to find a

way to contact the codebreakers in a place where we could cut them off from access to normal military channels." Sean still wasn't sure what Osaka had in mind. "What would you do with them if you did get access?"

"I would convince them it would be in the United States Navy's vital interest to know we have advance knowledge of the Japanese Navy's intent to strike Pearl Harbor. This would be the bait to get them onboard to act as neutral observers before our action with Nagumo. They could report what they witnessed to Admiral Kimmel, and you would have the most analytical minds in the area to bridge our two worlds."

Tony saw merit in this argument. However, there was one major element to consider. "How do you propose to get them onboard? Cruise right up to battleship row and send the Admiral's launch to pick them up?"

Oblivious to the sarcasm, Osaka finished his thoughts. "Since we can communicate with them in code, we ask them to keep this to themselves, and send them coordinates to a pickup point along our course. To allay their fears, I have historical personal information on them only their families or close friends knew of at the time."

"It's an interesting idea Commander. See if you can find a practical way to make it work. That is all."

Alicia could see that everyone could use a break so she grabbed the bottle of Jack Daniels Single Barrel out of Sean's hand. "If we wait for you to pour it, we might be here all day. Let's call it a wrap until we hear what the rest of the senior staff has to say."

"Amen to that. I don't want to know what else Sean has percolating through his gray cells." Tony took the offered glass from Alicia. "I mean I was half expecting him to suggest that we should all become vegetarians to get ahead of global warming."

Renée chimed in. "I was thinking NASCAR and the NFL, and see where that takes us first."

They all had a good laugh and kicked back their shots, except

Sean who was still waiting for his.

The staff meeting began in the Admirals Ready Room promptly at 0900, and Sean could tell the Captains appeared restless, so he got right to the point. "We're going to make a little side trip to pick up a couple of people I want onboard. Commander Osaka is working out how to locate and extract two codebreakers to act as witnesses to the Japanese aggression. We will keep you informed as it comes together."

This didn't result in any objections, so Tony stood up and went to the monitor to present the tactical plan against the Japanese carriers. "The Admiral's orders were to devise an attack plan as simple as possible." He then directed their attention to the monitor that showed the estimated position of the Japanese carrier force, the Enterprise Task Force, and the Seawolf positioned southwest of the Japanese fleet.

"On the morning of the 7th, we will close to fifteen miles southeast of the enemy's position. Our attack will begin with six Specter-equipped F-35's from the Enterprise, simultaneously delivering one 2,000-pound Paveway laser guided bomb to each of the carriers Akagi, Kaga, Soryu, Hiryu, Zuikaku, and Shokako. With the decks of the Japanese carriers clogged with fully fueled and bomb laden planes, each of the 2,000-pound bombs will be targeted aft of the carriers' islands. Judging by the results from the battle of Midway, the initial bomb blast will ignite secondary explosions that will rip the ships to pieces. We should be able to sink every one of them with a single bomb." Tony embellished the last sentence to drive home the implied loss of life for the Japanese sailors.

"After the attack begins, the Seawolf and Hampton will take out any Japanese attack subs in the area with Mark-48 torpedoes. We'll have the four uncloaked F-35s in reserve in case any of the carriers are still operational after the first strike. Our task force will close to within ten miles of the two battleships, Hiel and Kirasima. The

Missouri's 16-inch guns will fire a broadside delivering nine shells at each battleship, which at this range should severely disable both Japanese battleships. It's only necessary to inflict major damage on the battleships, not sink them.

"Once the Japanese carriers are destroyed and the battleships disabled there won't be any way for the survivors to retaliate. This will force the support ships to assist the battleships and then turn for home. Our action against the carrier force should also end the threats against Wake Island and the Philippines.

"If everyone is on target, our total armament expenditure will be six laser-guided 2000 pound bombs, two Mark-48 torpedoes, and eighteen 16-inch armor-piercing shells." Tony finished his preview of the battle, and waited for questions.

The first came from Captain Frederick Johnson who will be holding Alpha Whiskey on the cruiser USS Chancellorsville during the battle. "With our current predicament brought about by the malfunction of Specter to begin with, do you think it wise to put our ships so close to the Japanese battleships? Why take the chance of another Specter failure that would leave us vulnerable to their return fire?"

Tony was ready with an answer. "As a precaution, we will have missiles targeted on the Japanese battleships, ready to fire if there are any glitches with Specter. If we engage the enemy outside the range of their 14-inch guns, we would have to launch missiles we can't replace to make sure of a first shot kill. By using the Missouri, we can resupply 16-inch shells from existing stocks of this era."

"I'm not in disagreement with the plan, but if we leave their support ships free to return to Japan unharmed, our existence would be exposed to the Japanese leadership." This came from the youngest and most aggressive commander in the task force, Commander Regis Goddard of the destroyer USS John Paul Jones.

"What are they going to say? I would be surprised if they did return home knowing they did nothing, while the center of the

Japanese Navy blew up around them by a force they couldn't see. Besides, I don't see the point of needlessly killing Japanese sailors who are no longer a threat to the fleet at Pearl, or us. The destruction of the six carriers will be good enough. Any way you look at it, the Japanese high command will be clueless and probably in a state of panic. If we limit the carnage to their attack forces, it might come in useful later."

Captain Brewster voiced his contempt. "I'm still opposed to any involvement whatsoever in a conflict we have no business being a part of, and I want it on the record." He still felt slighted about the loss of his command of the Enterprise, his usual dour disposition now even more combative.

Fed up with his increasingly resistant attitude, Sean raised his voice. "Captain Brewster, do you feel your disagreement with this action will affect your ability to carry out your duties?"

The veins in Brewster's neck throbbed when he answered. "As a Captain in the United States Navy, I will follow any lawful orders I am given Admiral. However, I also feel duty bound to voice my moral objection to the road you are determined to drag us down. All of you are so blinded by what you see in front of you, you won't consider we are being manipulated to an evil purpose."

Sean had enough. "Nobody here, especially me, wishes to use the power our task force represents to become the next tyrant on the world stage. Your objections have already been noted Steve. Now be quite, and let Captain Knox finish."

With a click of his mouse, Tony added symbols that showed the positions of Japanese submarines Renée had identified in the waters south of Pearl Harbor. "As you can see, they sent most of their submarine fleet to provide surveillance."

Using a pointer, Tony pointed to the five submarines closest to the harbor entrance. "These carry the midget subs the Japanese launched into the harbor as part of the attack. The historical archives provided their day-to-day positions, which will allow us to take them out on the afternoon of the 6th as our position will converge with theirs right about here." Tony next pointed to a position roughly twenty-five miles south of the harbor.

"Captain Turner, the Hampton will be out front of the task force to the limit of Specter's capabilities, where after confirming sonar contact, you will launch your torpedo attacks on the submarines. Once again, I want to preserve our limited amount of Mark-48 torpedoes, so make sure you don't miss. I don't think during some future emergency you would want to have to reload with useless Mark-14 torpedoes from 1941 and their 80% chance of failure."

"Thank you Tony. It looks like you covered all the angles. Any questions?"

Without any comments from the rest of the senior staff, especially from Brewster, who Sean kept a hard eye on, he moved ahead. "Honestly, I like all of you have spent an inordinate amount of time over the last three days thinking about how and why we are here. The trouble with this line of curiosity is that none of us signed on to the Navy to become a philosopher. Therefore, as our oaths demand, we are going to defend the United States of America. What this means is once we destroy the Japanese carriers, we will continue on to Japan to take out their leadership to end the Japanese threat, once and for all."

Then we will return to Hawaii to meet with President Roosevelt and convince him that with his support, we can end the war."

This was too much for Brewster. "It's bad enough we're going to follow through with an unauthorized attack on Japanese warships, and you also want us to single-handedly go to war with Japan? I agreed to strike the carriers to save Pearl Harbor because there isn't time for any alternative, but what's your excuse for not returning to civilian authority immediately after the battle?"

Captain Brewster's complaint drew a nod of approval from Captain Frederick Johnson of the cruiser USS Chancellorsville. "That's a lot to chew off, even for you Admiral. Why not contact

Pearl after we dispose of the carriers?"

Alicia chose to answer for Sean. "Because the truth of the matter is, it will take too long to sort out through the normal political channels who we are and what we did. This will give the Japanese time to recover, and more importantly, how long do you think it will take the Japanese to discover we exist. Once we acknowledge who we are to anyone from this era, the clock will be ticking."

Captain Gordon Lincoln of the cruiser USS Princeton spoke up. "Do we have the fuel to travel the distances required for this to work?"

This gave Sean a chance to push his agenda forward. "Tony already crunched the numbers and found we have the necessary fuel to cover the distance."

This was news to Tony, but he recovered quickly. "I've kept track of our fuel expenditures," Tony confirmed, as he pointed to the Captain of the fleet replenishment oiler USNS Laramie, Lt. Commander James Peck. "With those numbers, my preliminary estimates show we could complete the mission with a thousand miles or so to spare. However, if we are forced into alternative actions that extend the distances, we'd be in trouble." He hoped the figures he rattled off were close to the mark.

Commander Steven Holmes of the destroyer USS Decatur was next to voice his opinion. "The way I see it, this is all conjecture until after the 7th anyway. Let's take care of this business, and then we can worry about the repercussions. No one knows how this is going to turn out in the end anyway."

Renée broke in. "So Captain Knox, the bottom line is we destroy the Japanese carriers, cruise a few thousand miles to decapitate the Japanese Government, and then return to Hawaii to meet with a long ago dead president to convince him we have the answers to world peace. Does that cover the basics of your plan?"

Renée felt like she was in the middle of a scene from a movie. The only part missing is the one where somebody should have already died. Then with a start, she remembered the crew of the Orion. "What if, after we destroy the Japanese task force, Japan and the United States do not declare war? How can we justify an attack on Japan if they don't?"

"Good point," Tony replied. "Without the knowledge of the destruction of their carriers, Japan's Ambassador to the United States will present Japan's declaration of war immediately after the beginning of their scheduled attack on Pearl Harbor. This will be the final validation for our preemptive strike on Nagumo, as well as further validation of our knowledge of future events."

With this statement, the conversation turned to the individual ship responsibilities during the operation. All questions and dissent disappeared as their military training took over. It pleased Sean to see his staff so engaged. An hour later, the meeting broke up, and the Captains returned to their ships. Sean, Alicia, Renée, and Tony remained behind in the Ready Room.

Alicia figured to rehash the meeting was useless, so she moved onto the one unanswered component. "After we shanghai them, what happens if these codebreakers refuse to cooperate? I wish you had talked this through with me before you announced it to everyone else."

Sean tried his best to mollify Alicia. "I apologize for my lack of consultation with you, and for all the times I'll probably do it in the future. The fluidity of our situation will undoubtedly be dictating the need for ad hoc decisions. But I can assure you that if you find yourself in disagreement with any of these decisions, I won't have any problem reversing direction."

"God knows you have to be reactive under these conditions," Alicia deflected. "I don't mind as long as you understand what's good for the Goose is good for the Gander when I negotiate with the politicians."

As Renée listened to the two of them come to an understanding, she imagined them as a married couple of twenty years. The kind of couple whose perfection would sicken anyone forced to spend too much time around them. She could visualize them talking through, with complete logic, the next sexual position they would attempt. This picture forced her to stifle a laugh. Instead, a loud snort escaped through her nose as she looked away.

Sean gave her a stern look. "Is there something you'd like to share Captain?"

Momentarily embarrassed, Renée quickly recovered. "Of all the things I dreamed could happen to me in my life, helping to formulate plans to change the course of history was not on any of my to-do lists."

"Nor mine," Sean agreed. "All of history was created and written down by people just like us, each one with their own perception of the events they played parts in. Even the ones who came down as the greatest of heroes or worst of villains, started out as unknowns. Who is to say that some of them were also out of their time and space? It would be hubris to believe we are the first."

Thankfully, a knock on the door interrupted their conversation.

"Enter," Sean ordered.

In walked an excited Osaka. "Is this a good time Sir?"

"That depends Commander." Sean motioned Osaka into the room, and informed the others, "Commander Osaka is here to explain to us how he plans to bring personnel from Pearl aboard our ship. Am I correct Commander?"

Nervous as he was before knocking on the door, Osaka now felt a desperate need to visit the head. Instead, he awkwardly stood, frozen in place.

Sean sat down and impatiently ordered the Commander, "Any time you're ready."

Then a switch went off in Osaka's head, and in rapid-fire he spit out his report. "Remember how I told you how I studied the codebreakers personal biographies as part of my hobby working on historical ciphers? When I went through some of my old files, I was able to find out where one of them was on 7 December. Turns out Lt. Commander Edwin Layton was fishing with Lt. Jasper Holmes, who also works in the encryption unit, about thirty miles to the east of Pearl."

"How does his position on the 7th help us get him on the 6th? I'm not following you." Sean wanted him to get to the point. "How do we know which boat he'll be on, and where it will be?"

"They went out fishing together for three days every three months. It helps us because they left on the 5th. The family papers I read also talked about how Lt. Commander Layton kept the same routine, which should put them south of Molokai on the 6th. If we sent a directional radio signal to this area of the ocean, we should be able to make contact. With our capabilities, we can grab them off their boat with a rapid deployment team from the Enterprise."

Tony backed up Osaka's idea. "Now there's a plan I can agree with. If we are going to accept risk, my vote is to send a launch from a mile off to rendezvous and pass ourselves off as naval personnel who need them for some made up emergency. That way they come willingly, hopefully without either of them having a heart attack when they find out who we really are."

Sean had heard enough. "We need a set of American eyes from 1941 to witness the Japanese aggression, as well as our capabilities. We're going with Tony's idea."

Sean walked up to Osaka and reached out to shake his hand. "Nice work Commander."

"Thank you, Sir." Osaka shook the offered hand a little too aggressively, before he released his grip and saluted. "Will that be all?"

"Yes Commander." Sean returned the salute then watched as Osaka left the room with a bounce in his step.

"Okay, thank you all for your input," Sean concluded.

" Tony, if there isn't anything else to discuss, inform Commander Thornton we have a job for one of his SEAL squads. I also need to get an update from Dr. Cutler on whether Specter will remain operational. By the way, have we gotten anything out of Dr. Safire on why he sabotaged his own project?"

"What, I'm not supposed to go to my cabin now?"

Alicia and Renée said at the same time, "What?"

Sean laughed. "Ignore him." Then to Tony. "Seriously, Dr. Safire."

"He's conscious, but they haven't gotten anything but paranoid ramblings out of him as of yet." This bothered Tony. He didn't believe Strangelove was the vegetable everyone thought he was. His instincts told him the whacked out scientist wasn't through messing with their reality.

Sean moved on. "We will be seventy-five miles south of Molokai by 0600, and according to Osaka's estimate, we can intercept the fishing boat by 0800. If all goes well we can plot a course to intercept the Japanese submarines by 1000, with almost a full day left to position ourselves to meet Nagumo.

"Inform Alpha Whiskey to prepare for action early tomorrow morning. I want everyone well rested and ready at 0500." Sean was way past done with this meeting. "If there isn't anything else, let's get to it."

As they finished, the CIC Officer called for Tony. "One of the cloaked F-35s has picked up surface contacts to the east, at a range of two hundred miles. He's continuing east for a visual sighting."

"Thank you Commander." Tony hung up the phone and relayed the information to Sean.

Sean put on his coat and made ready to leave. "Tony and I are going to the CIC. I'll call you as soon as we identify the contacts."

"What makes you think we want to stay here?" Alicia admonished as she and Renée grabbed their coats and headed out the door ahead of the boys.

Tony and Sean gave each other a look. "Women!"

When they entered the CIC, they could hear the voice of the F-35 pilot reporting. "The ships are the destroyers USS Porter and USS Selfridge, escorting the heavy cruiser USS Minneapolis. They are on a course that will take them south of the task force."

Renée wrote down the names. "I'll confirm their prewar status, and see if we have any information about their destination."

"Good," Sean replied. He then ordered the CIC Officer, "Maintain our course and heading. I'd like to get a look at these ships, and it wouldn't hurt for our sailors to see something solid from this era. Has there been any contact with the Seawolf?"

"No Sir. Captain Daily's next scheduled report isn't due for another two hours."

"Thank you. Carry on."

"We've got some time, and you wanted an update from Dr. Cutler, so why don't I go over to the Missouri and see firsthand what's going on." That and Tony wanted to make sure Brewster wasn't fomenting any dissension.

"I agree." Sean thought for a second and asked Renée. "Maybe you'd like to go with him?"

Renée smiled at Tony. "That's okay. He doesn't need me to be in the way. Besides I've got enough to do here."

Though Tony would have enjoyed the company, she was right. "I'll be back in a couple of hours." He grabbed his hat and coat, and with a shrug of his shoulders that suggested, "It's your loss," left the CIC.

Before Alicia could object to the way Renée handled the opportunity, Sean interceded. "It would be best if we let the children work out their own problems, dear."

"I was only…"

"You were only going to tell her what to do."

"We women have to stick up for each other, because if all we did was wait around for the man to make a smart move we'd die of old age."

Sean didn't miss the not so subtle dig at his own approach to relationships, but decided silence was his best option. He settled into a chair instead.

"You two know I'm still here, don't you?" Renée then mimicked the whine of a distraught teenage girl. "I never get to do anything fun."

After they stopped laughing, Alicia whispered to Renée, "We'll talk."

After Tony landed on the Missouri, it wasn't a problem keeping his time short with Brewster as the hatred was mutual. After several tense moments, he left the bridge and headed to the hangar where he found Dr. Rebecca Cutler and Dr. Forrest Phelps glued to their computers.

"Dr. Cutler, it has been two days without any further issues with Specter. Would it be safe to say there's nothing else for you to find and we're out of the woods?"

"Well Captain Knox, I can tell you we have been able to isolate the Enterprise servers from Specter's computers, and we've closed all the pathways through the switch to protect it. If there are any infected work spaces in Specter's program, we've narrowed down where Dr. Safire could have hidden them."

Rebecca then remembered who she was talking to and added in plain English, "In other words, we have better control over how Specter accesses the programs on the other ships. Therefore, if there is something we haven't found yet, you don't have to worry about frying the electrical systems if it goes rogue again. I've run two kick-ass antivirus programs, and all they spit back to me are simple unrelated programs some bored assistants installed to show their dislike for Dr. Strangelove."

"Just once I'd love to talk to a computer geek who could tell me everything was fine and there was nothing to worry about," Tony stated in frustration. "I know it isn't fair to compare a groundbreaking prototype like Specter to your basic operating systems, but it sure seems like they all need twice as much work to keep them operational than it took to design the damn things. All I want you geniuses to tell me is will this multi-billion dollar technology do what it was built to do."

Tony was in full rant mode. "Since they sold the first PC, it is all about the sale of the latest, fastest, most powerful computers while they fail to fix the thousands of problems their last wonder created. Microsoft my ass, more like Microshit as far as I'm concerned. I know none of this is your fault Rebecca, but will they ever make a computer work as advertised? Or will the next cluster fuck they create end civilization in mushroom clouds or, as in our case, make like Dr. Who and send more people and ships into the twilight zone?"

"For all the problems caused by the computer revolution, Captain," Dr. Phelps countered, "you have to agree they have dramatically freed humanity to explore any area of knowledge you can imagine. I can only envision the horror of your college life, having to study in a library full of *books*."

Rebecca thought Dr. Phelps scored with that one and had to suppress a quick laugh.

"You may be right about the ability of computers to share information, sport. I've witnessed dozens of programs like Specter developed for the Navy over the last twenty years. Not one of them worked as promised when first delivered, and every one of them was billions over budget when they finally did," Tony rebuked. "The bottom line is, we have to make life or death decisions based on our dependence on Specter, and you can't tell me all is well."

"I share your frustration with the situation, and I share your contempt for the way computer programs have a tendency to glitch up. The difference between you and me is I blame the assholes who write lazy code."

Rebecca paused for a moment to enter a new set of commands into her computer before she continued. "You'd be better off if you directed your anger at men like King Gates and the tentacles he has permeating every aspect of the computer world. What other company but his has the balls to dump a piece of shit like Vista on the world market and still rake in billions of dollars in profits."

"Let's get back on track here," Tony urged. "Tomorrow morning we are going to place our ships within point-blank range of the 14-inch guns on two Japanese battleships. I would prefer they not see us, or we will witness up close and personal the damage an armor piercing shell can do."

Tony finally noticed Rebecca's attire and hesitated. "By the way, I should compliment you on the choice of colors you're wearing today, and I do appreciate they are covering up more of you than usual." Having focused on Specter, Tony had missed the red, white, and blue ensemble she wore in multiple layers. He now took in the chiffon outfit only partially covered by her white lab coat, accented with four-inch blazing red pumps and huge blue hoop earrings.

"I figured under the circumstances lady liberty was the order of the day. And don't worry, Forrest and I will monitor Specter throughout whatever you have planned for tomorrow. But before you go, I should let you know we are working on a theory based on the weather conditions when Specter failed. We think water penetrated the coils, which acted as the perfect conductor when the lightning strikes hit the shield. Compounded by Dr. Strangelove's virus that overloaded the generators, a one-in-ten billion event might be the reason we are here. The only way to know for sure would be to replicate the same environment. It could either send us back or possibly fry all of the electrical grids or more likely send us to some other place in time."

"You're starting to give me another headache Dr. Cutler. The situation will have to be dire for us to test your theory and roll the dice in an electrical storm." Looking at his watch, Tony realized he needed to get going, and ended the conversation with one final thought. "Once again, the Admiral would like to remind you of his order to get enough sleep and food. How long has it been since you did either one of those? And remember, all I have to do is ask the Marines over there if you lie."

"Don't worry, Forrest got here half an hour before you did, and I'll leave as soon as you get out of my way so I can go get a bite to eat before you come and tuck me in."

Tony laughed at the image of himself as a lecherous older man bending over to tuck the young flag draped scientist into bed and was glad he never sired a daughter. "Seriously, before I leave, I know you both will do your best to make sure we don't get screwed tomorrow. I'll see you in the morning." With confirmation from one of the Marines that Rebecca was following orders, he left to return to the Enterprise.

Over the next two hours, the mood on the Enterprise changed as the crew prepared to become active participants in a war their grandparents had fought. Ironically, they joined the Navy after growing up with images of the mighty German battleship Bismarck and the battles of Leyte Gulf, Midway, and Pearl Harbor.

Tony's own musing carried him to memories of when he used to go to sleep dreaming about the Battle of Leyte Gulf. "What if Admiral Halsey hadn't run off after the Japanese Carriers and was positioned in the San Bernadino Strait to intercept Japanese Admiral Takeo Kurita's battleships. That would have been the last battleship-to-battleship engagement in history."

Most of his fantasies revolved around the strategies of epic sea battles, and now fate had given him a front row seat.

The Seawolf reported in on time with nothing out of the ordinary, outside of an overflight by a two-engine plane, which that far out to sea could only be an American PBY Catalina reconnaissance flying boat.

In the CIC, Tony addressed an issue with Sean that worried

him. "Most of the gun crews have had only limited training on the 16-inch guns, and I think it would be wise to engage in a little gunnery practice. I know we'll be close enough that it will be almost impossible to miss, but I'd be more comfortable to find out any problems with the turrets now than when we need to depend on them. The only live-fire exercise the Missouri has had was during sea trials, and that was over two months ago. Hell, some of the gun crew haven't been with the ship long enough to have fired them at all."

It made sense to Sean. "I agree, but include the destroyers and cruisers, except limit their expenditure to six rounds each from their 5-inch guns."

Tony turned to the CIC Officer. "Inform the Captains of the Princeton, Chancellorsville, John Paul Jones, Decatur, and Missouri, to prepare for a live fire exercise to commence at 1600 and order Alpha Whiskey to clear our CAP an additional fifty miles out during the exercise."

At 1600, and after the cloaked F-35s flying CAP reported the extended area clear, Tony witnessed for the first time since he was a Lt. Commander, the sight and sounds of the Missouri's 16-inch guns hurling nine tons of armor piercing destruction downrange. Though the other ships practiced with their 5-inch rapid-fire guns, no one paid them any mind as everyone focused on the violence unleashed by the Missouri's three gun turrets. Looking out on the geysers of water created by the 16" shells through their binoculars the accuracy of the Missouri's gun crews impressed both Sean and Tony. Fifteen minutes later, all was silent again.

Satisfied the gunnery would be sufficient for the upcoming battle, Sean left the bridge. With most of the next day planned and set into motion, it was time to get some sleep. He hadn't had a full night's sleep since they left San Diego. He stopped in on Alicia in the Admirals Quarters to encourage her to do the same.

"Why don't you take a break and join me in a little nap?" Sean immediately realized how this sounded.

"Sounds like a great idea," Alicia teased as she stretched out on the couch. "Renée has a sleepover with some friends tonight, so you know what they say, *when the kids are away…*"

Alicia may only have been teasing, but Sean suddenly felt a powerful urge to take her. Three times over the years, they had gotten close to crossing the line, but duty always intervened. This time the rush of pent up passion short-circuited his commitment to duty, grabbed at his tired mind, and led him over to her. There wasn't any need for conversation as he bent down and placed his lips on the surprised Secretary of Defense. Though her first instinct screamed to pull away, instead she eagerly surrendered.

For the first time since Sean was a teenager, a violent flash of heat permeated his body and buckled his knees. Fortunately, as if choreographed, Alicia threw her arms around his body and pulled him down on her. Their limbs became entangled as they desperately worked to remove the clothes that separated their bodies.

In one swift motion Sean rose from the couch and with Alicia's legs wrapped tightly around his body he staggered into the bedroom; pieces of uniforms marked the path. Sean landed her on the bed and with a passion he didn't know he possessed quickly went about exploring her body from head to toe. As he stared at her naked body, for the first time in his career, he cared little about how his own personal desire affected his command. Neither of them had a conscious thought for the next four hours as energy neither of their sleep deprived bodies had any right to expend flowed freely.

Fortunately, no one needed their attention during this long overdue coupling. Afterward, as they lay in each other's arms, Alicia was the first to break the silence.

"After all the stress of the last two days, it's nice to know I could feel the most simple of pleasures. Look at me." She lifted her shaking arm from under Sean. "I couldn't raise my body off this bed if the ship sank underneath us."

"Hey, I resent the implication anything I just did was simple." Sean couldn't resist a little humor about the various positions they had found themselves in. He also realized he didn't want to minimize the moment and added, "It's amazing it took science fiction to finally do what would have come naturally for others a long time ago."

Still wrapped in each other's bodies, neither made the effort to let the other go. Finally, Alicia recognized the vulnerability of their situation and rolled away from Sean.

"Now would not be a good time for this kind of news to get out. As wonderful as this has been, we better get dressed and return to reality." She thought about what she just said, and laughed. "Reality seems to be a rather overrated concept at this point, don't you think?"

"Not if what we just did is real, it's not."

Alicia quickly jumped out of bed and started to get dressed. All at once, the atmosphere in the room soured. It was as if they both understood this was a one shot opportunity and sneaking around like a couple of teenagers wasn't an option. After she finished dressing, Alicia leaned over and gave him a quick kiss. "It was worth the wait. Thank you."

Moments later, after she disappeared from the bedroom, Sean felt an incredible sense of loss. "Reality sucks."

Sean was still in the shower when Renée arrived. "I brought along the rest of the charts we haven't looked at yet." She put them on the table excited to share what she discovered. "I pulled information on President Roosevelt, his cabinet, US Army Chief of Staff General Marshal, and the Commanders at Pearl for you to review." Renée handed Alicia a flash drive.

Though Renée was all business when she updated Alicia, she could sense something had changed. "If I didn't know better I would think that you went to your happy place." She didn't expect Alicia's reaction. "Oh my God. You're blushing."

"Some nap," Renée thought with a smirk. "It's about damn time."

At that moment, Sean entered the room in a bathrobe towel drying his hair. "I can't believe how well that…" He stopped short when he looked up to see Renée sitting next to Alicia. Catching on quickly by the expression on Renée's face, he beat a hasty retreat back into the bathroom.

Alicia gave Renée a, *You better knock it off or I'm going to claw your eyes out*, look.

Five minutes later, Sean returned fully dressed and without any reference to the obvious, headed to the door. "I'll let you know when we're closing on the Minneapolis and her escorts, which should be in another hour or so."

The second the door closed behind him, Renée began to laugh. "When we flew out from Washington, I could tell by the way you talked about Sean you always wanted more from the man than you were letting on. I'm glad to see it has finally happened."

"What are you talking about?" Though she attempted to sound serious, Alicia couldn't keep the glimpse of a smile hidden from her friend.

Renée was relentless. "That's all right. I'm not going to say another word, because I know you'll eventually explode if you don't tell me."

Ten minutes later, she knew everything.

At 1930 hours, Tony stood on the bridge of the Enterprise with Captain Folger at his side. It was a clear night with a three-quarter moon, and visibility out to four miles. Reports from the CIC counted down the distance that separated the Enterprise Task Force from the World War II era Cruiser and Destroyers. Both men trained their binoculars to the southeast and strained to see through the darkness.

Captain Folger was first to pick something out of the darkness. "I think I've got them."

Tony looked to where the Captain pointed, and as his eyes adjusted, he began to make out the shapes of the two destroyers running ahead of the cruiser.

Sean, Alicia, and Renée watched from outside the Admirals Quarters as the small squadron glided by a mere two miles south of the task force, which allowed a full profile of the Minneapolis and her destroyer escorts.

Throughout the fleet, sailors on and off duty found any place possible to get a glimpse of these ancient warships. Those who knew the history of the USS Porter thought about the crew and that a Japanese submarine had torpedoed her with great loss of life less than a year later.

Sean hoped by allowing these ships to get close, his sailors would embrace the idea that their involvement could save the flesh and blood of their ancestral shipmates. As he looked out over the Enterprise flight deck, he observed large numbers of sailors with binoculars. He watched their animated gestures as the ships appeared and then slowly fall silent as the squadron disappeared into the night.

As the ships faded from the radar screen, Tony looked down at the charts spread out in front of him. He estimated the Seawolf should make contact with Nagumo's carrier force within the next two hours. When they made contact, the battle he planned would enter the opening stage.

"Charles, I'll be in the CIC waiting to hear from Captain Daily." Tony wanted to be there when the Seawolf sighted Nagumo's fleet.

"Captain's off the bridge!" the Officer of the Watch sung out.

⊰⊱

Brisk debate had continued on the Seawolf throughout the day, punctuated by two crewmembers who needed to be separated when one particularly religious zealot condemned the decision to become involved. He proceeded to punch the crewmate who, in the course of disagreeing, had asked the fundamentalist a simple question. "Is this the same God who sanctioned Catholic priests to molest young boys?"

Captain Daily knew action was the best cure for a restless crew, so he put all hands to battle stations to focus their attention. At a depth of one hundred and fifty feet and onboard the 21st Century's most quiet propulsion system, he knew the Japanese destroyers couldn't pick up the Seawolf on sonar. However, he wanted the crew to operate as if they were on the hunt of a modern warship to keep them sharp.

At 2330 hours, Captain Daily was contemplating how weird it was going to be when they sighted the Japanese ships. After another fifteen minutes passed, he was about to refresh his cold coffee, when the sonar operator reported multiple contacts.

"Take us to periscope depth." When the Seawolf reached the proper depth, Captain Daily scanned the surface and abruptly stopped. He backed away and turned to his XO. "You need to see this."

The sight of the Japanese Fleet's forward screening ships greeted the Commander. They had made contact with Nagumo's fleet. "I count six destroyers leading two heavy cruisers closing in from the northwest, about 35 degrees and 6500 yards off our port quarter."

"Reduce speed to ten knots," Captain Daily ordered. He wanted to allow the Japanese to pass to starboard.

"I now have two more heavy cruisers, followed by two battleships." The XO swung the periscope thirty degrees and shouted, "Good God! I count three, four, five, six carriers! I'm seeing the main show two miles astern of the battleships!"

Captain Daily took over the periscope. The view was surreal, silhouetted in the moonlight like ghosts from another era. They seemed to pass endlessly until all six of the carriers cruised through his view, with three destroyers bringing up the rear. Sonar broke the spell to report a submerged target off their port side on the same course as the Seawolf, three thousand yards out. It was one of the three reconnaissance submarines attached to the Japanese fleet. Daily ordered the ship's periscope lowered, and set a course to shadow the fleet. After the Seawolf was two miles behind the last of the ships, he sent the flash message to end any doubt as to when and where they were in history.

This realization put Captain Mark Daily in a melancholy mood. "This *is* for real," he thought. "I am probably not going to see my wife and kids again."

Sean was in the Admirals Ready Room going over the battle plan for the twentieth time when the CIC reported the news. He thought about what could be in store for them on what would surely become one of the strangest days a person would ever experience. He didn't have time to delve very far into the implications because his thoughts were interrupted by a voice from the bedroom.

"I figured you might want some company tonight. You seem to have run out of problems for the day. Maybe we can take advantage of your free time."

It took only a moment for Sean to decide he could live with being a teenager for one more day. His feet voluntarily followed the sultry voice to the bedroom where the rest of the night passed exploring new ways to further their growing bond.

Chapter Four

A Date Which Will Live in Infamy

The next morning 6 December 1941 at 0500, found Sean in the CIC with Tony and Lt. Commander Osaka studying the plan to intercept the codebreakers. The task force had closed to within fifty miles south by southeast of Oahu, and were about to alter course to take them west of Lanai close to the southern coast of Molokai. It was then the Hampton reported a submerged contact five thousand yards north of the fleet.

Osaka pointed to the maps. "Admiral, according to the chart Captain Aslan supplied, the contact is the Japanese submarine I-16. It's one of the five carrying midget submarines, and is on a heading for Pearl."

"Do you want to take her out?" Tony asked, eager for action.

"Let's leave it alone for now," Sean answered with a smile, acknowledging Tony's need to blow something up. "Let's bring the codebreakers aboard first. We'll still know where it is when we head toward the Kauai Channel."

The CIC Officer interrupted their conversation. "Admiral, Alpha Whiskey has picked up several small contacts 25 miles off the southern coast of Molokai."

Sean ordered the CIC Officer, "Inform the task force to set a course to take us to 3 miles south of the contacts."

"Yes Sir."

Tony turned to Osaka. "Your boat should be in the area where we have identified multiple contacts. We will be close enough to launch the SEAL squad in the next hour, after you confirm their location."

"Aye Aye Captain."

At 0600, the SEAL squad gathered in a recess on the Enterprise's port side and waited to enter the launch that would take them over to the fishing boat. So they wouldn't look out of place, they dressed in basic Navy khaki uniforms, which had not changed much since World War II.

Tony approached the squad and yelled out to the imposing man who was shouting orders like a drill sergeant. "How can the Navy expect to get the most out of its elite forces when they still have wheezy old men from WWII to lead them? Oh I get it, you're the one responsible for us being here in 1941. You missed the good old days."

Without slowing down or turning around, the man responded sarcastically. "Until it can actually train some officers to replace worthless screw ups like the Admiral's Chief of Staff, I'm afraid this man's Navy might sink beneath the waves under the weight of their stupidity."

When the SEAL squad noticed Tony's rank, all four members snapped to attention. This interruption in his preparations caused the imposing figure to slowly turn around to face Tony, and as he did, gave a look of menace that had terrorized many a new member to SEAL Team 7.

Tony returned the glare for a few moments, to the discomfort of the rigid sailors, until a big smile suddenly spread across his face. However, his smile didn't bring any noticeable change in attitude in the SEAL squad leader's threatening demeanor.

"You come down here to wish us luck? Because if you did, based on whatever it is you and your friends on the bridge have cooked up, I'd rather you didn't. You guys realize how many ways we can get screwed with the shit you're trying to pull off?"

"As a matter of fact, I think we're pretty clear about how thin the ice is underneath us. Besides, it seems to me you have it pretty cushy these days, Thorny, not at all like I remember you back in Iraq in 2003."

Tony turned to the still frozen SEAL squad. "At ease gentlemen. Did the Commander tell you about how he single-handedly saved Baghdad during the Iraq War by storming the Mukarayin Dam to keep Saddam's people from blowing it?" Tony knew Commander Michael Thornton, Thorny to his friends for obvious reasons, used past missions to show his squad how many ways a mission could blow up in your face. "Or was it the Polish GROM?" [Polish Special Forces who helped secure the dam]

This brought a quick chuckle from one of the men.

"Corporal Harris, recheck all your gear," Thorny barked in rebuke, as he gave Tony a slight nod to follow him. When they were out of earshot, he relaxed. "What the hell are you guys trying to do?"

Commander Thornton was in the 22nd year of his service to the Navy, and in his day, he was on the short list of those expected to accomplish the impossible. Known throughout the SEAL community for his abilities to combine sheer brute force with acute battlefield awareness, he was a legend in the Navy, and every SEAL in the service wanted to serve under his command. Now in his mid-forties, the man still had a physical presence of a coiled snake, except this snake was six foot three, 260 pounds, and could bench press 340 pounds.

"To tell you the truth, this part of the operation should be a piece of cake," Tony assured him. "The mission is exactly what it sounds like. Get a couple of geeks off a civilian charter and bring them aboard. But seriously, I have the unpleasant feeling your squads will be in the thick of it before too long."

"What I want to know, is do any of the brainiacs on the Missouri have any ideas about how to get us back home?"

"We have the best person working on it, and based on my read of the woman in charge, if she can't get it done, no one can. I'll try to keep you in the loop as much as possible. I've got to get back on the CIC." Without another word, Tony turned and started to walk away.

"What? You're not going to wish us luck?"

Without breaking stride, Tony disappeared, leaving Thorny to smile for the first time.

At 0630, Lt. Commander Osaka worked the ship's short band radio to send out his message directed toward Molokai. Within ten minutes, he received the response he was looking for.

"This is the Flying Tuna, Captain Fletcher speaking. I have the men you are looking for onboard – over."

Osaka had a difficult time controlling his excitement. "Thank you Captain. Please maintain your course and speed. Let Commander Edwin Layton and Lt. Jasper Holmes know a Navy launch is on the way to pick them up – over and out."

Twenty minutes later on the Enterprise bridge, Sean listened to the SEAL squad's conversation as the launch approached the Flying Tuna.

"Good morning, gentlemen. What's with the rush to get hold of us?" asked Lt. Commander Edwin Layton, dressed in a battered shirt, dungarees, and a fishing lure festooned hat.

"I'm sorry, Sir, but I'm not at liberty to say," the stoic SEAL in charge replied. "Your questions will be answered when we return to our ship."

"A Date Which Will Live in Infamy"

"What ship? All I see is empty ocean." This wasn't making any sense to the Lt. Commander. "Whose orders are you acting under?"

"Sir, we are under strict orders from CINCPACFLT to retrieve you and Lt. Holmes. My orders further state you don't have the option to refuse."

While the conversation took place, two members of the SEAL squad boarded the fishing boat; their presence drove home the point the codebreakers didn't have a choice.

With a shrug, both men boarded the launch.

Their sense of unease built as the launch sped them away, violently pounding up and down on the ocean swells while the man guiding the launch remained oblivious to his passengers' discomfort. After ten minutes of this, Lt. Commander Layton couldn't take it anymore. "I demand that…," was all he got out when the launch pierced Specter's cloak and the task force magically appeared out of nowhere.

"Holy shit!" Lt. Commander Layton yelled in disbelief above the screaming engine. "Where the hell did these ships come from? Holy shit! Look at the size of that aircraft carrier, Jasper!"

"You see it too? Thank God, I thought the pounding we're taking jarred my brain loose," Lt. Jasper Holms nervously joked. "Look at the ship closest to us. Have you ever seen a silhouette like that?"

"Who the hell are you guys?" Lt. Commander Layton demanded. "And how can warships appear out of nowhere?" Once again, their answer was only silence as they passed the destroyer John Paul Jones and made their way to the port side of the Enterprise.

Onboard the Flying Tuna, the Captain watched the launch and was curious why the ship it belonged to was nowhere in sight. With his attention on getting underway again, he blanched when out of the corner of his eye the launch vanished. "What the hell?" His instincts told him it was not far enough away to lose sight of, yet with the rest of the fishermen aft and no one to confirm what he thought he saw, he chalked the mystery up to crazy Navy secrecy.

The size of the Enterprise blocked Sean's view from the bridge as the boat came alongside. "Contact Captain Knox and Commander Osaka in the CIC and have them greet our guests and then to escort them to the Admirals Ready Room."

"Yes Admiral," the Bridge Communication Officer acknowledged.

"I feel like Jody Foster making First Contact with an alien world," Tony joked as he and Osaka reached the flight deck.

Tony could hear colorful language emitting from the obviously upset, shanghaied scientists as they approached the flight deck. When they saw the rank on Tony's shoulders, they shut up, stopped abruptly, saluted, and stood at attention.

"At ease gentlemen," Tony responded as he returned the salute. "Sorry to interrupt your fishing trip on such a beautiful day."

Lt. Commander Edwin T. Layton stood five feet seven inches tall, and, unusual for an intellectual, possessed a sturdy body with a face that reminded Tony of Dano in the 1960s original TV series Hawaii Five-O.

Layton was about to comment on the size of the Enterprise flight deck, when he caught sight of the Missouri. "Excuse me Captain, but who *are* you guys, and where did that monster come from?"

His counterpart, Lt. Jasper Holmes, looked more the stereotypical geek, being dumpy in appearance, with a set of black-rimmed glasses on a face ravaged by a bout with adolescent acne. Dates had to be hard to come by for the intelligence officer.

Before they could ask another question, Tony interceded. "I am Captain Anthony Knox, and this is Lt. Commander Daniel Osaka, our Information Warfare Officer, the one who contacted you."

After they shook hands and the two guests introduced themselves, Tony continued. "There will be plenty of time for questions. Please come with us." While they walked, Tony could feel the ship heel to port as the task force turned west toward open waters.

Sean stood up when they entered the Admirals Ready Room, and both men once again came to attention and saluted.

"At ease gentlemen. Please be seated. I'm sure you have many questions."

"I'm Lt. Commander Edwin Layton, and this is Lt. Jasper Holmes." Under the circumstances, Layton spoke directly to what was on his mind. "Excuse me Sir, but who are you? I counted eight ships in your group, and I can honestly say none of them belongs to the US Navy I know. What's this carrier's tonnage anyway? She looks close to one thousand feet long. In addition, I noticed her smoke stacks are missing. What's powering this ship?"

"I am Admiral Sean Phillips, and this task force is part of the United States Navy. The ship you are on is the USS Enterprise CVN-65, which displaces close to one hundred thousand tons, and you are correct, she is one thousand one hundred twenty-three feet long." Sean dodged the power question by redirecting the conversation. "Now, I've answered your questions, could you please answer one for me? Commander Osaka told me you two possess the best scientific minds at Pearl. Is he right?"

Lt. Holmes nervously answered Sean's question. "Within the island's scientific community, I guess you can say that's true with regard to our math skills."

"You have Commander Osaka here to thank for your presence, or to blame if things go wrong. Commander, please explain why you picked these gentlemen out of your hat."

Osaka opened his laptop on the table and motioned for them to look. "I am an encryption officer like you, with the major difference being what my computers are capable of." Osaka then opened one of the files, which displayed Japanese military codes from 1941.

"Either of you recognize this?"

"What are we looking at?" Layton's eyes ignored the content and remained glued to the little box that popped up full color pictures.

Osaka glanced at Sean, who shook his head no. "I'm sorry Commander Layton, but if you could focus on what's *on* the screen."

"Who are these people?" Layton thought as he fought to calm his racing mind before he answered. "These are the Japanese naval codes."

Osaka clicked the mouse. "Now what do you see?"

At this point Sean decided it was a good time to leave the three math geeks alone. "Rather than confuse you more than you already are, I'm going to leave you with Commander Osaka who will show you around the Enterprise after he answers a few more or your questions.

"Commander, a word."

They walked out to the corridor where Sean advised the Commander. "Spend the next hour or two to get a feel for if you're right about their usefulness. However, leave out any references to what we are up to. I have ordered these two Marines to stay with them until I am convinced they won't be any trouble. If you feel a need to impress them, keep your show and tell to information no later than the fifties. Also, do not tell them what powers this ship."

"Yes Sir. Is it all right to show them the attack on Pearl Harbor to give them a sense of urgency?"

"Yes. I think it would help explain to them why they are here."

"Thank you Sir." Osaka wished he felt as confident as he sounded, social conversation not being one of his strong suits. At least he knew nobody understood these men as he did.

When they re-entered the room, Sean gave a nod to Tony. "It's time we went to the CIC to check on the locations of our friends." With that, they left Osaka alone with his guests.

When they arrived in the CIC, Alicia and Renée were already

there listening to communications from Captain Marlowe Turner on the attack submarine USS Hampton, one mile ahead of the group. For the next hour, they waited impatiently to reestablish contact with the Japanese submarine.

At 1000 hours, the Hampton reported they had reacquired the I-16, three thousand yards off the Hamptons port bow.

Sean didn't give it second thought as he addressed the CIC Officer. "Give Captain Turner the go ahead."

"Yes Sir"

Captain Turner looked over at his weapons officer who reported, "I've fed the coordinates into the submarine's targeting computer. Ready to fire Captain."

Turner didn't hesitate. "Fire." With this order, one Mark-48 torpedo sped out of the tube and ran straight and true towards its target.

"Twenty-five hundred yards and closing… Two thousand yards and has acquired target…" This went on for the next minute and a half without another word spoken among the crew.

The crew on the I-16 had no warning. One minute they were alive and planning the strike on Pearl, the next an imploded mess plummeting to the bottom of the ocean.

From the deck of the John Paul Jones came a roar as the sailors witnessed a large column of water shoot up into the morning sky a half mile off the ship's bow that announced the torpedo's detonation. This was not a simulation.

As the John Paul Jones passed over the area where the Mark-48 torpedo exploded, the crew watched an oil slick develop, with objects popping up to the surface, including a body or two. The sailors, who were so vocal watching the geyser, were now silent as the grim reality of the first sinking of a Japanese warship by American action in World War II hit home.

Moments later in the Enterprise CIC, "Sir, Captain Turner reports the I-16 destroyed." Sean heard this with a sense of detachment he found disturbing. He looked over at Alicia and Tony, and he could see in their faces a similar reaction to the submarine's destruction.

"Feels unreal, doesn't it?" Renée observed. "Part of some badly written movie, the kind so badly written it's lacking in any suspense, and you always know what's going to happen next."

Alicia looked at the video feed of the bodies drifting by the John Paul Jones. "Except those bodies are real."

Tony added his own feelings about ordering the death of others. "It reminds me of how I felt when we launched cruise missiles into Bagdad from five hundred miles away and thinking how sanitized we've become in our ability to kill people.

"Politicians don't have to deal with the brutal reality of the horrific damage they unleash. I'm still pissed off Bush junior banned media coverage of the soldiers who returned home in coffins from Iraq and Afghanistan, and how the American public allowed this disrespect to their sacrifice. Thousands of soldiers died while the public went about their lives with a sticker of a tiny yellow bow on the back window of their BMWs, as if that made them some kind of patriot."

As the impact of what they started sunk in, they spent the next few minutes in silence, reflecting on the world they had left behind.

Alicia broke the somber mood. "Well, here's hoping we make a difference this time around."

Once again, Sean turned to what was next. "I think we've given Osaka enough time with our guests." He started to walk to the door. "Let's go see if he is right and we can make use of their presence."

Sean, Alicia, and Tony returned to the ready room where they found Osaka still at his laptop and the codebreakers in animated conversation. The three men rose to salute, but Sean motioned for them to remain seated. "I see you've got their attention

Commander." Sean peered over their shoulders to see encryption codes.

"Both Commander Layton and Lt. Holmes are quick studies Sir." Daniel was obviously pleased with himself about how the two men seemed at home. Then again, it didn't matter what environment you put mathematicians in as long as the equations challenged their curiosity.

"Have you informed our guests what we need from them?"

"No Sir, not yet."

"No time like the present," thought Sean. "At 0720 tomorrow, the Japanese will launch close to three hundred bombers and torpedo planes off the decks of six aircraft carriers two hundred miles north of Oahu. Show them the footage Commander."

Osaka opened the file and began to play the documentary footage of the destruction of battleship row that culminated in the annihilation of the Arizona.

The look of disbelief on their faces told Sean all he needed to know. He let the images sink in before he continued. "When the last wave returned to their carriers, every battleship in the United States Pacific Fleet were either sunk or heavily damaged, and over twenty-four hundred sailors, Army personnel, and civilians were dead. Over eleven hundred dead remain entombed in the bowels of the Arizona lying on the bottom of the harbor. It was blind luck our carriers were at sea during the attack, or there wouldn't have been anything within three thousand miles to counter the Japanese.

"You two were part of the team that allowed the Navy to read the Japanese encryption codes accurately, which led to their defeat at the Battle of Midway in June of 1942," Sean concluded.

"You're saying this all happens tomorrow morning?" a visibly shocked Lt. Holmes asked.

Tony took over. "We've tracked their force since yesterday morning, and we're on our way to their launch position now. If all goes as planned, the bulk of the Imperial Japanese Navy will be on the bottom of the ocean by 0800 tomorrow morning."

Sean got to the point. "We brought you here as observers to witness the Japanese Carrier force preparing to launch this attack, to certify our response, and act as our liaison with Admiral Kimmel and General Short. Do either of you have any objections to carrying out this role for us?"

It was Lt. Commander Layton, who answered for both men. "Everything you explained is way above our pay grade, and I honestly don't know what to believe. Why did you choose us? We are nobodies in the greater scheme of things. If what you say is true, and I can't say I believe you at this point, what choice do we have as officers of the United States Navy?"

He hesitated before laying open his own fears. "Besides, what would you do with us if we refused? You have shown us movies that detail the destruction of the 7th Fleet, which if they were fake would do Cecil B. DeMille proud. All of this, while aboard a ship that should not exist, and all you want from us is to watch you destroy the Japanese force so we can verify it happened? If I read the situation correctly Sir, regardless of what we say you will not allow us off this ship until you've met the threat."

Tony liked Lt. Commander Layton's pragmatic thinking. "You have read it perfectly Commander. Even if the forces at Pearl had time to sortie against the Japanese, the odds are they would be destroyed as well."

"I appreciate your quick decision," Sean acknowledged. "Commander Osaka will see you to the cabin we have prepared for you. I am sorry to inform you, but these two Marines will have to accompany you wherever you go, and you will be restricted from certain areas of the ship. Commander Osaka will be available to give you any information you need pertaining to the United States war efforts, but that's as far as he can take it for now. I'll leave you in his capable hands, as I have further duties to attend to."

When they returned to the CIC, Alicia offered up her own assessment. "Osaka read these men well. It looks like we have the right people to bridge our two worlds. I'm beginning to think we might be able to pull this off."

Both Sean and Tony shot Alicia a look as if asking, "Are you trying to tempt the fates?" Although they easily destroyed the first Japanese submarine, they both knew from experience nothing went as planned once weapons of war were unleashed.

As they continued west, the Hampton identified the next target along their course, and once again, the Japanese submarine I-18 was right where it was supposed to be. The Hampton expended another precious Mark-48 torpedo with the same results. Two more of the midget carrying submarines were disposed of as the task force passed directly south of Pearl Harbor. Tony felt little excitement in what amounted to shooting ducks in a barrel.

The historical archives showed the last of the five midget carrying submarines, the I-22, sitting on the ocean floor at a depth of one hundred and thirty feet, two miles from the harbor entrance. Tony contacted Captain Marlowe Turner of the Hampton, and they both agreed, though the risk was greater, to deploy divers from the Hampton to attach mines to the Japanese submarine to keep from using a fifth Mark-48 torpedo.

Forty-five minutes after they detached from the group, the Hampton came to a rest one hundred and fifty yards from the bottomed submarine. Three divers exited the Hampton, swam over, and attached two mines to the hull. After completing this task, the third diver snapped pictures of the midget sub attached to the I-22 behind the conning tower to document the mission. Within twenty minutes, all three divers were back on the Hampton, and she backed slowly into deeper waters. When the submarine was clear of the I-22, the crew felt the detonations that signaled the destruction of the carrier of the last hostile midget submarine assigned to enter the harbor on the 7th.

By 1300, the task force passed the western end of Oahu, and turned north through the Kauai Channel. After he called Dr. Cutler for an update, Tony decided to take another walk around the Enterprise to gauge the crew's readiness for the upcoming action. Along the way, he picked up strains of music from belowdecks, and as the song became clearer, he recognized the sound of Benny Goodman's Blue Skies. He reached the enlisted mess and found the song was playing on the overhead speakers to a roomful of sailors, who upon seeing the Chief of Staff enter the room, rose to attention.

"At ease, gentlemen." Tony walked through the mess hall to the end of the chow line and grabbed a plate.

"So where did you find this golden oldie? One of you steal it from your grandmother?" This elicited a laugh from those present.

From the head of the line, one of the sailors spooning potatoes onto the next plate spoke up. "No Sir. We picked up a radio station out of Honolulu, and we figured, *When in Rome*... They played some trippy songs earlier that rocked by some girl band called the Andrew Sisters."

Tony felt old when he remembered how his grandmother spent Sunday mornings listening to the sounds of Glen Miller, Benny Goodman, Ella Fitzgerald, and of course one of her favorites, the Andrew Sisters.

"This reminds me of my first days afloat, when I served under an old salt of a Captain named Reggie Harris. Keep in mind this was the seventies and my generation was rocking to the Doors, Led Zeppelin, and the like. He showed the same disgust for our music as most of you Rappers have for mine. Listening to this music takes me back to those days and how old he seemed to me because his music and mine were worlds apart."

When his plate was full, Tony found an open seat at a table with what looked like sailors right out of boot camp, bringing them to a nervous silence. He picked out one especially spooked youngster and asked him, "What made you decide to go to sea sailor?"

"I'm third generation Navy, Sir. My grandfather served twenty-one years, the first four of them fighting in the Atlantic aboard the USS Scorpion, a WWII Gato Class Submarine. He used to tell me stories all the time about how he was part of the original crew on the first nuclear submarine, Nautilus. I wasn't focused in school, so I hoped by joining the Navy my grandfather loved, I could find something in it as well. I sure never expected this. Do you think we're ever going to see home again?"

Tony knew every conversation with the crew would include the sailor's last question. "Considering not a person among us could have possibly foreseen being here in the first place, I can equally say there isn't any reason to believe we can't somehow find a way home. The older I get, the more I realize it isn't how you get to where you're at, it is how you make the best of the moment you're in. Maybe this is the lesson we need to embrace. Who knows, maybe there is a higher power looking over our shoulder to see how we measure up, and if that is the case, we must be some very special people to be picked for such a job."

"What's it going to be like when we meet the Japanese tomorrow, Captain?" This question came from a sailor five feet five inches tall, and by the look of his pale complexion, a strange candidate for surface duty.

Tony guessed this was not his first choice. "You wanted submarine duty, didn't you? What happened?"

All the sailors stopped short at the Captain's intuition as the embarrassed sailor answered. "I had a little trouble in the flood tank and they don't give many second chances, Sir."

"Well if it makes you feel any better, I joined to be a fighter jock, and look how things turned out for me. You've got to figure life has something different in store for you, and instead of Dolphins on your uniform you might someday become some future ship's Chief instead."

The conversation continued until Tony finished his meal. "Get plenty of rest because tomorrow is going to be unlike anything you've ever been a part of."

"We're used to that being the case every day Sir." This gave everybody a laugh.

As usual, every word Tony shared with the sailors over dinner spread would throughout the ship. Even some of the doubters softened their criticism when they heard exaggerated stories of the Chief of Staff as just one of the boys, or in the case of the female sailor's, more of a calming father.

The sailors in the mess hall all rose to attention as Tony left the room.

When he reached the cavernous hangar of the Enterprise, he found the plane crews were all business preparing the F-35s for the next day's mission, while in the Pilot Ready Room the aircrews went over their attack profiles to ensure their timely delivery over Nagumo's carriers. Each of the two thousand pound bombs loaded onto the planes had the name of its intended target scribbled on them, continuing a tradition that became fashionable during World War II.

On his way up to the flight deck, Tony thought about how difficult it must be for the younger sailors who needed their world to make sense. It wasn't lost on Tony that he was more comfortable with the sailors of the lower decks than the privileged class he came from. Then there was Sean, who was just the opposite, he came from little, yet was at ease with power. There was no better place than the military to allow two people from such diverse backgrounds to cross paths as equals, let alone develop their friendship.

When he reached the Admirals Ready Room and opened the

door, he noticed something different. He looked over at Renée seated at the conference table and then at Sean and Alicia, who were sitting close together on the couch.

"Dr. Cutler seems to have her people under control," Tony began. "She thinks there might be a way to get us back home, but based on her explanation, I wouldn't count on it." He stopped for a moment and looked around the room as if something was missing. "I can't put my finger on it, but something is out of place."

Renée gave him a look, as if to say, duh.

Now that he thought about it, Alicia had barely left Sean's side over the last thirty-six hours. Tony was so busy he didn't notice the subtle changes in their relationship. When the realization hit him, all he could do was awkwardly stand there.

Alicia decided she should throw the dumbfounded Captain a rope. "What's the matter, Tony? You look like you've seen a ghost."

"With the way things are going, I wouldn't be at all surprised if I started seeing ghosts, with Johnny Depp leading the way, turning us all into Disney pirates. I hear Tortuga is lovely this time of year. I see congratulations are in order, and come to think of it, I am a Captain with the legal right to make an honest couple out of you two."

"Very funny," Sean replied. "I think our lives are complicated enough without announcing to the crew we have become King Phillips and Queen Elizabeth II."

"I don't know Sean," Alicia countered. "King Phillips has a familiar ring to it, but I'd like to change mine to Marie Antoinette."

"I think you both know what I mean," Tony muttered. "An open admission of you two spooning would limit your ability to appear unbiased. In addition, it would encourage people with views similar to Captain Brewster's to imagine you are conspiring to assume dictatorial authority. You think Marc Anthony knew what he was getting into the first time he crossed swords with Cleopatra. We all know how that worked out for the Egyptians." Tony couldn't resist the analogy.

Sean laid the issue to rest. "Alicia and I made the decision that news of our relationship would not go any further than the two of you."

"Just your luck," Renée added. "You finally get to consummate a relationship twenty years in the making, and then you have to deny it."

"We can't risk discipline among the crew breaking down." Sean then teased, "Besides Tony, you couldn't marry us anyway. How could you be my best man if you did? But seriously, we've had a full day, and…"

"You can say that again!" Renée couldn't resist the poke.

Sean gave her a look. "We all need to call it a day."

Renée got up and left, followed shortly by Tony.

Sean looked at Alicia. "Did I hear somebody say something about spooning?"

By 2330, the task force closed in on the coordinates where the Japanese would launch their strike. The Seawolf had sped ahead of the enemy fleet during the night and rejoined the Enterprise Task Force at 0300 the next morning, 7 December 1941.

Reveille sounded throughout the task force at 0330, which gave the crew an hour to prepare before ordered to battle stations. After a subdued breakfast, Sean, Alicia, Tony, and Renée joined Captain Folger and Commander Barrish on the bridge. Captain Daily reported in at 0500 that the attack submarines had repositioned four miles to the east where the Japanese would launch their assault. Thus began for Tony the most excruciating wait since he had to attend church, when his most inspired prayer was, "Please let this damn thing end."

At 0530, per Sean's orders, Osaka arrived on the bridge with the two codebreakers. "Thank you Commander Osaka. You can assume your duties now."

"Aye Aye Admiral." Osaka saluted and left the bridge.

Tony noticed the codebreakers look awkwardly at each other. "Relax gentlemen. You're about to become witnesses to living history."

"You'll excuse me Captain Knox, if I appear to be nervous," Lt. Commander Edwin Layton answered. "But the closer we've gotten to your target time, the more difficult it is to believe in my own sanity. I keep thinking this is part of some whacked out delusion."

Lt. Jasper Holmes shared these sentiments with a nod of agreement.

"You'll get used to the feeling. I've discovered over the last four days it gets easier with time. Just relax and prepare to be amazed."

The morning broke clear and bright, so with binoculars focused to the north, the Japanese scouting force came into view exactly at the location preordained by history. One mile behind the heavy cruisers, battleships, and destroyers appeared the six Japanese flattops with scores of personnel preparing the planes for action.

The group watched the activity on the Enterprise flight deck as the first two F-35s were loaded onto the catapults. At 0540, Sean gave the order to launch the strike force. The F-35s shot into the air, gaining altitude as they headed north. During the next ten minutes, the rest of the attack force of eight F-35s launched and joined them. With the cloaked task force on an opposing parallel course with the Japanese fleet, the Missouri moved to the starboard side of the Enterprise so she would be starboard to starboard with the battleship Kirisima when she fired her 16-inch guns.

On the bridge of the Akagi, all of the doubts Admiral Nagumo felt about this mission faded away with the launch of his first attack wave only minutes away. There hadn't been any sightings of reconnaissance overflights or radio intercepts revealing their presence to the Americans. Now it would be up to his well-trained pilots to capitalize on their surprise. He looked on with pride at the precision of the choreographed movements as the crew positioned the tightly packed armed and fueled planes on the flight deck. For the first time in weeks, a slight smile appeared on his face.

The lead Japanese destroyers were now to the south of the Enterprise Task Force, which had reached the mission distance of ten miles. As the lead group of six cloaked F-35s circled back at 0555, all eyes were on the Japanese fleet. The flight leader, Air Wing Commander, Captain *Dash* Nelson, counted down the seconds to 0600.

Over the bridge speakers, they listened as he reported his bomb released and tracking along the laser beam fixed on the aft section of Nagumo's flagship, Akagi. The other five cloaked F-35s dropped their bombs within seconds of his, while the reserve package of the four uncloaked F-35s flew five miles to the west.

On the flight deck of the Akagi, a young member of a plane crew un-chocked the wheels of a Kate dive-bomber. After signaling the pilot good luck, he looked to his right and saw a bright red point of light on the deck. When he looked up to find the source of this oddity, the sight of a plunging two thousand pound bomb registered its proper horror before it penetrated the unarmored flight deck of the carrier to the hangar deck below.

The explosion rocketed back upward, vaporizing the sailor and detonating thousands of pounds of bombs and fueled planes as it blew them into the air like toys. In the hangar deck, a raging inferno erupted triggering a string of explosions that gutted the carrier. The blast was so intense it penetrated the carrier's island, killing everyone on the bridge. Before Admiral Nagumo could realize what happened, he became the first famous warrior of WWII to have his name erased from history.

The same result repeated on the remaining five Japanese Carriers, as one by one bombs ripped through the Shokaku, Zuikaku, Hiryu,

Soryu, and Kaga, tearing the core of the Japanese strike force apart.

From high above the blazing carriers, the pilots of the four F-35s in reserve could see they wouldn't need to deliver their payloads on the infernos below. They continued to circle with a front row seat to what followed.

Everyone on the bridge stood mesmerized by the sight and sounds of the massive carriers as they blew apart in rippling waves of explosions until the roar of the Missouri's 16-inch guns caught their attention. Firing as one, the recoil of the nine guns pushed the Missouri sideways through the water as they unleashed eighteen thousand pounds of armor piercing metal down range.

The shells covered the ten miles in seconds, and slammed into the upper decks of the Kirisima, with one shell penetrating its number two forward 14-inch gun turret. The force of the explosion launched the entire turret off the deck and out a quarter mile in front of the ship. In rapid succession, six more shells tore into the structure, turning the once graceful ship into a splintered wreck. Stunned by the sheer brutality, Sean continued to watch through the lens of his binoculars as the Missouri increased to flank speed.

After a course change to take the Missouri between the Japanese carriers and the rear guard of cruisers and destroyers, the rest of the task force increased their speed to match the Missouri's turn to get at the second Japanese battleship. Onboard the Princeton, gun crews locked their Harpoon missiles on the trailing Japanese warships as a precaution.

The escorting ships of the Japanese task force began to pour rounds of undirected fire into both the air and at imaginary surface targets. The Japanese ships in the front, heeled sharply to port and headed back along the same track as the American ships. It was apparent in the way the Japanese maneuvered that they also assumed there were enemy submarines in the area responsible for the attack on their carriers. Halfway through their turn, a large eruption of water shot up signaling the Seawolf's destruction of the I-19 submarine. A second waterspout shot up behind the charging Japanese ships that signaled the Hampton's first kill. Ninety seconds later the third Japanese submarine met the same fate.

The Missouri closed the distance on the battleship Hiei, and a second devastating salvo whistled like a freight train through the air before it slammed into the Japanese battleship. When one of the shells penetrated her forward magazine, a catastrophic explosion sent wreckage hurling hundreds of yards into the air. As the smoke cleared, there was only a view of the stern section of the ship, vertical in the water, while its massive propellers spun wildly in the air.

The sight of the shattered battleship mesmerized Sean. He recalled the Battle of Jutland, and its witnesses who described the destruction of the Battle Cruiser HMS Hood in such a manner. With the image of the Hiei's destruction burned into his consciousness, he turned away and ordered the fleet to retire to the west to recover the F-35s that had ripped the heart out of the Japanese Navy with only six cast iron bombs.

Still with a sense of awe at how quickly they decimated the Japanese fleet, Sean turned his attention to the two equally shocked codebreakers. They hadn't had a chance to gather their thoughts, when Sean broke in.

"As you witnessed, without a formal declaration of war, planes from the Japanese carriers were about to launch a strike directed at our forces stationed at Pearl Harbor, which would have resulted in the destruction we showed you earlier." After saying this, Sean realized that from here on, nothing of his past memories now existed. They were truly on a new path.

What remained of the Japanese strike force spent the next hour dropping depth charges on phantom submarines, which only served to kill survivors from the sinking ships. Still hidden under Specter's cloak, the sailors of the American task force watched as the

"A Date Which Will Live in Infamy"

Japanese ships tried to pick up their comrades in the oil-polluted waters. Through his binoculars, Sean could make out the state of disbelief on the survivors faces from the sudden destruction, which to them must have come straight from the gates of Hell.

Back at Pearl Harbor, one of the radio operators on duty picked up a chorus of distressed communications in Japanese from north of the island. He rushed to inform his senior officer, who verified the intercepts, and ordered PBYs [flying boats] to the area.

An hour later anti-aircraft fire greeted them from the remnants of the Japanese fleet. This stopped the rescue effort and they began a hasty retreat. With the confirmation of Japanese warships in the vicinity and firing on the PBYs, Admiral Kimmel ordered Admiral William Halsey's USS Enterprise CV-6, which was 200 miles west of Pearl, to converge on the coordinates. Then he ordered his battleships to sortie. Halsey's carrier planes arrived an hour later to the sight of a large debris field mixed in with large patches of ocean still ablaze from thousands of gallons of spilled fuel.

The confusion only increased, when the first American ships arrived on the scene, and discovered hundreds of bodies in Japanese naval uniforms in the debris field. It was only after they were able to pull the few survivors out of the water and lead them off to interpreters that the full extent of what happened came to view. A powerful Japanese strike force was in American waters. The only logical explanation for their presence and the firing on the PBYs was to attack the American fleet at Pearl Harbor. The bigger question was what happened to them?

The scene at Pacific Fleet Command was chaotic, as conflicting reports came in throughout the day. Finally, Admiral Kimmel reported to Admiral Nimitz that a naval engagement had taken place. When Nimitz in turn informed President Roosevelt, Japanese Ambassador Kichisaburō Nomura had just presented Roosevelt with the Declaration of War.

Confusion reigned throughout the day as no one could supply a satisfactory explanation to who had destroyed the powerful carrier force. This mystery then rippled its way out, creating shock waves all over the world. When the news made its way to Washington, and thus reached the foreign spy networks in London, Berlin, and Stalingrad rumors began to circulate that the Americans had developed a new super weapon. In war-torn Europe and Asia, propaganda machines began to pump out false accounts of the event. While this was underway, the Japanese Government made the decision to continue invasion plans for Wake Island, but decided to put the invasion of the Philippines on hold until they learned what had destroyed their carrier fleet.

For the rest of the morning off to the west and under the cloak of Specter, the Laramie refueled the task force. When she completed the task, Tony and Lt. Commander James Peck calculated how much fuel they had burned since leaving San Diego, and how much they had left. They checked their figures against the sea miles they needed to travel, and were satisfied they had enough fuel to travel to Japan and back.

In the Enterprise CIC, Osaka looked over decoded messages sent by both the Japanese ships and the American response throughout the day. Sean and Alicia joined him after the F-35s recovered back to the Enterprise. Satisfied, it was time to put the next phase of his plan into action, Sean motioned to Alicia for them to return to the ready room, and informed Tony and Renée to meet them there.

When they arrived, Renée offered them a cup of coffee while Tony rattled off the battle stats. "The task force has reported no damages suffered. Six bombs, three torpedoes, eighteen 16-inch shells, and poof, six Japanese carriers, three subs, and one battleship sent to the bottom with nary a scratch on us. Who knew it would be so easy to change the history of a major US defeat with so little expenditure of our resources. So, are you two still clear about how you want to follow up our success?"

Sean nodded in the affirmative, as he picked up the phone to call the CIC. "Commander Osaka, I need you to bring your new friends to the Admirals Ready Room, now. No, go ahead and leave everything where you are. Just bring them."

After he put the phone down, he answered Tony. "I don't think anything else makes sense. We cannot allow the Japanese Government any breathing room now that their Navy can't defend itself. It's unfortunate so many died today, but without such a bold statement about our capabilities, there wouldn't be any grounds for dialogue."

There was a knock on the door and in walked Osaka with Lt. Commander Edwin Layton and Lt. Jasper Holmes. Sean immediately got to the point. "I needed you here to observe not only what the Japanese intended, but also our ability to dictate whatever strategic or tactical action we feel is necessary to protect US interests. What you witnessed today will give you enough information to convince President Roosevelt and his military Commanders of our capability to put an end to the war quickly, and remove the threat of Japanese Imperialism in the Pacific. Therefore, I need you to decide which of you will return to Pearl to deliver a note to this effect to President Roosevelt, and who will stay here with us."

Tony could see the indecision in the two codebreakers. On one side, who would want to leave such a historically incredible event, and the other bursting to share with their contemporaries what they witnessed. Tony realized if left to them to decide, it would take longer than they had. He pulled a quarter from his pocket and flipped it in the air. "Commander Layton, heads you stay, tails you go."

Lt. Holmes wasn't sure if he was disappointed or happy when it landed heads.

Tony flipped the coin over to Jasper Holmes. "Here's a little souvenir to show off when you get back to Pearl."

Lt. Holmes noticed it wasn't silver and looking closer read the date, "2012?"

"Yeah, it has been around awhile." Tony enjoyed messing with the Lieutenant.

Sean needed time with Tony, Renée, and Alicia to work on the language of the letter Lt. Holmes would be delivering to the President. "Commander Osaka, please return our guests and keep them comfortable for the next couple of hours."

"Yes Sir," Osaka acknowledged as he escorted the codebreakers out of the ready room.

"Tony, inform the senior officers I want them aboard the Enterprise at 1300 hours."

While Tony executed this order, Renée opened her laptop to record the first draft as Alicia began to rattle off the points she felt needed to be covered. It would be her task to compose the final draft to the President. Alicia had thought long about the impact they would have if they saved the battleships at Pearl Harbor. However, she had not planned on her emotional reaction to the sight of the Japanese fleet being ripped apart. Within this reality, the scope of so many deaths made her change the tenor of her message.

Mr. President,

This letter is to introduce you to the impossible idea that we can achieve world peace within the next six months. I am Secretary of Defense Alicia Calhoun, Rear Admiral Retired UH, the civilian authority attached to a task force of advanced United States naval warships, the likes of which you cannot imagine. By now, CINCPACFLT has informed you of the destruction of a Japanese naval force, two hundred miles north of Oahu, by unknown forces. You also know by now, from information supplied by Lt. Jasper Holmes, who we are and how with stealth and overwhelming superiority we managed to carry out this destruction. Let me assure you at this point that our intentions are in unison with the interests of the United States. Our ultimate goal is to return our forces under your command as our Commander in Chief. However, before this can happen we will be out of touch…

At this, she paused to ask Tony, "How long exactly will it take for us to return from Japan?"

"To have enough fuel, we need to set our speed at fifteen knots to cover the seventy four hundred miles. We should be back in eighteen days if everything goes to plan."

Alicia continued where she left off.

…we will be out of touch for eighteen days, after which it would be my honor to meet with Prime Minister Winston Churchill and yourself in Hawaii. We would like to discuss how we could help end the carnage taking place throughout the world. I will reveal who we are and where we came from along with some of the capabilities at our disposal. I assure you that you will find them exceptional. Germany will announce a declaration of war in the next few days and I can only urge you to minimize your deployments in response to their declaration, though you should mobilize your forces. Over the next eighteen days, I implore you to restrain your impulse to take any aggressive actions. Maintaining restraint will be to the benefit of both the United States and Great Britain if you were to do so.

Concerning the Atlantic supply lines, my advice would be to limit all shipping, including coastal traffic, over the same period. Germany has already stationed U-Boats off the United States eastern seaboard to wreak havoc on the merchant ships that will be defenseless to their depredations. Believe me when I say you will lose hundreds of sailor's lives, while thousands of tons of shipping will needlessly wind up on the sea floor if you do not heed this warning. When Mr. Churchill expresses his displeasure with the idea, you can tell him England will quickly benefit from this momentary delay of materials.

I would also like you to understand the importance of keeping the Russian government in the dark about this communication until we can meet with you and the Prime Minister. If you agree to my proposal, please keep both Mr. Churchill's and your staff's information about this communiqué to a minimum, with only General George Marshal and British General William Donovan informed of its content. We will be monitoring radio traffic over the eighteen-day period, and will make earlier contact if the situation warrants it. I look forward to meeting you, Mr. President, on the 25th of this month.

Alicia Calhoun

United States Secretary of Defense

Civilian Authority aboard the USS Enterprise CVN-65

"I like the way it reads, especially that you don't show any more cards than necessary. What do you think, Tony?" Sean was impressed with the way it teased Roosevelt's curiosity. He knew the President wouldn't refuse to agree to the meeting, and once he relayed the contents to Churchill, he was sure they would be on Oahu when they returned.

Tony had concerns. "Your promise to come under Roosevelt's authority will give those who might agree with Captain Brewster's position little to argue about. Nevertheless, you better be ready to explain what those terms mean, and under what context you will present them. I agree with your suggestion about the German U-boat threat. We should add one other important issue in the letter that affected the submarine forces for the first year and a half of the war. The Navy's Mark-14 torpedoes were defective. We should alert him to ask the Navy to conduct tests to expose the problems. For one thing, the damn torpedoes ran ten feet deeper than programmed and the contact exploder is defective.

"With our own supply of torpedoes finite, the Mark-14 will be our only alternative ordnance when we run out. Besides, maybe we'll earn some of their trust when they find out the torpedoes are worthless, though I doubt they'll listen."

"That's a good idea Tony, and along those lines we need to set up a strategic supply command to project what materials from 1941 we can convert to our future uses. Get our staff on it [the Admirals Staff schedules fleet resupply] with orders to receive weekly reports of their future supply needs from the rest of our command. This way we will be ready to present a list when we return to Pearl.

"As it stands now, we have been at sea for only seven days so we shouldn't have any problems for the next month. Nevertheless, even if Roosevelt is agreeable, we have to figure it will take time to upgrade their stocks to make them usable to our needs. For the sake of simplicity, until we do meet with the President, we should keep our military requirements to the minimum."

They spent the rest of their time on the final draft, so when the senior staff arrived and received copies, there was little conflict over its contents. Sean could see Captain Brewster arrived looking for a fight, but even he could find little fault with the plans. With general agreement reached, the conversation turned to the tactical planning for the attack on the political leadership in Tokyo.

Sean's voice was firm and clear as Renée passed out pictures gleaned from the historical database of wartime locations where the Japanese ran their operations. "The plan calls for a direct course to Japanese waters, ignoring any hostile contacts along the way to ensure complete surprise when we launch our strikes. Captain Aslan has compiled the geographical maps and landmarks we will need to supply the attack crews with their targets. Our goal is to destroy both the military government and their command and control. The best time to hit their leadership would be the middle of the day while the government is in session. Our main objective is Prime Minister Hideki Tojo and as many of the Japanese Army General Staff as possible.

"As much as I would like to avoid collateral political damage, there isn't any way to achieve a complete decapitation without endangering the lives of the few moderates in their government.

"This brings me to secondary targets. The Japanese Navy has only seven remaining carriers in their inventory, some anchored at Atsugi naval station. This base is accessible to attack with little deviation from our planned course. This information might prove useless if they choose to deploy them after our destruction of the Japanese task force, but my gut says they will keep the rest of their military assets close to home until they can get more details about what happened.

"Once again, the plan calls for limited use of missiles and torpedoes, so the screening force will be in reserve. Your role will continue to be to protect the Enterprise in case Specter experiences any glitches. I hope I do not need to remind you we can't be overly complacent about Specter, as the initial plan only called for it to provide coverage for a two-week exercise, so we can't count on its continued health over a still to be determined amount of time. If we are successful in the removal of the hierarchy of the Japanese leadership, we'll return to Hawaiian waters, and leave the rest of the Japanese naval and merchant shipping for the US Pacific Fleet to mop up."

When Sean finished his briefing, the assembled senior staff went over the details of the operation for another hour with few changes. When they finished, he ended the meeting. "We will put Lt. Holmes in the water with some rations and a radio to contact the ships and planes in the area. That's all for now."

Twenty minutes later Lt. Holmes sat in a lifeboat bobbing in the Pacific swells, picked up thirty minutes later by a PBY, and returned immediately to Pearl Harbor.

For the next hour, Lt. Holmes met with Admiral Kimmel and General Short. Their lack of knowledge of the epic destruction of the Japanese carriers in their own backyard, along with his unbelievable description of the fantastic naval forces who carried it out, made it impossible to give a lucid account to Washington. They only had Holmes's word this unknown force was on its way to Japan.

When the interview was over, Admiral Kimmel turned to his Chief of Staff. "Freddy, I want you to get the Seventh fleet ready to sortie."

General Marshall had other ideas. "Belay that order Captain."

He then turned to Admiral Kimmel. "This is way above our pay grade This is going to the President before we do anything. Besides, if there is a futuristic naval force out there destroying naval units of a nation that just declared war on us, I think we should stay out of their way."

Marshall's interpretation of the situation disturbed Kimmel. "You're not in the least bit curious as to who these people are and where they came from?"

"Like I said, this is above our pay grade."

After the meeting, Admiral Kimmel forwarded Alicia's letter to the President, and then sent for the Captain of the submarine USS Dolphin SS-169 to discuss the reference to the Mark-14 torpedoes. "I don't think there is anything to this, but take the Dolphin out for a live fire torpedo exercise."

"The usual compliment of three?"

Admiral Kimmel thought about it for a moment before he answered. "Fire off your full load of 18." With the identity of their benefactors a complete unknown, Kimmel didn't need to be caught with his pants down if the allegations were true.

"Yes Sir."

Late on the afternoon of the 7th, the communiqué describing Lt. Jasper Holmes's stay on the Enterprise reached the hands of

President Roosevelt. Secretary of State Cordell Hull, Secretary of War Henry Stimson, and his confidant Harry Hopkins were at his side trying to make sense of what happened.

The President was not having one of his better days. "Now that you've all read this incredible letter, can any of you tell me what the hell is going on? Do we have naval forces in the Pacific I have not been informed of or not?" President Roosevelt was not accustomed to being the last to know about anything under his authority. "Who the hell is this so called Secretary of Defense Alicia Calhoun and what exactly is this task force she refers to?"

Secretary of War Henry Stimson shrugged. "I've been in touch with Admiral Kimmel, and if you believe the story of a Naval Intelligence Lt. by the name of Holmes, who was found floating 200 miles northwest of Pearl Harbor, we're dealing with a United States naval force from sometime in the future. If we hadn't confirmed a Japanese naval task force lost six carriers and two battleships in the blink of an eye, I'd put the man in a psych ward."

Secretary of State Cordell Hull added what he knew. "The Japanese are adamant the attack on their ships was unprovoked. They claim our ships and planes attacked their ships without warning. However, there hasn't been any response to our queries about why the Japanese were so close to the Hawaiian Islands with such a large force considering they declared war against us."

"Lt. Holmes also described aircraft, alien in capabilities, catapulting off a massive carrier and then disappearing." Secretary of War Stimson delivered this news as if he didn't believe anything he was hearing out of Pearl. "He claims he and a Lt. Commander Edwin Layton were shanghaied off a fishing boat and ferried to a task force of ships which were invisible until they were right on top of them."

"So, am I to infer by the tone of your voice, you don't think we should give these reports any credence?"

"I'm more concerned, Mr. President, that all of this could be misdirection formulated by both Japan and Germany to have us chasing after ghosts."

The President shook his head no. "I've already gone down that road Henry. There haven't been any intelligence reports in either the Pacific or the European theater suggesting any mass redeployment, so I'm inclined to keep an open mind until I hear from Lt. Holmes directly. In her letter, this Alicia Calhoun claims they defeated the Japanese with stealth. If there is truth to this claim, I can't say I am displeased with the results of their actions. It's obvious the Japanese were about to launch a surprise attack on Pearl, but I'll be damned if I will travel to Hawaii and meet with these unknown benefactors."

Harry Hopkins spoke up. "Mr. President, I don't see how you can refuse. Although we have ordered a complete blackout over the event, you have to get out in front of it. Whatever this force represents, they do appear to be on our side. However, the one thing I am in agreement with our mystery benefactors is we need to mobilize our forces now."

The President took a moment to ponder what he heard before he decided. "I can see all of the arguments have their merit. However, if this mysterious fleet of ships does exist, what do you think they plan to do over the next eighteen days? It seems to me, they could cover a lot of ocean in that time."

"If they were headed toward the West Coast, why would they ask you to be in Hawaii?" Secretary Stimson took a moment to look at a map of the Pacific before he added, "There is the possibility their objective is to relieve the Marines under attack on Wake Island, or if this was a perfect dream, they are on their way to Japan to finish the job."

This got a chuckle from everyone in the room.

"Henry, as you suggested, order Admiral Kimmel to send a task force centered on three battleships from the 7th Fleet to Subic Bay in the Philippines and put MacArthur's forces on alert to the possibility of a Japanese attack. Further, order the Admiral to deploy Admiral Halsey's Enterprise Task Force to Wake Island. The remainder of the 7th Fleet will remain stationed at Pearl Harbor to protect the waters around Hawaii. And see to it our forces are mobilized."

"Yes Mr. President."

"And Henry, has Admiral Newton's Lexington Task Force been diverted from Midway?"

"That is correct, Mr. President."

Roosevelt leaned back and massaged his chin with his right hand. "I'll draft a letter to Winston to see if he's up for a little trip."

Secretary Hull impatiently looked at his watch and advised the President, "You better make it quick. You are due in front of Congress in the next hour to deliver your response to the Japanese declaration of war. Also, do you intend to postpone the convoy shipments?" Cordell needed to know if Roosevelt would follow the letter's advice about the U-boat threat.

"I'll get Winston to agree to the halt they requested, and then based on what happens when we meet in Hawaii, we'll see."

Within these issues, there was still the question of how to explain to the American public a believable version of events to counter the Japanese claims of a US preemptive strike. An hour later, they arrived at the Capital building and focused on the Japanese aggressions in Asia. With the Japanese attack on Wake Island confirmed, the President convinced the reluctant American Congress the time for peaceful negotiations was past.

In Tokyo, when Prime Minister Hideki Tojo received the news they had lost all but one of the eight capital ships involved in the attack without the loss of a single American ship, he met with his senior military staff to revise their plans. Japan only had three fleet sized and four escort carriers remaining after the debacle, which forced the leadership into a defensive position. Without a rational explanation of what they were up against, the need to protect the supply lines to the troops in China became the priority. Convinced it was Japan's divine right to rule all of Asia, no one in the room would take the risk to advise reversing the war declaration.

With offensive operations now out of the question, the need to keep their naval forces close to home to repel attacks on the home islands became their only practical option. However, this did not resolve the main reason Japan attacked the United States in the first place, the need to access oil fields in Indonesia. This was critical because of the oil embargo placed on Japan by the United States for their aggression in China. As it stood, Japan would run out of the precious commodity within the next two months, and when the oil ran out, the dream of creating a Japanese empire in Asia would end. If they could not find a way to counter this unknown threat, they would have to accept the humiliation of a withdrawal from Manchuria and China.

The Japanese decided to keep their submarines deployed in Hawaiian waters to monitor American warships deploying from Pearl Harbor. With so many available targets it was miraculous the Japanese submarines didn't inflict any losses. However, this followed historical norms, in that the Japanese military throughout the war misused this weapon. The Japanese submarines also failed to target merchant ships to disrupt supply routes, choosing instead to use this valuable asset to ferry troops and material. This was an even greater blunder, considering the Long Lance was the most dangerous torpedo of the war, with a longer range to target, better accuracy, and it packed a more powerful punch. It was the best weapon Japanese technology produced throughout the war.

The one operation in the Pacific Theatre the Japanese still pursued was the attempted occupation of Wake Island. The difference this time was the American 7th Fleet was able to respond. Unfortunately, the first American casualties of the war occurred on the 8th when the Japanese submarine I-22 sighted the USS Lexington. Minutes later, a spread of four Long Lance torpedoes were on their way toward the aircraft carrier. Two of them found their target. Six hundred pounds of explosives ripped into the ship's forward port side and opened two large gashes in the hull of the ship. Almost immediately, the Lexington took a list of fifteen degrees to starboard. Escort destroyers raced to attack the Japanese sub. Soon the telltale oil slick rose to the surface to announce the I-22's destruction.

When Admiral Kimmel received the report on the damages, he decided that to reinforce the task force would leave the rest of the 7th Fleet spread too thin to adequately defend the expanse of ocean between Hawaii and the West Coast. The aircraft carrier USS Yorktown CV-5 was due to arrive after her detachment from the Atlantic 6th Fleet to supplement the 7th Fleet, but it was days away.

On the 8th in Berlin, Adolf Hitler called a meeting of the Reichstag to announce Germany's declaration of war on America in support of their axis partner. In his speech, he went on a rambling tirade about the decadence of the American society. Afterward, he ordered Admiral Dönitz to send Germany's U-boats operating in the Atlantic to the American East Coast to wage unrestricted warfare against their newly declared enemy.

In Moscow, news of America's entry into the war brought a rare smile to Joseph Stalin's face. He knew it would open the door for massive material aid to the battered Russian Army that burned up its soldiers the way their tanks burned fuel. Led by Generals who lacked command experience because of his purge of the nation's military leaders in 1938, the Soviet troops marched into a meat grinder reminiscent of the battles of WWI.

The mystery of who destroyed the Japanese fleet preyed on Stalin's mind. His spies could not offer the slightest information on the weapons the Americans used to defeat the Japanese Navy so decisively. Because of a strong faction of leftover depression

"A Date Which Will Live in Infamy"

era socialists populating the American government, Stalin's spies usually knew almost everything that went on in matters concerning American intentions.

The next afternoon at Pearl Harbor, Tuesday the 9th, Admiral Kimmel received a report from the Captain of the Dolphin that verified the inadequacies of the Mark-14 torpedo. Only two out of the eighteen torpedoes fired against the Kahoolawe cliffs detonated. Ordnance specialists recovered the dangerous unexploded torpedoes and returned them for inspection. Along with orders to check the contact exploders, they were also to look for any other design flaws. This information confirmed the torpedo's uselessness and effectively neutralized the American submarines until the problem was rectified. Until they could recall the affected submarines to reset their torpedoes, Admiral Kimmel decided to notify his submarine Commanders to act only in a reconnaissance capacity.

Commander Submarines Pacific Rear Admiral Robert English argued the problem was probably in how the Dolphin's crew set the torpedoes before firing it. From his perspective, his argument made sense, considering he sent submarines out for the first eighteen months of the war without a single test to either validate or refute their claims. It took the Admiral's death in a plane crash in 1942 for a new commander to listen to his Captains and take the time to discover and correct the deficiencies. Thankfully, this time his stupidity would not be repeated.

Also on the 9th, several reports from the German U-boats in the waters off the American East Coast created confusion among the German General Staff. There was a shortage of ships sailing from America to resupply England, which left the U-boats to sink only a few stray freighters along the Eastern Seaboard amounting to less than ten thousand tons. Combined with the United States victory in the Pacific, it didn't make any sense to either Grand Admiral Erich Rader, the overall Commander of the Kriegsmarine, or Admiral Karl Dönitz who commanded the U-boats. Before Germany declared war on the United States, a steady flow of materials passed from US ports to England. Logic dictated these shipments should be increasing.

When told of this news, Hitler laughed and reiterated his belief the Americans didn't have the stomach for war against his master race and proceeded to announce these thoughts to his enraptured audiences. The faces of the generals standing behind him, betrayed completely different ideas about their new enemy.

On Wednesday the 10th, Dr. Rebecca Cutler came over from the Missouri and was on her way to a meeting with Sean to discuss an idea she was working on. It was risky, but she thought worth the effort. When she arrived and turned down the offer for coffee, she absent-mindedly wondered if all retired sailors suffer from ulcers drinking so much of the acidic brew. She also noticed Sean looked more relaxed than usual and thought her timing might be right for what she wanted to ask.

"With your permission Admiral, I'd like to take Specter off-line for a couple of hours so I can run some simulations."

Sean noticed Rebecca was once again dressed in black. "Unless you have a new problem that threatens my ships or crew Doctor Cutler, now would not be the time. Am I to infer by your wardrobe that there is a problem?"

"Believe it or not, when I put this on last time, I was in a good mood all day. Therefore, I'm thinking reverse psychology, at least until something bad happens while I wear it. Another reason for the funeral wear is when we go into battle, it will be me that is responsible if Specter malfunctions and sailors die.

Rebecca paused for a moment and looked as if she forgot something. "Getting back to whether or not there is a problem. Yes and no."

In a measured voice, Sean asked her, "So, do you have some way for me to figure out which one it is?"

"Exactly! I spent the last two days designing code to set off a series of random anomalies in Specter's programming to see if I can replicate what happened. There's only one problem with what I found."

"And that problem is?"

"If this program is connected to the field generators, my anomalies would definitely wreak havoc on all of your systems and quite possibly send us off into space. With Specter disconnected I can mess with its brain and not get bitten."

"Off into space?" Her convoluted reasoning made Sean sorry he asked.

"When you think about it Admiral, there's a whole lot of space compared to terra firma. From purely a scientific perspective and a *gee, wouldn't it be weird* point of view, think of how bizarre it would be if the astronomers watching pictures from the Hubble telescope all of a sudden saw our task force orbiting the moon."

Sean started to respond, but found he had nothing. "Excuse me for a minute." He picked up the phone and called Tony. "I could use your help."

It only took a few moments for help to arrive.

"Good afternoon Rebecca," Tony grinned, pushing the familiarity. "What's so important you two needed *my* help?"

Sean ignored the extreme elements of Rebecca's concerns and explained the basics of what Rebecca wanted to do. "I think it would be the perfect time to test the task force with an exercise, the premise of which would be our response to the loss of Specter. We detach both the Seawolf and the Hampton to the west and south, out to twenty-five miles. Then launch Seahawks to the north and west to drop sonar buoys. If we pick up any submarine activity, we alter course. The question is, *Doctor* Cutler," Sean's emphasis on Doctor was for Tony's benefit, "can you give me your assurance Specter can be brought to operational status within fifteen minutes notice?"

"I could bring Specter back on line Admiral, but if I run into any altered programs at the same time you need Specter, it will take time to purge them."

"I like the idea," Tony added. "We're nine hundred miles from Wake with nine hundred miles of ocean between us and Japan, and only the occasional Japanese submarine to avoid. I for one, would feel better if *DOCTOR* Cutler," Tony smiled when Rebecca noticed the dig at Sean, "knew as much about Specter as that crazy son of a bitch Safire."

"Then that's how we'll proceed. Dr. Cutler, I assume you need to be back on the Missouri to run your tests. Can you be ready at 1800 to disengage Specter?"

"I will make it so, oh Fearless One."

"Tony, while she's getting ready, order Alpha Whiskey to widen the distance between the screening ships when Specter disengages to give us more room to maneuver."

Rebecca was about to leave when she remembered another reason for her visit. "I went down to Sickbay this morning and pleaded with Dr. Strangelove to tell me what else he screwed with. All the bastard did was give me the most-wicked laugh you could imagine and finished by flipping me off. I wonder if he really is crazy. This morning was the first time since his meltdown I thought I saw his usual disgust with my presence."

"We'll deal with the doctor later. Without access to Specter, he isn't a threat. And Dr. Cutler..."

"Yes Admiral?"

"Please do your best to keep us on the water."

Sean's comment drew a smile from Rebecca and a puzzled look from Tony.

"Don't ask."

"A Date Which Will Live in Infamy"

Tony was in the CIC of the Enterprise with Lt. Commander Daniel Osaka studying a chart that marked their present position, now twelve hundred miles west of the Hawaiian Islands. Since the previous evening, intercepts from Wake Island confirmed the Marines were fighting a desperate struggle against superior odds, and Halsey's task force wouldn't arrive for another two days.

Tony noticed Commander Osaka was doing his best not to ask the obvious question of why didn't the Enterprise go to their aid. He decided to use it as a teaching moment. "Do you know the reason we decided not to intervene on Wake's behalf?"

Osaka didn't need to be asked twice. "I only understand it wouldn't take much for us to sink the light cruisers and the troopships."

"Take a look at this chart again Daniel, and tell me if you see the same picture Japanese intelligence would."

"I understand the Admiral wants to keep the Japanese confused about our location, but I also thought one of our major objectives was to destroy the Japanese Navy along the way. Doesn't it bother you that if we arrive a day before our namesake Enterprise, we could save lord knows how many Marines? What if the Japanese sink the Enterprise because we didn't respond?"

"Of course it bothers me. You should also consider how many more we can save if we do manage to decapitate the Japanese Government." Tony figured this would be a good time to add a little real world education. "Do you seriously think they would just sit still and ignore our attacks from Pearl Harbor to Wake and then to Japan? If we attack their ships along the way, Tokyo would make the logical conclusion they would be next, and go underground.

"We need to focus on the big picture. If we terminate the fanatics, the next leaders might be more willing to negotiate a quick end to their aggressions, which would leave us with most of our ordnance still intact for use in Europe. Besides, if we sink carriers in their home waters, with the Japanese ignorant about how, there's no way they'd risk assembling another task force. Under those conditions, tactics demand you scatter your assets in the hopes you can gain more time to figure out your enemy to counter their moves. If they don't suspect they are our target, we will have a better chance to decapitate the leadership."

After Osaka took a moment to let what Tony said sink in, the logical Information Warfare Officer in him still had to ask, "So you're telling me that when you went against civilian orders and rescued your downed pilots in Iraq, you looked at the big picture?"

Tony smiled while he answered the Commander. "I never said all tactical thinking is in absolutes. Sometimes you will find yourself in command of a situation where the fur is flying and you need to be flexible enough to go with your instincts. You're lucky if when that moment arrives you've already gained enough combat experience to allow you to make an informed emotional decision. The major difference is, if you fail in the attempt, you can probably kiss your career goodbye. Sometimes even success won't allow you to keep your neck if you pissed off the wrong Admiral or politician."

By 1800, the attack submarines and F/A-18Fs were in position. Armed with pages of checklists, Rebecca turned Specter off, but to her surprise, the program wouldn't respond to her commands. Fifteen minutes later, after every attempt failed, she contacted the technicians who monitored the generators on the other ships. She was further frustrated when they also were unable to take their generators offline. Rebecca was just about to take the risky step of turning off its power supply and crashing the program, when Specter responded to her original commands and shut down.

"Okay catch-up time. Dr. Strangelove – one; Team Rebecca – zero."

For the next hour and a half, Rebecca and Dr. Phelps ran the series of simulations, which included conditions that mirrored the simulated attack on the Reagan. They uncovered corrupted commands written into the code, which went from sophomoric to diabolical. Rebecca realized the time she asked for would not be nearly enough to disable all the extraneous programs Dr. Safire had taken years to imbed. After Rebecca was sure of the ramifications, she contacted Sean.

"I think you'd better sit down Admiral. Dr. Strangelove has wired Specter into more of your ship's systems than I thought possible. I have to hand it to the crazy bastard how he managed to corrupt so many of the subroutines. It ranges all over the network corrupting everything from fuel line valves to your missile launchers."

"You're telling me we could lose control of our weapon systems?" Sean's mind conjured the nightmare friendly fire aimed at the Enterprise would create.

"Not now they can't. That was the first malware we removed, and with more time, we can deal with all of the other little nasties we found. One of the corrupted commands we found in the links were between the Aegis radar systems and the missile systems they directed. If any of those missiles launched, they would have targeted the nearest ships, and not the incoming threats in the air.

"Fortunately, Dr. Strangelove spent a lot of his talent on the corruption of the satellite uplinks that tied everything together. He couldn't have known at the time that they would be useless. This leads me to speculate they were only backups to the ones he used on the surge protectors. The uplinks were his primary trigger. All I know is Dr. Strangelove is as big a whack job as I've ever run into and it will take us at least a week to sort it all out and purge the corrupted codes."

"I guess I should look at the bright side. You discovered this before we launched the strike on Tokyo and shot ourselves in the ass. We have five more days until we're in heavily trafficked waters. Would it be possible for you to do the rest of your work during the night and keep Specter operational during the day?"

"As much as I'd like to please you and say yes, no we can't. Once we start to remove his codes, there's a good chance this alone could activate other sleeper programs that would wreak havoc. We'd be chasing ghosts instead of a systematic purging. In other words, it's all part of his plan."

"I'll inform Captain Knox of the problem. Is there anything else he or the other ship Captains should be made aware of?" Sean was worried they would have to set back their timetable for the attack until Rebecca could assure him Specter would function without turning on them.

"Yes there is, and it's a big one. You know how we speculated about reproducing the environment that brought us to this little party. Well, I now know we can. I'm not saying the odds of our return back home would be anything but minuscule, but I think the chances are better than I thought before. What I am sure of though, is we need to be where we first arrived for the greatest chance of success."

"Thank you Dr. Cutler. Let me know if there are any other surprises to brighten my day."

The evening of the 10th, a travel weary Lt. Jasper Holmes arrived at the White House where he gave his report to the President. After the an hour of explaining in detail for what to Jasper seemed like the hundredth time since he left the Enterprise, he could see this put the President in a high state of agitation. "Winston was rather perplexed at the information I supplied in my letter to him. He insisted I tell him how we so handily defeated the Japanese at Pearl Harbor and how much he looked forward to my explanation of the secret weapons we used. The irony in all of this is, it is usually the Prime Minister who surprises me with his intelligence sources. All we have is the eyewitness testimony of a Navy Lieutenant found floating in a raft. The press will have a field day if any of this leaks out, George." President Roosevelt referred to General George Marshal, the overall Commander of the United States Military.

"His description of the size of the carrier and alien planes makes me believe the Lieutenant has read too many comic books. Both the Prime Minister and I are sure, once we reach Pearl, there will be a logical explanation about what happened, and who was responsible. Though for the life of me I have no idea what that might be."

Lt. Holmes was fascinated that they were discussing all of this as if he was no longer in the room. "The powerful really are different," was the only conclusion he could draw. Without a word he got up from his chair and left the room without a single recognition he was even ever there.

After conferring with Alicia and Tony, on Thursday the 11th, Sean ordered Captain Renée Aslan to return to the Missouri. He wanted eyes on Captain Brewster to observe and report on his ability to command.

Renée regretted her orders after only one day of Brewster's hospitality, which consisted of treating her more like an Ensign than a serving Captain in the US Navy. Every conversation with him, which Renée soon learned to avoid, included liberal portions of God's wrath against the actions they were taking.

Renée could tell most of the officers and sailors showed little respect for their new Captain. However, she did discover the crew had a strong rapport with their XO, Commander Carl Eddington. Renée observed a junior officer in quiet conversation with the Commander not long after Captain Brewster had given him a contradictory order that left doubt in the sailor's mind about how to respond. On a ship with over fifteen hundred souls, doubt is dangerous. Renée noticed the conflicted officer relaxed after a few minutes of conversion with Commander Eddington.

On her second day onboard, Renée made a point to run into the XO in the Officers Mess. After observing how the Missouri functioned under Captain Brewster's command, she decided the time was right to approach him away from Brewster. "I've noticed since I've been onboard that most of the senior officers look to you for guidance instead of Captain Brewster."

"The crew was used to the way Captain Folger handled the ship. I'm sure once everyone gets used to Captain Brewster's style of command, things will go more smoothly." Eddington knew better than to criticize his Captain in front of a superior officer, even if he thought he could get away with it.

Renée didn't let him off the hook. "It doesn't take a trained psychologist to see the morale on this ship has declined dramatically since Captain Folger was in command. I looked up Brewster's service record and found out he came straight off the cruiser San Jacinto after only eight months of command. He had almost no command experience in carrier operations and the scuttlebutt was he didn't seem interested in learning either. Then there's that little problem he has with females in the Navy."

The Commander answered this question with the confidence of one who knew it would be coming. "Of course there isn't a squid on the Missouri who wouldn't give anything to have Captain Folger back in command. Even if Captain Brewster were more charismatic, it wouldn't matter. Either way, the Navy doesn't give you the choice of whether or not to obey a senior officer."

Renée could tell that by the way he parsed his words she would have to take a more direct route. "Would you feel the same if morale sunk so low as to put the ship and crew at risk? Remember, we can't just send a fitness report to Admiral Hendricks at USPACFLT outlining Captain Brewster's incompetence."

"I get your point Captain Aslan," Carl answered with a smile. "But I know you've seen the same things in Captain Brewster I have. Excuse me if I'm out of line for saying this, but the only reason I can think you're pushing me to assess him is you want me to do something for you."

Renée could see the Commander was enjoying himself. While he talked, Renée noticed how self-assured the 40-year-old Commander seemed to be. He was not as handsome as Tony, but he did have the same ability to charm a woman. She noticed the solid build on a six-foot frame with green eyes that he kept focused like a laser. Commander Eddington emitted a masculine intensity she found attractive.

"All right Commander. The Admiral ordered me to tell you if you see Captain Brewster spread disapproval of his orders among any of the crew, to inform me immediately."

"Yes Ma'am." Eddington hesitated for a moment, and then decided Brewster's connections couldn't do him any harm now. "In my opinion, Captain Brewster isn't fit to command a Captain's launch, let alone a capital ship in the US Navy. Nevertheless, it is also because of his lack of mental acuity that he doesn't have the brains to pose a threat to the ship. However, I will report if I hear of anything contrary to the Admiral's orders."

"Thank you for your cooperation Commander."

Renée winced and wrinkled her nose before she continued. "By the way, how can you eat this? The food on the Enterprise is five star compared to this crap."

"I don't know. I've gotten rather fond of chipped beef, packaged potatoes, and soggy vegetables. Although a bottle of White Lightning would be nice to set it all off."

"Yeah, if we were watching a NASCAR race. Look, they're making another left turn!" Renée quipped.

While Renée quizzed Eddington, Rebecca was now in her fourteenth straight agonizing hour of working through the maze of pathways composing Specter. She compared the frustration with the video game Myst. After she successfully interpreted the clues and reached what should have been a solution, the assholes who designed the game merely sent you on another obscure quest, ad nauseam. She thought, "Dr. Safire must have been a big fan of the game."

This was the end of the second straight day without meaningful sleep, and most of the other technicians had already burned out from her constant demands. Forrest was sound asleep in the corner of the room, oblivious to everything.

Her team had spent most of the time removing the covert missile override commands embedded in the programming before they focused on the numerous nuisance coding. It quickly became clear to Rebecca it would take all of Comstock's technicians months of dedicated effort to give Specter a clean bill of health. This left only one option. Any time the task force wanted to operate the advanced weapons systems, they would have to shut down Specter on every ship and F-35 involved.

On the 13th, as the WWII aircraft carrier USS Enterprise CV-6 Task Force 8, accompanied by the Colorado class battleships USS Maryland BB-46 and USS West Virginia BB-48 bore down on Wake Island, the Japanese abandoned their efforts to take it. This gave Tony more ammunition to poke holes in Lt. Commander Osaka's previous arguments to intercede.

Throughout the day, Osaka listened to radio intercepts in the Enterprise CIC. Off the east coast of British Malaya, Japanese bombers sank the British battleships HMS Prince of Wales and HMS Repulse, which sent 840 souls into the Abyss. These two British capital ships became the first battleships in history sunk by air attack while operating on the high seas. "Oh well, apparently we can't save everybody," he thought.

Intercepted communications verified confusion still reigned in the Japanese Government. The Japanese Naval Command ordered the redeployment of their warships still in home waters in an attempt to protect the supply lines necessary to support the large Japanese Army in China. Further, the Japanese naval command ordered the remaining reconnaissance submarines to withdraw from Hawaiian waters and return closer to home to supplement

"A Date Which Will Live in Infamy"

their beleaguered surface forces.

The Japanese Army didn't have the necessary oil to continue operations in China for much longer. Without the means to take it by force, Japan's only option was a return to the negotiation table without any cards to play. The United States Navy now controlled the waters from Wake Island to the west coast of North America. In effect, Japan lost the war with the United States before it had a chance to start, and the further Japan collapsed their naval forces around Japanese home waters, the more obvious this became.

Chapter Five

The Head of the Dragon

On the evening of the 15th, and now 300 miles southeast of the Japanese homeland, the senior staff met on the Enterprise to go over the attack plan they would launch the next day.

Tony stood in front of the monitor pointing to a spot one hundred miles off the coast of Japan. "We'll launch the F-35s at 0730 without Specter's cover. Because of our uncertainty over Specter's reliability, we will carry out this mission in the clear.

"There will be three F-35s attacking the Japanese Diet [Japan's bicameral legislature], and three going after the Japanese Imperial General Headquarters. They will reach their targets at 1115 and release their bombs. The remaining four F-35s orbiting offshore will launch follow up strikes as needed or attack targets of opportunity at the Naval Station north of the city.

"The strike craft will recover to the Enterprise by 1500 if all goes well. Just in case, we will have four F/A-18s flying CAP to defend against the unlikely event one of their Zeros gets to close. We will remain on station until 1800 hours to analyze strike video and communication intercepts to determine if further air strikes are required. Are there any ques…?"

Captain Brewster jumped in before Sean could finish. "What do think will happen when thousands of witnesses see our 21st Century craft in the air over Tokyo blowing their leadership to pieces? I'll tell you what will happen. Instead of fighting each other, the threat we pose will unite them to destroy us."

"That's a little extreme even for you Steve." Tony tried to suppress his sarcasm, but had to add. "I mean, do you really think they take Godzilla that seriously?"

Brewster shot back. "Mock me if you want, but how else do societies react when they are threatened by forces they can't explain? Was the panic created by the War of the Worlds broadcast an anomaly or a small sample of what will happen when news of our existence becomes common knowledge to the entire world?"

Sean was about to counter his argument when Captain Daily jumped in. "No one in this room is unaware of what we're up against. We're damned if we do, damned if we don't. We settled this argument when we decided to attack Nagumo, so why are you still trying to tell us the sky is falling? Give it a rest already."

"I think that's enough for now." Sean was grateful for Daily's intercession. He knew he needed Daily's support to give the younger destroyer Commanders a clear-cut example to follow. "Report back to your ships, and good luck to us all."

The next day, Tony was on the bridge, while Sean and Alicia sat in the Enterprise CIC with Lt. Commander Layton, and Lt. Commander Osaka. As the F-35s launched on schedule, the Seawolf swept the area twenty miles to the west, with a couple of fishing trawlers the only shipping to report. The Hampton patrolled to the south, also with little to report. To protect the task force, Seahawks with sonar buoys from the Enterprise and the cruisers searched for Japanese submarines.

While the strike package formed up, the Imperial Japanese Army General Staff happened to be meeting to figure out how to acquire the oil they desperately needed to continue their quest for Asian dominance. Arguments broke out between those who had opposed war with the United States and the militant Army leaders lined up with Prime Minister Hideki Tojo who were obsessed with realizing the dream of an Asian Empire. As was the case for the last ten years, the militants used intimidation to shout down the dissenters.

While this argument continued, three F-35s closed in on their location at five thousand feet and opened their bomb bay doors, ready to drop their payload.

In the Japanese Diet [legislature], a debate mediated by the President of the Privy Council Hajime Sugijama mirrored that of the military leaders. Sugijama argued, "The only advantage we had is now lying on the bottom of the ocean without having inflicted any damage on the Americans." Then he did something unheard of by one who wasn't trying to commit suicide. "To continue this war with the United States will lead to the destruction of Japan. It is time for serious negotiations, even if it means withdrawing from China and Manchuria." This brought a howl of disgust from the militants in the Diet.

Just when violence seemed inevitable, in rapid succession three two-thousand pound bombs ripped into the chambers. As the building imploded under the enormous blast, the destruction didn't discriminate between the pragmatic and the fanatical.

While they struck the Diet, the three bombs that targeted the Army General Staff turned out to be overkill. The first bomb hit dead center, killing everybody within one hundred yards of the blast radius. The two remaining bombs only acted as exclamation points to their deadly precision.

With the primary targets destroyed, the pilots of the four reserve F-35s headed north to the naval station. They found two aircraft carriers moored in the bay, and paired off to release two bombs over each of them. The pilots watched in satisfaction as both ships erupted in giant fireballs, which put two more nails in the coffin of the Japanese Navy.

After the strike package recovered to the Enterprise and they reviewed the video footage from the F-35s, Osaka worked throughout the afternoon with a Japanese interpreter transcribing intercepts that confirmed the Japanese Government was in chaos.

After receiving permission from Sean, Lt. Commander Layton sat in. He was still there when Sean stopped by to get Osaka's take on the Japanese response.

"What are you hearing?"

"If you don't mind a simple Japanese analogy Sir, it reads a lot like the panic in the 1973 Japanese movie where Godzilla battled Megalon in the hills outside of Tokyo. The Japanese Imperial Command has issued orders and then within an hour issued new orders to countermand the previous ones. It's obvious there's a power struggle going on for the Emperor's ear between the Army and Navy."

"Godzilla? That's the second time I've heard that same lame analogy."

"Sorry Admiral, but the exaggerated eyewitness descriptions about futuristic planes flying at great speeds reminded me of the Godzilla movie."

"Moving on," Sean stated with irritation. "Is there any indication who is taking charge yet?"

"No Sir, just confusion."

"Fine. Let me know if anything changes." He made to leave when he remembered the other reason for his visit. "Commander, I would like both you and Commander Layton to join Miss Calhoun, Captain Knox, and me for dinner tonight at 1900 hours. Dress whites will not be required. Also, please inform Captain Aslan on the Missouri. I want her there as well."

"Yes Sir!" Osaka had trouble keeping his voice from cracking at the thought of sharing a table with his admiral.

Satisfied with the strikes, at 1800 Sean ordered the task force to set course back to Hawaii.

An hour and a half later during dinner, Lt. Commander Layton couldn't contain his curiosity. "Why did you change tactics Admiral? When you launched your aircraft before the attack on the 7th, they disappeared almost immediately. Yet today I followed them well out to the horizon." Layton didn't know they had sailed most of the last six days without Specter's cover.

"You should know a magician never reveals his tricks," Tony joked.

Sean changed the subject, and turned to the political fallout created by their decapitation of the Japanese Government. "As much as I'd like to tell you more about our capabilities, I'm more interested in your opinion about today's intercepts. Any thoughts about what faction winds up in control of the Japanese Government?"

"Back at Pearl we knew most of the officers in the Japanese naval command spent time either as students in our universities or as military attachés to the United States. Because of this Western exposure, they would be the ones most sympathetic to negotiations. Therefore, if you did remove the hierarchy of the Army's high command, you probably created an opportunity for senior Naval Commanders to rally the moderates of the Japanese Diet who are still alive. Admiral Yamamoto carries a lot of weight, and he was against war with the United States in the first place. There would be room for dialogue.

"The Army attracted thousands of young officers indoctrinated into the Shinto warrior mentality and assassinated anyone who tried to compromise with the West. There's a real chance with the leadership splintered, there will be a real bloodbath to see who controls the Emperor."

Renée agreed. "You should know that from our historical perspective, near the end of WWII the Army came close to assassinating Hirohito, which backs up your assessment. It could still happen."

"This is why we targeted their Army Command structure. Even if the Japanese Navy can't control the government, we created an environment where the Japanese will be so busy trying to sort out what happened they won't have time to look outward. They have to fear we might still be right off their shore ready to launch further strikes.

Sean stopped to take a bite of his dinner. "Either way, we've left them without the means to affect an acceptable defense, let alone room to launch any further offensives. Even if they wanted to, without a Navy and a source of oil they lack the means."

Lt. Commander Layton thought for a moment and then shook his head in disagreement. "As much as I'd like to buy into your optimism, I find it hard to believe they'll give up on the idea that they have the right to dominate Asia. They believe in this in the same way the United States has justified dominating the Western Hemisphere under the Monroe Doctrine, which by the way is one of their justifications to claim Asia."

"I'm afraid you are now in Miss Calhoun's territory." Sean motioned for Alicia to take over.

She ably took the hand off. "I'd be inclined to agree with you, except most of the fanatical commanders of the surviving Japanese Army are spread throughout Asia without the means to return home quickly. It would require the Japanese Navy to transport enough of their soldiers back to Japan to maintain the Army's control over the government. Do you think under the current situation, the Navy is in a hurry to transport them back?

"If the new Japanese Government decides to continue the war, they'll be hard pressed to without oil, which they should be running out of by the time we return to Hawaii. The bigger question now is how President Roosevelt and Prime Minister Churchill will react when they meet with us. We do have some ideas about how to straighten this whole mess out and to help the political leaders of this era move onto a more enlightened path."

Lt. Commander Layton took a few moments to digest the meaning behind Alicia's statement. "If I accept you did come from the future, I have to assume I've only witnessed a small portion of what you're capable of. With the exception of the Missouri and Enterprise, I haven't seen any other of your other ships in action, so obviously their role is to protect the carrier. Therefore, I assume they have greater firepower than the single gun mounts I see on their deck. Speaking of superstructures and hidden capabilities, there is my repeated question about what powers the Enterprise. It must be important, because you ignore the question every time I've brought it up."

Sean bluntly headed off his question. "The mystery of the propulsion technology at the heart of the Enterprise is one of the secrets we will give up when we feel we've done everything within our ability to see that the powers we possess are not abused. In the meantime, we can use our advantages to bring enough stability to the world to reduce the need for them."

"Isn't it contradictory to use weapons of war to create this society you speak of?" Lt. Commander Layton demanded. "If the nations of the world want to continue to build weapons of war, what makes you think you can throw a magic switch to stop it?"

"This is only one of the many paradoxes we have to deal with," Sean agreed, as he leaned back in his chair. "We don't flatter ourselves with the belief we can change basic human nature. All we want to do is try to gain some time on the historical time clock to better the odds. For better or worse, the history we remember changed once we released the first bomb on the Akagi. We hope as hostilities end, we can enlighten the political leaders of this era to open up their minds to some truths. For example, do you agree with the current segregation policy of the United States and the discrimination that goes along with it?"

The sudden change in the conversation confused Layton. He

took a moment before he responded. "I was born in a small town in Illinois and life was the way it was, never changing much from day to day. I didn't give race much thought and that didn't change much when I spent four years at Cal Tech. My only interaction with Negroes came after I entered the service. When I think about it, I guess I should have given more thought about why they always seemed to work in the mess hall or as stewards for the officers. Based on my lack of personal experience in this area, I can't give you much of an answer to your question."

Sean was seeking a reaction. "Could you imagine the people of the United States electing a black man as a United States Senator or even President?"

Alicia quickly squeezed in her own agenda. "Or, how about women who share equal opportunity with their male counterparts in government and business?"

"Yeah, that's another one of those disasters we speak of," Sean joked. "Women not only achieved equal rights in the future, they raced right by us, so you better learn how to cook and change baby diapers Lt. Holmes."

Alicia gave Sean a look that both Tony and Renée couldn't help laughing at. "You better modify that statement somewhat Sean, or Alicia is going to spend plenty of time reminding you just how much smarter she is than you."

"You're right Tony. Misogyny in any form is unacceptable."

Alicia took a moment to gauge Sean's seriousness before letting him off the hook. "One of these days I hope we will finally reach parity so jokes like that are merely funny, not a reminder."

Lt. Holmes was thoroughly confused at the whole exchange and chose to keep his mouth shut.

Seeing his confusion, Sean decided a quick primer course. "Over the next sixty years, equality for women and civil rights for minorities were the only positive evolutions Western societies could look at with pride. You have probably already witnessed some of this by the diversity onboard this ship. Do you think it would be possible to force these changes now?"

This line of reasoning and where it was going continued to baffle Lt. Commander Layton, who answered carefully. "First off I'm not political, so I don't think you're talking to the right person to answer that question. However, if you want my opinion about if I would have a problem working alongside a Negro or a woman, here it is. Mathematics doesn't care about the color or gender of the theoretician."

"Well said," Alicia applauded.

It was getting late at the end of a long day, so Sean put his napkin on the table, which signaled the end to the dinner. "Now, I don't mean to be rude Commander Layton, but we have some issues to deal with that quite frankly would bore you."

As he shook Layton's hand Sean turned to Lt. Commander Osaka. "Would you be kind enough to escort Commander Layton back to his cabin?"

Osaka knew this to be an order. "Come on Commander Layton. I have a few questions I'd like to ask you."

Despite the bums rush, Layton smiled. "Thank you for the invitation and the interesting conversation. Good Night."

"And we thank you for your insights," Sean replied.

After they left Sean turned to Renée on a different matter. "Your reports from the Missouri indicate few of the crew share Brewster's views. In fact, you said most of the senior officers respond better to Commander Eddington."

Alicia interrupted with a little girl-to-girl wink. "*She* told me the *Commander* seems to have taken a little from Tony in the way *he* handles the crew. *She* also says *Carl* is capable and can take command in an emergency. Is that about right?"

Clueless to Alicia's innuendo, Tony got up from the dinner table to pour coffee.

Renée glared back at Alicia with a covert negative nod before she answered Sean. "Based on the crew's responses to him, I stand by what I said in the report."

Sean was not aware Alicia and Renée had discussed the possibility of Eddington taking over as Captain of the Missouri. "All that aside, there is another reason we chose to send you over to the Missouri. It isn't Commander Eddington we want to replace Brewster with, it's you."

Before the surprised Renée could respond, Alicia cut in again. "We couldn't very well tell you our real agenda when we sent you. It might have made you find excuses for Brewster out of guilt you were there to take his command away. This way we got an unbiased report, and when the moment comes, you won't be conflicted."

"To tell you the truth after watching the creep in action, I would have recommended a grease monkey from engineering as more qualified to command sailors. It will be an honor to command the Missouri if you feel it necessary. Thank you both."

"What about me? Don't you think I had any say in their decision?" Tony whined.

"I'm sorry Tony. Your support is always welcome," Renée said with an appreciative smile.

Sean effectively ended the celebration and got back on point. "Great, now that's settled, we need to discuss how we intend to shake up 1940s international politics."

Alicia dove right in as she reclined on the couch. "It would be best to keep any thoughts except those that deal with the defeat of Germany and Japan out of our first meetings with Roosevelt and Churchill and leave the rest for another day. I said it before and I'll say it again, if we can end WWII quickly, the Cold War will not have a chance to begin. This in itself could hopefully kill off those of the Industrial Military Establishment before they can put a strangle hold on our economy. Now, let's say we remove Stalin and the Cold War never begins. What's next?"

"Unlike you Alicia," Tony argued, "I don't have the use of a crystal ball to see into the future. My best guess would be Germany would still lead the world in precision automobiles and Soviet leaders will remain holed up in their Dachas while their citizens stand in bread lines. England will still believe the sun doesn't set on their empire and the French will still be the French, contemptuous of everybody else."

Tony continued with his rant. "Regardless of what you think, even if we manage to stop the current carnage in the world, I don't believe we will all join hands and sing Kumbaya. Two generations from now the same corrupt, power hungry menaces will re-emerge to send us back down the same rat hole. Reptilians – 1, Believers in Nirvana – 0, and the world turns. I admire your altruistic attempt to save humanity from itself, but you better than most people know this cycle hasn't changed since man left his caves for a mud thatched village."

While still lying on the couch Alicia countered his cynicism. "I'm sorry Tony, but I have to believe there is a time in the future when we can evolve past our instincts to render our species extinct. Neither Sean nor I believe our presence here can magically turn a switch and all will be well, though you have to admit, our even being here is magical. If we could calm the waters enough to give the world a chance to survive the next century, there could be a renaissance of the human spirit. It has happened before."

Tony wasn't so easily convinced. "We left a place in time where special interest groups in constant conflict with one another swallowed the individual whole. Instead of honoring the legacy of the independent American individual portrayed by the likes of John Wayne, governmental rules and regulations buried the dream under six feet of paperwork. At the same time, we stripped the world's resources bare, while we attempted to procreate ourselves out of existence to support the voracious need for mega-corporations to expand their sales base.

"I do hope you are right," Tony continued. "But none of this begins to address the other elephant in the room – Captain Brewster and his merry band of fundamentalists. Their need for Armageddon to occur in their lifetime will only become more obsessive with us as the poster child of evil. We all watched these nut jobs capitalize on the Indian-Pakistani war to drive up their memberships in the *How can we help end the world for Jesus* club. All because they realized their own dreams of the good life had faded into the mists of time and they got bitter about it." Tony despised the violence of the Christian right as much as he did the Muslim extremists. "As far as I'm concerned, all religious fanatics are cut from the same cloth. Believe as I do, or my God demands I blow you up."

Alicia knew the drill, but couldn't help herself. "Once again your cynicism knows no bounds. It's less about religious fanaticism and more about the lack of a decent life. Look where all of these zealots come from. You don't see reports on CNN of domestic terrorists from Beverly Hills setting off IUDs on Rodeo Drive for God's sake. In the Middle East most of their human fodder is fed radical ideology from birth with the goal to remove any semblance of European influence from their midst. Their success has simply spread to Afghanistan, Pakistan, and any other *somethingstan* in the region. And I know you don't want to hear it Tony, but without the need for oil, nobody in the Western World would give a rat's ass."

Surprisingly, Sean didn't come to her defense. "Alicia, I don't disagree with most of what you said, except for one simple fact. Gandhi, Mandela, Martin Luther King, and I can list others who brought about revolutions through the sheer will of their personalities without resorting to carnage. They understood how to use the media to amplify the brutality of their societies' oppressors. This shined the spotlight on every injustice until the tipping point of world opinion brought down the offending government.

"Violent overthrows almost always lead to a cycle where the deposed become the terrorists and the violence continues. Ethnic rivalries have been a way of life for millenniums throughout most of the world. Regardless, the bottom line is everyone responsible for crashing those jets on 9/11, or who were happy it happened, lost any compassion I might have had for their plight."

"Yeah, what he said," Tony added in his most childlike manner.

"You're a big help Sean," Alicia reproached. "He's going to be insufferable for the next few days."

"I'm sorry. I don't know what came over me." Though thoroughly entertained by the conversation, Sean was tired. "I'm done. Most of this can wait until our next staff meeting, which by the way I want to schedule for the 24th at 0900. And Tony, have the staff work up the list of supplies we will need to get us to the North Sea and back."

Tony, though disappointed the conversation had run its course, went straight to an issue bothering him. "Speaking of which, it's going to put a lot of miles on these ships to cruise all the way to Europe and back. Have you given any thought to cutting a few thousand miles off the trip by going through the Panama Canal? The sooner we reach the Atlantic, the faster we can reach Europe."

"That's going to depend on how our meeting with Roosevelt and Churchill turns out. The politics of what we need to accomplish all resides on the Atlantic side. Again, this can wait. I'll see you in the morning, except for you Renée. I want you back on the Missouri."

Roosevelt was in a meeting with Churchill at the White House when he received the first reports of the attack on Tokyo and the devastation of the Japanese leadership. Decipherers were verifying this as it became apparent the Japanese were preparing for the defense of the home islands against further attacks. Regardless of the mystery surrounding how their invisible paramours accomplished it, the news added a boundless energy to the Prime Minister's step that made him almost unbearable to be around.

"This means certain defeat for Hitler. With Japan neutralized, we can focus all our forces in Europe to defeat Germany. You also won't need to waste the power of the 7th Fleet in Pacific waters, when they could be better used to protect the Atlantic convoys from the German U-boats."

President Roosevelt was more cautious. "Slow down Winston. We still don't know if the Japanese Government is willing to leave Manchuria and China, which was the main point of contention in the first place. Until we know if they are willing to re-engage in negotiations to remove all of their troops from occupied foreign territory, the 7th Fleet is staying where it is.

"And in case you've forgotten, there's a force roaming the Pacific which took down a one of the world's most powerful nation in days, and we don't have a clue what their motivations are. For all my intelligence people know, they could be aliens from another planet.

"Think about it, Winston. A naval task force of incredible power drops in from nowhere, and in three weeks destroys Japan's ability to wage war. Who is to say what it is they will want next or if it is contrary to our interests? They have weapons my people cannot explain, let alone defend against.

"And for God's sake Winston, could you please put on some clothes? Marshal and Donovan should return soon, and Marshal's prudish sensibilities don't need to see your cherubic nakedness."

Churchill didn't hear much of what President Roosevelt said, because British dominance in Asia was no longer threatened. Still, he could not let go of the idea Roosevelt was holding out on him.

"I don't see why you can't let me in on what weapons you have deployed, Franklin."

"For the last time Winston, I am as much in the dark as you." Roosevelt was grateful when at last General Marshall arrived.

When Churchill and General Donovan had returned to their hotel, Churchill's sense for the melodramatic took hold. "How can I know if the President's letters were sincere, or if he's covering up a major weapons breakthrough while we're left in the dark? If the United States military has the capability to defeat the Japanese in 9 days, why wouldn't they have offered to use it against the Nazis?" Churchill expressed with sadness his relationship maybe wasn't as special as he once thought. "And, how did our own intelligence miss something so big?"

General Donovan had nothing to add, so he remained quiet.

Joseph Goebbels, Hitler's Minister of Propaganda, was having as bad a day as Churchill's day was good. The German High Command received conflicting reports out of Japan about the struggle for control of the government. On one side was Admiral Kantaro Suzuki who sent a letter that, in its ambiguity, hinted at the possibility of rapprochement with the United States.

Yet at the same time, a strongly worded letter arrived from the Commander of Japanese Army forces in China, General Korechika Anami, stating Japan had everything under control. He also assured the German Government that he looked forward to Japan's continued alliance with Germany. In this letter, he requested any information the Germans could supply as to the nature of the enemy that struck with such deadly stealth.

The only information the German network of spies in America and England could supply was that Roosevelt and Churchill had disappeared from public view shortly after the attack on Japan. German intelligence speculated, based on ship movements in the area that the two leaders were meeting somewhere in the Hawaiian Islands.

Japan's political chaos took the pressure off Russia's southern frontier, and worse still, allowed the American military buildup to focus on Europe. The German military leadership's plans were based on it taking at least three years for the United States military to build up to the necessary levels to force a beachhead in Europe. They based this estimate on the late entry of the United States into

World War I, while for three years the French and British were fighting on the continent.

Hitler did not waste any time to bring the war to the Western Hemisphere. He ordered every available U-boat sent into the Atlantic sea lanes. He also ordered the German capital ships in Norway and France to prepare for convoy interdiction. Even Goebbels, the master propagandist, could not find a way to spin any of this as good news. Everyone in the German Government, except Hitler, now believed the declaration of war with the United States was a mistake.

In the Soviet Union, Stalin began to purge the senior members of his government and military, as he grew paranoid about how his *allies* had managed to render Japan impotent. His first target was Lavrentiy Beria, head of the NKVD [forerunner to the KGB], for conspiring to keep Stalin in the dark about the American new wonder weapons. In his twisted logic, he assumed his spies, compromised by the decadence of the Americans, had known this wonder weapon existed.

While paranoia consumed the despots, onboard the Missouri Renée reported to Brewster, who promptly reminded her of the difficulty of her position.

"So how was your dinner with the Admiral, *Captain* Aslan? Did you all finish planning how to imprint your egos on history?"

"Dinner was wonderful. It was a nice opportunity to spend some relaxing moments with those I care a great deal about. I hope your evening went as well." Renée chose not to feed into the man's attempt to instigate an argument on the bridge. However, she did take a moment to look around and noticed there were a few new faces. She made a mental note to ask Eddington about it.

"I'm sure you have somewhere you need to be," Brewster said in a dismissive manner and drove the point home by turning his back on her to talk to one of his new bridge acolytes.

"I'll be in the CIC if you should need me." As Renée left the bridge, a chill shot up her back that brought up the thought, "Maybe I should keep my side arm close."

As she made her way to the CIC, she thought about the dangers. "As Captain Eddington reported, a few in Brewster's command who had previously served under him share his narrow view of the world: all white, all male, with subservient women barefoot and pregnant in the kitchen. For some ungodly reason, every one of them believes their version of God must be crammed down the throat of everybody else. Too bad if they piss all over the Constitution and deny you your *certain unalienable Rights endowed by* your *Creator* as long as they have the opportunity to direct you to the light. Yes, I definitely have to pack my side arm."

It blew Renée's mind how some of the great humanists had their teachings twisted into a language of ridicule and hate. This inability is also responsible for maintaining the idea that a woman's place is still in the home, and their highest ambition should be to head the local PTA. In other words, these same people resented her rank because she was a woman.

"At least the Navy I serve has taken great leaps in equality since the days of the Tailhook scandal back in the 80s, but it is still the last bastion of the *good old boy* way of thinking. That is why I jumped at the chance to serve in the diplomatic corps. The only tool necessary was a quick mind, and if foreign diplomats hit on me, I just walked away instead of having to share close quarters with the bastards for the next six months aboard a ship."

Renée spent most of her time in the Missouri CIC where the testosterone levels were easier on her sensibilities than the swinging dicks of the Air Wing she left behind on the Enterprise. She especially enjoyed her conversations with Commander Carl Eddington who dropped in from time to time.

After eating her dinner alone, she headed to her bed in the

Admirals Quarters. Right before she fell asleep, the image of Tony on the Central California beach appeared along with a sense of jealousy about Sean and Alicia's relationship. She wondered if there would be a happy ever after for any of them as she drifted away.

Roosevelt and Churchill now ran the governments of both the United States and Great Britain from the island of Oahu while they waited for the 25th to arrive. In an attempt to take advantage of Japan's political confusion, Churchill convinced Roosevelt to send an ultimatum to the Japanese Government. In it, he promised further attacks against the heart of their government if they did not return to the negotiation table to discuss terms of their withdrawal from China.

They had transmitted this message through back channels the day after the strikes on Tokyo. Three days later, the Japanese cabled their response to Washington, bearing the name of Prime Minister Kantaro Suzuki. It contained a request to resume negotiations and return Ambassador Horinouchi to Washington to meet with Secretary of State Cordell Hull.

"Looks like the Japanese Navy's in charge for the moment, Franklin, and the bastards are looking to save a little face." Churchill could read between the lines and figured the Japanese Government was looking for a way out.

Neither man knew Japan was close to a civil war between the Army and Navy during the two days it took for the response to arrive. Two factors decided the outcome. Most of the surviving Army Generals were in Japanese occupied countries. This left only a junior cadre of Army staff officers who survived the attack on Tokyo, to fill the political vacuum and fight to continue hostilities with the West.

The second factor was a meeting the new Prime Minister Kantaro Suzuki had with the Emperor. In it, he laid out the limited options that remained open to the Japanese military. With the majority of the nation's naval strength destroyed and less than two weeks of oil left to supply both the military and the civilian population, they didn't have the resources to continue offensive operations. This reality, along with threats from Supreme Commander Admiral Yamamoto that he would deny support to the Army in China if the generals did not concede to negotiations, left the Emperor little choice but to side with the Navy.

In the United States, Congressional leaders were concerned about the lack of useful information supplied by the President and his Cabinet. Restricted by his own lack of information, Secretary of War Stimson was constantly in and out of meetings with Senate Majority Leader Alben Barkley and Speaker of the House Sam Rayburn.

Fortunately for the President, his party controlled both houses of Congress. His friend and adviser Harry Hopkins, whom everyone referred to as the deputy president, managed to keep a lid on the events taking place in the Pacific. Hopkins even floated the rumor the President was in secret negotiations to reach a settlement forcing Japan out of China. Harry Hopkins never missed a chance to make political hay out of any situation.

━━◆━━

On the morning of the 21st, Alicia was sitting on the couch in the Admirals Ready Room shuffling through pages of typewritten notes she had worked on the night before. In these notes, she hoped clarity of purpose would magically appear. Unfortunately, every time she found a route through the historical data, there were flaws that disrupted the flow. This made her devote too much time on minor issues and lose the big picture. Her brain had absorbed so much conflicting information from the seventy years since WWII she short-circuited and tossed the papers to the floor in frustration.

"Who are we to think we have the wisdom to alter the course of history successfully?"

"The devil is in the details," Sean said from across the conference table, reading copies of the same pages. "As much as I hate the use of outlines, I think in this case it might be useful. You might want to give it some thought."

While down on her knees, Alicia stopped picking up the papers and looked up at Sean. "It isn't so much the sequence of events I'm worried about, as much as the idea that for every question I think I have an answer to, how much does that solution come into conflict with something of equal importance.

She rolled onto the floor exhausted. "Think about our situation for a minute and then tell me you are not concerned about our lack of professional expertise when it comes to issues like what our impact on the world economy might be. On the other hand, if instead of preventing a Holy War within the next fifty years, we trigger one now. That fact alone is enough to upset any plans we are foolish enough to make."

"If we're not consumed by doubt now and then about what we're trying to accomplish, I'd be worried," Sean answered as he rose from his chair.

He picked Alicia up off the floor and they both sat on the couch. "The way I see it, the direction our country was headed when we went poof, meant poor disenfranchised kids like me had as much a chance to be educated to their potential as winning the lottery. As tough as it was for me to break through the *raised by a single mother* stigma in the sixties, at least there were after school programs to pick up the slack. Shop classes and the President's Physical Fitness programs kept me moving in the right direction. Not only have all these programs been shit-canned, single parents are raising fifty percent of the kids in the United States in 2014. Any doubts I have turn to rage when I think about all of the wasted potential.

"The reason I bring this up is because it was the so-called *economic experts* like Summers, Bernanke, and Paulson who looked the other way when other *economic experts* raped and pillaged Wall Street. We will make mistakes, but at least we'll be on the side of the angels."

"Okay, I get it," Alicia acknowledged with a frown and a bit of sarcasm. "Any idiot could do a better job, and we are the only idiots available. However, how do you tell Roosevelt that everything he knows is wrong? 'Excuse me Mr. President, but your policies will lead the country down the road to absolute ruin.'"

After a moment of thought, Alicia continued with her rant. "I could argue his policies did more to shift the responsibility for taking care of our senior citizens from the family to the government. The biggest growth industry in 2014 was assisted care and nursing homes families shuffled their elderly off too. No one cared to make the time to listen to the wisdom of their experiences, so all of their aches and pains became a burden and their years of wisdom useless. I know this because I was responsible for putting both my grandmother and mother into those institutions. I witnessed firsthand the depression that pervades even the most beautiful of these places. It opened my eyes to the fact that we threw away a valuable resource we can never get back."

Sean noticed tears had welled up in Alicia's eyes, with a single stream trailing down her right cheek. Before it could reach the corner of her mouth, Sean reached over and wiped it away. "You never talked about your mother before."

Alicia recovered enough to offer up a weak smile while she clutched Sean's hand. "Probably because we never had anything in common. You know, daddy's little girl. After my mother died, I realized I never gave our relationship a chance."

She wiped the rest of the moisture from her eyes and straightened up. "Did you know that the public schools no longer require civics classes as part of the basic curriculum? It isn't any wonder that seventy-five percent of high school graduates can't name the United States Senators of their own state or the three branches of the Federal Government."

Sean smiled at the way Alicia segued away from the brief glimpse into a painful memory. He knew it would be best to leave it alone for now. "I think from the perspective of how to manage the growth of the Federal Government, you're on the right track. However, when we meet with Roosevelt and Churchill for the first time we have to find an immediate connection, such as the defeat of Hitler and the restraint of Stalin's ambitions. Stick with these related goals and it should buy us time to address the hundreds of others."

Sean then cut to the chase. "So what's the carrot we're going to dangle in front of two of the most manipulative leaders in modern history to get them to agree to hand over control to us?"

It was Alicia's turn to smile. "With Roosevelt, it's simple. Let him have all the credit for arranging a quick peace. In Churchill's case, all we need to do is agree with his assessment that Joseph Stalin is evil, and when we remove Stalin, we will give him the credit as the savior of Europe. Nothing beats good press when you deal with politicians of any era. I plan to play as much as possible on these weaknesses.

"Now leave me alone to work on this."

"Yes ma'am," Sean popped off a quick salute and a wink. He could tell Alicia had what she needed and felt a little sorry for Roosevelt and Churchill.

Still at work in the hangar, Dr. Rebecca Cutler had done all she could to limit the effects of Dr. Strangelove's manipulations to Specter's program. To move forward, she felt it necessary to gain a different perspective on the problem. She needed to talk to Dr. Safire.

Fifteen minutes later Rebecca took a seat next to Dr. Safire's bed in the Missouri's Sickbay and began to play a little game. "I found the codes you inserted to redirect the missile launchers." She smiled at the surprised look he gave at this news and in a coy voice continued. "I also removed dozens of other gremlins you loaded, so there will not be misdirected communications, faulty steering commands, or inaccurate course headings to worry about."

Rebecca could see the tension building up in the scientist, so she continued to provoke him. "By the way, *I* would have done a much better job hiding those codes. Nobody would have uncovered them."

Her last statement hit the right nerve, as Dr. Safire fought against his restraints in an attempt to attack her while he screamed. "You think you can undo in a mere matter of weeks what I spent five years of my genius meticulously building? If you think that, then you are as moronic as all the other monkeys I have had to deal with. I've buried enough corrupted coding in Specter to keep your team of monkeys busy in the lab for years." Then Dr. Safire's look turned murderous. "That is of course if you had years, or who knows, maybe we'll all be dead tomorrow?"

When he heard the outburst, the Sickbay doctor rushed into the room and sedated the ranting scientist.

Rebecca, with the knowledge there was still more of his evil buried in the program, became more determined to disable the threats and rub it in his face.

On the way to the hangar, she thought through everything he had said. "Dr. Safire didn't rant about their current situation, so he wasn't responsible for their trip through time."

The morning of the 24th, now only eight hundred miles northwest of Oahu, the senior officers sat around the conference table reading the pages Alicia had prepared to present to President Roosevelt and Prime Minister Churchill.

Sean knew Captain Brewster would continue to be a pain in his ass, so with Alicia in agreement, they decided beforehand that if the rest of the senior staff agreed to the plan it would be the right time to relieve Brewster.

As if given a cue, Captain Brewster immediately began to raise objections. "You've spelled out a secular future history. I don't believe any of this is in God's plans, so there is no way I will support a plan so blasphemous." The Captain stood up and nervously walked around the table.

"Please let the others finish reading through the Secretary's brief Captain, and when they are finished, you can have your say." Sean decided that until he heard from the rest of his staff it would be best not to provoke Brewster.

Brewster returned to his seat, and when everyone else had finished, Sean turned to Captain Daily of the Seawolf first. "What do you think, Mark?"

"To tell you the truth, I wish I was back at home in bed next to my beautiful wife listening to what trouble the kids got into today. But seeing how that's not going to happen, do you think you can convince Franklin Delano Roosevelt and Winston Bloody Churchill to let us interject ourselves into international politics without a fight?"

Sean could hear in Captain Daily's voice how much he missed his family. "Believe me, I'm sure most of us feel the same way about missing those back home, and yes I do believe they can be convinced to support our proposed operation after they view the evidence. When we have them here for the meeting and give them the irrefutable proof Captain Aslan has spent the last two weeks compiling, they'll jump at the chance to finish Hitler."

Alicia broke in at this point. "Convincing Roosevelt to become the peacemaker is an easy sell, and with Churchill's knowledge of Stalin's brutality to back up our documentation, this is the easy part. What I want from all of you is whether you think the concessions I've spelled out in return are workable."

Brewster jumped in. "I most certainly do not think they are, and I for one oppose every one of your hair brained schemes. I'd rather sink every last one of these ships than see us involved in the Devil's work."

Sean and Alicia waited patiently to see what the other Captains thought.

Commander Steven Holmes of the Decatur, the most junior of the warship Captains, was the first to offer up his take. "I know I don't have as many years of service as most of you, but in my opinion, I don't see what other choices we have. First off, does everyone agree that if we let the world slide into the mess we left behind, it would be a complete abdication of responsibility on our part? I'm only thirty-six and already feel old from the constant push and pull we've gone through as a nation, tossed from one crisis to the next. Before I could get my head wrapped around yesterday's disaster, three more acts of depravity would crop up the next day. That's the truth of what we left behind. Nothing worked. I don't have an issue with trying to change this, even if we fail."

Now it was Captain Gordon Lincoln of the Princeton's turn. "The way I figure it, the minute we arrived in 1941 everything changed, which included if those we left behind still exist. We can talk all day about the chicken or the egg, but the truth remains the same. We are here, and I think it would be selfish of us if we didn't try to make the world a better place with the knowledge we possess."

"Thank you Captain Lincoln," Alicia was happy for the support. "Both the Admiral and I, contrary to the tradition of absolute military authority, want you to cast a vote on this proposal, with a simple majority to decide. Raise your hand to signal approval."

Nine hands shot into the air with Captain Brewster the only dissenting vote.

Sean turned to him and in a deadly serious voice informed him. "I've also come to the conclusion, Captain Brewster, that you are unfit to command the Missouri, and I am relieving you of your command, effective immediately." This statement brought the room to a quick silence.

"You can't expect me to turn over command a second time in

two weeks because I don't agree with your attempt to usurp God's will. I haven't done anything to warrant my removal as Captain of the Missouri."

"That's where you're mistaken Steven. As your commanding officer, I have the law on my side if I believe you are unfit for duty. As your immediate civilian superior, Secretary of Defense Calhoun has the authority to overturn my decision if you still feel there's room to argue."

Alicia picked up the book of naval regulations and turned to the page on dereliction of duty that spelled out her underlying authority. When she finished reading, she slammed the door shut. "You will remain on the Missouri. As long as you choose not to interfere with the safe operations of this fleet, you can maintain your freedom of movement there."

With a nod from Alicia, the Marine standing at the door opened it, stepped aside, and came to attention. To the further amazement of everyone in the room, Captain Renée Aslan entered the room, followed by Commander Carl Eddington.

Alicia stood up and announced, "Captain Aslan will assume command of the Missouri with Commander Carl Eddington as her XO."

"You're turning my command over to a woman?" Brewster's voice cracked, his rage making it difficult for him to keep control of himself.

Sean stood up and looked over the room of officers before settling his gaze on Brewster. "Captain, I want you as well as everyone in this room to know it isn't your disagreement with my orders that has forced me to relieve you. It's more the irrational method you apply to your arguments. I don't mind if you believe a flying cow is the God you choose to worship. I do mind when your opinions are a manifestation of the beliefs you would force on all of us.

"That and you're a misogynist on top of it. I've learned a lot since you came aboard about your interaction with the female officers under your command. You have a history of going out of your way to use your authority to abuse them. The Navy can't move fast enough to rid their ranks of cultural dinosaurs like you."

As he spoke, Sean passed copies of the report to the Captains to drive home the point Brewster was being relieved because he was an ineffectual Captain under wartime conditions, and for no other reason. Based on their looks, Sean was happy to see their agreement.

Brewster stormed out of the room into the waiting arms of Marines who escorted him off the ship. Captain Aslan took Brewster's place at the table, and the meeting continued for another thirty minutes.

After the Captains left, Lt. Commander Osaka approached Sean. "Admiral, with Captain Aslan transferring to the Missouri permanently, I would like Ensign Gloria Layworth transferred to the Enterprise to assist me."

Sean turned to Renée. "Any objections, Captain Aslan?"

"No Sir."

"Good, make it happen."

"Yes Sir," Renée replied.

"Thank you Admiral, Captain," Osaka acknowledged before he saluted and headed for the door.

Sean had some final thoughts for Renée. "Speaking for myself, I want to thank you for the great job you did gathering the information Alicia used so skillfully. You certainly have the talent to become a political operative if you ever decide to lose your moral center." Sean's joke got a laugh from both Tony and Alicia at the thought of Renée shilling for some beltway politician.

"Considering it was one of the many roles I played as Alicia's attaché, Admiral, I'm still trying to wash the dirt out of my soul. I am grateful for the experience, though. It feels refreshing to be back in command at sea, even under these conditions."

Tony and Alicia silently observed the respect Captain Renée

Aslan showed in the way she addressed her superior.

Sean looked at his watch. "It's time we made contact with the President."

Tony followed Sean and Alicia down to the CIC, where Osaka was already waiting. Five minutes later, Admiral Kimmel CINCPACFLT was on the other end.

"Good morning, Admiral Kimmel. This is Rear Admiral Sean Phillips aboard the USS Enterprise. I am sure you have many questions about who we are and where we came from. Unfortunately, you will have to be patient for one more day. Is the President available?"

"Give me a few minutes to…" Before Admiral Kimmel could say another word, another voice impatiently interrupted.

"This is President Roosevelt. To whom am I speaking?"

"This is Admiral Sean Phillips. But I'm not the one you need to talk to." Sean handed the phone to Alicia before the President could voice a complaint.

"Good morning, Mr. President. My name is Secretary of Defense Alicia Calhoun, the civilian authority of this task force. I know this may sound confusing, but please bear with me for a minute so I can explain."

"I don't care who you are if you can explain how you destroyed the Japanese ability to wage war in under two weeks. The Lieutenant you shanghaied and left on the open sea gave me an unbelievable description of what you did. The letter you left for me was cryptic to say the least, and to tell you the truth, you have those who know of your existence worried about your intentions. Who are you and who do you serve?"

"All you need to do is come aboard our ship tomorrow to have all of your questions answered. I don't see how I can convince you of anything, without proof to back up what we tell you. I want to invite you aboard our carrier at 1500 tomorrow at the location of the sunken Japanese carriers."

The Head of the Dragon

"I'm sorry, but there isn't any way either the Prime Minister or I could agree to such a risky idea. It would be irresponsible for us to do so."

Alicia had prepared for this little dance. "If we wished to do you or the Prime Minister any harm, we certainly wouldn't need to bring you aboard to do so. And correct me if I'm wrong, but isn't Churchill just dying to get a look at our ships?"

"You have to give the woman credit," Roosevelt thought. "Churchill did spend the last three days badgering me with inane conjecture about what this unknown power represented."

This was one of the reasons Roosevelt did not want Churchill there during this conversation. He would have agreed to anything to get a look. "What assurances can you give us that you won't use the opportunity to disable our governments? After all, based on what happened in Japan, how do we know we're not next? You do seem to have the ability to strike anywhere without warning."

"If we meant either the United States or Great Britain any harm," Alicia answered calmly, "then why have we focused all of our attention on destroying Japan's ability to make war? We sunk their ships and decapitated their government. Now we are talking to you, not shooting at you. Neither of you have anything to fear from us.

"I appreciate the position you are in, and I promise that neither of you will be disappointed. This is all I will say for now and I thank you for your time. I hope you will agree to see us tomorrow – out." Alicia made a slicing motion across her neck to the operator to end the call immediately.

An unnatural quiet permeated the CIC. Tomorrow they will enter the 1940s in the most real way, face to face with two of the most powerful leaders of the 20th Century.

The establishment of radio communications with their mysterious benefactors brought more questions than answers to the President's mind. "Admiral Kimmel, Commander Layton said there was a battleship Missouri in their task force. When I was at the launching of the battleship Washington earlier this year, I seem to recall that the Missouri was on the list of the next class of battleships. This doesn't make any sense."

Roosevelt was Secretary of the Navy in World War I, while Churchill served the British as First Sea Lord. The two men's combined knowledge of the history of sea power was expansive.

"How can a battleship we haven't built yet be a part of their forces?"

Roosevelt met with Churchill at their hotel to fill him in on the conversation he had with Alicia. They spent the rest of the day debating if they should agree to her request.

"I understand your reluctance Franklin. However, you must admit she has a point. I think by their actions they have earned the right to expect some faith from us."

The President wasn't convinced. "Or their plan all along was to destroy the biggest threats first and then work their way through the rest of us. I still maintain there isn't anything we know about who they are, and more importantly, whose orders they are operating under. Everything we know about reality is an illusion if they did come from the future. If they didn't, where did they develop their technology?"

Churchill had his own concern. "All I know for sure is England is going to run out of war materials in thirty days, so we better come up with something to get that convoy underway."

After another hour discussing the pros and cons, they agreed they didn't have a choice in the matter. If they were to understand what they were dealing with, they had to enter the lion's den.

The next morning at 0600, they boarded the USS California BB-44, a 32,300-ton Tennessee class battleship, for the nine-hour trip to where the Japanese carrier fleet went down. Neither of the men were happy with the lack of control they had over the situation.

⟶⟥⟵

Brewster was noticeably missing when the Seahawk with Captain Renée Aslan, Commander Carl Eddington, and three Marines set down on top of the hangar. As soon as it lifted off, a second Seahawk unloaded a detachment of five more Marines sent to supplement those on the Missouri. Irritated at this breach of protocol, Renée barked an order to Eddington.

"I want you on the bridge. When you get there, reassign every last person Brewster added since he took command. I don't care how innocent any of them may appear to be. Until I have a chance to talk to all of the senior officers, I only want this list of personnel Captain Knox gave me anywhere near the bridge or a secure space." She handed him the list and started walking toward the stairs that lead down to the deck.

"Where are you going? And what if Captain Brewster is on the bridge?"

Renée stopped and turned back to Eddington with a determined look. "If he is on the bridge, take command. Take some of these Marines with you. I'm headed to his cabin, where I'm sure he is either packing his things, or preparing to do something stupid."

"If that's the case, shouldn't you bring a Marine or two with you?"

"Why, you think he needs protection?"

Commander Eddington was about to question his Captain's logic, when he realized it would be a good time to shut up and start acting like her XO. "No Ma'am. I'm sure you will show the proper restraint when you find Captain Brewster."

"Use your radio if you run into any problems the Marines can't handle, Commander."

As Renée approached the Captains Cabin, she slowed down and

took a deep breath before knocking on the door.

"It's open, *Captain*."

Renée entered the room and was immediately struck by the austerity. "You have to give the man credit," she thought. "He certainly maintains the image of piousness right on down to the small altar set up in the corner of the cabin."

"You were supposed to be on hand to transfer command when I arrived, *Captain*."

"And why should I bow down to *Admiral* Phillips and his acolyte *Admiral* Calhoun after the humiliation of being removed from two separate commands in the space of two weeks?"

"Because we all *bow down* when we receive a direct order from a higher ranking officer. The way I see it, Captain Brewster, is you have a choice to make. Either you can continue to preach dissension, in which case you will force me to keep you locked up in this room with an armed Marine as your constant companion, or you can find another way to make yourself useful. Personally speaking, I don't give a rat's ass which you choose. As a matter of fact it would make my life a hell of a lot easier if I didn't give you a choice."

Brewster's response took Renée completely by surprise. "You're absolutely right Captain Aslan. I haven't exactly been a team player since our unfortunate passage through time. Though it is true I don't agree with any of the actions the Admiral and Secretary Calhoun are so determined to take, there isn't any excuse to pass my criticism along to the crew. If you have something useful for me to do, I will cooperate."

This was the last thing Renée expected from him, and instead of reassuring her, his comments raised the hair on the back of her neck for the second time. Unprepared, Renée now had to think of something that wouldn't require his appearance anywhere he could do damage. The best she could do is stall for time. "I'm sure I can find something to suit your talents. In the meantime, you can keep your quarters and I will remain in the Admirals Quarters. For now, you need to come with me so we can officially transfer command of the Missouri."

"Yes Captain."

When they entered the bridge, Renée made sure to take note of the quick expression of anger on Brewster's face. He was just as quick to cover it up. "I see you've already made changes on the bridge, *Captain*."

"All I'm doing Captain Brewster, is returning the personnel you removed back to the positions their rank entitled them to."

This time, he smiled at the obvious dig.

After the announcement to the crew of the command change, Brewster left the bridge to return to his cabin.

Satisfied the bridge was now in order, Renée turned to her XO before she left. "I want you in the Admirals Ready Room in an hour."

When Commander Eddington arrived in Renée's quarters, he made a point of taking in all of the room before he voiced his approval. "Pretty fancy digs for a lowly diplomatic attaché. I'm impressed."

"So is that how it's going to be with you?"

"I'm sorry; I don't have the slightest idea of what you're talking about Captain.

"Oh my God!" Renée thought. "He only spent a short time around Tony, and here he is acting like a carbon copy of the man."

"Look, we have work to do. I don't trust Captain Brewster. I was expecting him to continue his confrontational attitude, and instead he apologized and wanted to become more of a team player. Fortunately, he's not smart enough to pull off the 180-degree shift. What have you got on the men he placed on the bridge?"

"I thought you might ask, so I pulled up their service records before I came here. Like our former Captain, their connections are all they have going for them. They also share common religious and political links between families, right down to the churches they attend."

Renée wasn't surprised considering that most of the officers in the Navy came from the same regional stock. "Great. So in effect we have a microcosm of the Christian right to help boost his twisted ideas. I'd like to put their Crazy-Christian asses on a large uninhabited island somewhere in the Pacific. They could fight it out with the other religious fanatics like al-Qaeda, Hamas, Hindutva, Taliban, Khalistan Sikhs, and the 'Sharia forced on all' Shi'ites, to see who would rule it. Supply them with strap on bombs, IEDs, RPGs, automatic rifles, and all the ammunition their little twisted hearts could handle. The TV networks could turn it into a reality show that would allow the world to watch as they blew each other to the afterlife they all so desperately want to get to and leave the rest of us the hell alone."

"Sounds good to me. In the meantime, what's the plan?"

Renée took a moment to think before she answered. "Until he does anything overt there's not much we can do. The Admiral made it clear to me until we have any evidence, the only thing punishing him will do is call into question our own motivations to those who lean toward his way of thinking. The last thing we need is to turn Brewster into a martyr."

"So what do we do with him in the meantime?"

"For now I want to keep all secure spaces off limits to him. Quietly inform those you trust to help monitor his movements, and let's see if we can find out what he has in mind. There is a reason for his complete shift in attitude. Until we find out why, I want one of us on the bridge at all times. I'll relieve you when the watch changes."

"Aye Aye Captain."

When he turned to leave, Renée once again admired the way he filled out his uniform. Since it had been some time since her last relationship, she felt a little weak in the knees. She smiled when she remembered the mental exercises she learned in the male dominated service on how to deal with her needs. "I know Carl is my subordinate, but Tony better get on the ball and make a serious play, or regulations be damned…" Renée stopped when she realized she was talking out loud.

The next afternoon, 25 December 1941, under skies bright and clear, the Enterprise Task Force waited at the location of their first battle. Though it was Christmas, it wasn't to the sailors of the task force who had celebrated the holiday only two months ago in December 2013. Tony had ordered the crew to store the ship's aircraft belowdecks, except two F/A-18Fs. There was a buzz of energy from the lowest ranked squid, all the way up to the senior staff. By 1300, those not needed to operate the ship or man its defenses were putting on their dress whites and preparing to line the decks.

At 1430, Sean was on the bridge with Alicia when the John Paul Jones reported contact with a battleship and its escorts fifty miles out. In case Alicia was nervous about negotiating with two of the most famous leaders of the 20th Century, Sean gave her encouragement as they made their way down to the flight deck.

"Remember they're flesh and blood, and you're every bit as sharp as they are. However, also remember these two are champion political manipulators and everything they say carries meaning. The biggest advantage you have is your gender. They're not used to negotiations with a woman, so don't be too proud to use it to your advantage, if you know what I mean." A picture of Alicia bent over so the elder politicians could sneak a peek flashed across his mind forcing him to stifle a grin.

Alicia gave Sean a look as if to say, are you kidding me? "What makes you think I'd have a problem dealing with any politician? Remember, I've held my own with Bill Clinton, the best snake oil salesman of our generation."

Sean had made the decision earlier to engage Specter for the event to magnify the aura of the task force. "I wish I could see the look on Roosevelt's face when we pull back the curtain," Tony quipped as he joined Sean and Alicia on the deck. "For me, it would be the sight of Churchill drooling over how Britannia could still rule the seas if he got hold of these ships."

"Come on you guys," Alicia scolded as she braced against the wind. "We're about to come face to face with history, and all you can do is brag about how much bigger yours is than theirs. Just because we don't agree with Roosevelt's policies and Churchill's imperial sense of entitlement, it doesn't diminish the fact these two men shaped modern human history. Besides I remember that not so long ago we all agreed that what Roosevelt accomplished was nothing short of miraculous."

Undeterred, Tony got personal. "Oh, you mean back in the day when we foolishly believed that our leaders would actually try to measure up to Washington, Lincoln, and the other Roosevelt. That they would live up to the oaths they swore to, and the only reason they ran for political office was the vision of improving on the ideals of a truly free and prosperous nation where anyone could grow up to be President."

Tony gave an exaggerated pause, with a finger in the air motioning them silent, and then added, "Wait a minute – I do believe the last one holds true. How else do you explain the second Bush?"

Sean ignored Tony's wisecrack and responded to Alicia's comment. "I'll have to admit it wasn't until I reached the rank of Admiral and got close enough to see how much vested interest there was in the coin of the realm, did I go over to the dark side."

"The dark side of what?" Tony asked with an exaggerated look of amazement. "If you look in the dictionary for the definition of the altruistic Boy Scout, your name would be right alongside Spiderman's. Just look at how you've spent twenty years with

The Head of the Dragon

Alicia, and just now got around to doing the big nasty is all the validation anyone needs to know your truth."

"Stop trying to provoke him, Tony." Alicia covertly winked at Sean. "Besides, hopefully in the near future I can spend some time discussing that very subject with my man. I bet he didn't tell you I proposed to him."

This shut Tony up as a hurt look crossed his face.

However, before he could protest that neither of them shared this news with him, Sean quickly interjected. "That's not quite how it happened. We both came to the idea of marriage at the same time. Besides, you can't tell me the idea is any surprise to you. You were going to marry us, remember?"

Tony was quick to recover. "Knowing you two, I suppose the date will be twenty years from now, and you'll pull a Tony Randall and have a baby in your sixties. Think of the hours of fun the little tyke will have playing with the teeth in the bathroom glass. Hell, the kid can change your diapers almost as soon as she gets out of hers. And if you ask me how I know it will be a girl, I think we both know who will rule your household of the future."

"Touché," was Alicia's only response.

Sean shrugged his shoulders in resignation.

Chapter Six

Meeting History

Roosevelt and Churchill anxiously waited on the USS California, quietly staring out to a still empty horizon as they neared the coordinates of the sunken Japanese fleet. A shout from one of the sailors nearby got their attention. He pointed to an oil slick off the port bow. Seconds later, a fleet of warships appeared out of nowhere a mile off the starboard bow, and square in the middle was the largest aircraft carrier they had ever seen.

"My God Winston, Lt. Holmes wasn't exaggerating. How in the hell did they build a carrier that big?"

The only thing the Prime Minister could see was the potential the Enterprise offered, if he could find a way to use it. After several minutes viewing the ships through his set of binoculars, he offered his assessment. "The battleship looks like it could be one of yours, but I've never seen anything like the other four warships." He looked through the binoculars again. "I only see single 5-inch gun mounts on what appear to be destroyers, and one fore and aft on the other two. Yet they have a full battery of 16-inch guns on the battleship."

Lt. Jasper Holmes experienced a sense of pride race through

him as he stared out at the Enterprise. After the grilling he received from naval intelligence, even he had begun to question what he witnessed while aboard the Enterprise. Now when he returned to Pearl he would have the satisfaction of rubbing their noses in it, rank be damned.

Right about then, the Captain of the California received a radio message from the Enterprise. "This is Captain Charles Folger of the USS Enterprise, and we are ready to receive the President and Prime Minister at their convenience."

Twenty minutes later, as the launch with President Roosevelt, Churchill, and their staffs approached the Enterprise a lone F/A-18F catapulted off the deck. The sight brought such a shock to the sailors handling the launch they momentarily lost control. It wasn't until after the F/A-18F shot straight into the air and disappeared from sight that they regained their senses enough to maneuver their craft alongside the Enterprise.

The sense of awe was shared over on the USS California and her escorts at the sight of the alien F/A-18F, the sheer size of the Enterprise, the modern cruisers, destroyers, and of course, the Mighty Mo.

Sean, Alicia, Tony, and Captain Folger waited at the top of the gangplank as crewmembers hoisted the polio stricken President aboard. Also in attendance were Commander Logan Barrish, Lt. Commander Daniel Osaka, and Lt. Commander Edwin Layton.

With the exception of Churchill, the rest of the official party was still unnerved as they followed the President aboard the USS Enterprise.

The sailors lined up on the eight ships of the Enterprise Task Force snapped to attention as Alicia approached the President and Prime Minister.

"It's an honor to have you aboard the Enterprise. I am Alicia Calhoun, and this is Admiral Sean Phillips, the Commander of this task force."

Sean approached the two leaders and saluted. "It is a pleasure to meet you both."

When all the dignitaries were aboard, the F/A-18F flying at over eight hundred miles an hour swept between the Missouri and the Enterprise at a height of thirty feet.

The President continued to watch the F/A-18F as he recovered from the sensory overload. Still staring skyward, he shook his head. "None of this is from the planet I call Earth. Who are you people?" Then with a sense of humor, he added, "I don't suppose we put this fleet together and somebody forgot to mention it to me."

"No Sir, the situation is a little more complicated than that," Alicia answered.

President Roosevelt shook her hand. "You must be the woman I talked to earlier."

"Yes, Mr. President. If you and the Prime Minister will follow me?" Alicia tried to lead them to the island, but Churchill wasn't ready to leave the flight deck.

He spun his cane in the air, his black bowler hat almost flying off his head. He grabbed it while he quizzed Alicia. "It's safe to say with what we've heard and now see for ourselves that you could conquer the world with your weapons. Would this be a presumptuous statement on my part?"

Sean interceded. "If you would follow Miss Calhoun to my wardroom, we can do our best to answer that and any other questions you have."

A childlike smile appeared on the Prime Minister's face. "Maybe if we went by way of the hangar deck?"

Tony thought to himself, "Yeah, wouldn't you just love to get a look at what we have stored there."

Alicia noticed the smile disappeared from Churchill's face, replaced with a scowl as if frustrated there wasn't more magic for him to steal a peak at.

With no response to his query, a disgruntled Winston pointed his cane. "Lead the way."

After they reached their destination and with everyone seated, Alicia continued to lead the conversation. "Once again, I want to welcome you aboard and begin by expressing our wish to help bring this unfortunate conflict to an end. As much as our timely arrival in these waters prevented a greater tragedy, it is sad so many Japanese sailors had to die. I know you have many questions, but I would first like to explain who we are and what we represent, which should go a long way in answering most of them."

Churchill interrupted. "Am I to understand you are in overall command of this force of ships? Is it Mrs. or Miss Calhoun?"

"My correct title, *Sir*, would be either Secretary of Defense Alicia Calhoun or Madam Secretary. And yes – I am the civilian authority. As I said on deck, Admiral Phillips is the overall Naval Commander of this task force.

"Let me begin by explaining we are part of the United States Navy's 7th Fleet, deployed out of San Diego Naval Station. On the second day of a secret naval exercise, we transported hundreds of miles away from where we were, and into another era, yours."

Earlier Tony had convinced both Sean and Alicia that to expose they were not in control of the time warp would be a mistake. He wanted those who became aware of their existence to wonder how powerful they were and when they came from.

The President was confused. "If you are a part of the 7th Fleet, why have I not heard of you or your ships? This also begs the question, shouldn't you be taking your orders from me, different era or not?"

"Great," Tony thought, "aboard only a few minutes and they already were trying to gain authority over something they didn't have the slightest clue what it was." If Tony had his way, he would tell the two leaders they were from another planet, and if they didn't shut up and listen, he'd eat their heads.

Alicia quickly motioned to a female Ensign, who dimmed the lights and turned on the monitor at the front of the conference table. "If you could be patient for a minute and watch the screen, we'll talk when it's over."

Though neither man responded, they did talk in hushed tones to their aides, until video images of the Japanese attack on Pearl Harbor grabbed their attention. Five minutes later, it ended when the bomb struck the Arizona's magazines, sending her to the muddy bottom.

Fifteen minutes of Discovery Channel video followed that showed the Japanese occupation of the Philippines, Indochina, and the Marianas Islands, complete with the subsequent brutality to the civilians and captured allied prisoners.

When it was finished and the Ensign turned the lights on, Alicia stood up. "These were real events documented in the historical records. However, because of our actions, they won't happen."

The shock of such severe losses through the clarity of the LCD screen seemed to unnerve President Roosevelt for a moment. He quickly recovered enough to ask, "Madam Secretary, if you wouldn't mind backing up for a second. I have an obvious question. How are you able to time travel, when did you come from, and can we expect more like you to follow?"

"I can assure you Mr. President this isn't the beginning of an invasion from the future. The probability of other arrivals is unlikely."

"When you say unlikely, does that mean you have the ability to summon others with your capabilities, and at the present you feel it is unnecessary to do so?" Churchill asked.

"What I'm trying to say Mr. Prime Minister is at this time I will not go into specifics about any of the technologies we may possess. I'd be happy to answer any questions not related to how we came to be here."

The President leaned back as if he had a *gotcha*. "Okay then.

How is it you have so many miraculous technologies at hand, yet you have as part of your task force a battleship I recognize as one we are now building?"

"If I may interject Madam Secretary," Sean offered. "In answer to your question Sir, you are correct. The USS Missouri is one of four Iowa class battleships built in the early 1940s. I won't tell you how old she is, but I will say she is the only battleship in the world currently in service where we came from."

Sean then motioned for Alicia to continue.

Alicia nodded toward the Ensign and the lights dimmed again. Images of the war in Europe exploded on the screen and ended in raw footage of the death camp at Dachau.

Alicia continued her narrative. "Over the four years those images represent, twenty-five million civilians and soldiers were killed or wounded throughout the world. In Europe and Asia alone, the devastation cost billions in capital and decades to rebuild the decimated societies."

Alicia again nodded to the Ensign.

The documentary continued with a May Day parade of Soviet Union military might, complete with formations of fighters and bombers flying overhead, and continued through brief histories of the Korean and Vietnam wars. The montage ended with the Yom Kippur War in 1973.

With the lights back on, and the effects of the last pictures still bombarding the overwhelmed leaders, Alicia dropped the hammer. "These are images of the world we left behind. From this conflict in the 1940s and through the coming decades, regional warfare became so commonplace that all the best negotiators could hope for was containment. The very idea of a peace treaty to signal the end of a conflict between waring nation's governments became an impossible achievement. A constant state of war existed throughout the world, creating human suffering on a scale you cannot imagine. Imagine the consequences of one hundred and ninety six nations, all with the hubris that comes from their own self-interests. In affect gentleman, the next great extinction was already well underway.

"On the bright side, seventeen men walked on the moon. Yes, gentlemen, they walked on the moon.

Alicia paused for a moment to take a sip of water. The fact that neither man had interrupted her so far surprised her. "Almost done. Focus," she told herself.

"I could go on for the next hour about how fantasies from the forties became glorious reality, but the truth is corruption, greed, and avarice took the shine off many of the greatest technological breakthroughs. With the ever present demand that giant multinational corporations grow their sales annually, there are now seven billion consumers chewing through the planet's dwindling resources.

"Apparently, it is perfectly moral to exploit the present without any regards to tomorrow's devastation. Or to put it in words you both can understand, nothing changed except the ability of governments to control every aspect of those under their rule. None of us before you can see this as being something we wish to repeat."

Alicia paused for a moment, and then in a tone that couldn't be mistaken as anything but passive aggressive added, "I think it would better serve you to think about the possibilities this unique situation has given you, rather than worry about the threat we represent."

"Why do you need our support?" Churchill asked, without a single reference to what Alicia had said. "With the unlimited power you seem to possess, what could you possibly need from us?" As was his nature, he immediately turned to search out advantages he could exploit.

Because of Churchill's apparent disdain, Alicia decided to have a little fun at his expense. "Mr. Prime Minister, we don't *need* your support, we want your support. Everything we will be attempting will be to your benefit, so why wouldn't you want to supply us?"

With her back to the table, she nonchalantly poured herself a glass of water and spoke in a low measured voice. "Or we could park our ships off your island nation and control all of Great Britain. Better yet, we could sit outside of Scapa Flow and sink every ship of the British Grand Fleet. Which one would be the greater humiliation to you and your countrymen?"

When she turned around, Churchill's face was red with rage. "There it is," she thought with satisfaction. "Time to turn it up a notch."

She stiffened her stance, stared directly at him, and in a stern voice admonished, "If all you hope to do is find and exploit our weaknesses, we are not going to get anywhere. If it isn't already obvious by our actions that our interests are connected, then you are not the man history honored."

This stunned the room into silence.

Roosevelt took hold of the situation when Churchill rose from his chair and looked like he was about to explode. "I recognize the point you make Miss Calhoun, though I think you could have spared us all the drama."

He leaned back with a smile and lit the cigarette attached to his gold holder. "I think we can agree it will take some time for us to become acclimated to the unique opportunities you represent. However, you have to respect our fears, whether founded or not, that you pose a threat. Why don't we focus on the here and now and see where it takes us. The bigger issues can be left for another day."

"Thank you, Mr. President. I think we can accommodate you there. Captain Knox, please explain to our guests your tactical plan to end the war in Europe, and what we need from the Allies to accomplish it."

Churchill was still angry and wanted to speak out, but Roosevelt motioned with his hand to wait. Reluctantly he relented.

Tony stood up and walked slowly to the head of the table. "We propose to cruise by way of the Panama Canal to New York, where we will help escort your convoy of supply ships to England. That is, if you followed our earlier advice to hold off sending them. After we safely escort them to England, we will target Hitler and the senior Nazi leadership. If we succeed, this will have the same effect on their government that we achieved against Japan." As he returned to his chair, he smiled at Alicia and out of view of everyone else, cupped his hands at belt level and moved them quickly up and down.

Alicia quickly looked away so she would not laugh. "Thank you Captain Knox," she acknowledged before she turned back to the table to continue.

"You can then send reasonable surrender terms to the surviving members of the German Government, with the threat of further strikes to follow if terms are not met within the next thirty days."

For the last time the lights dimmed and a slow motion image of a thermonuclear explosion filled the screen with all its destructive might.

A shocked Churchill was the first one of the guests to react. "Was this weapon ever used?"

Alicia motioned to Sean to answer.

"The first time was over Hiroshima, followed three days later over Nagasaki, which forced the Japanese to surrender."

"This brings me to Joseph Stalin," Alicia continued, "and why it is critical we deal with him next. Mr. Prime Minister, it was you who sounded the alarm about the threat he posed to Europe."

"The man is a bloody monster," Churchill responded. "But then again, for a country which looks with affinity to a ruler who went by the name of Ivan the Terrible, benevolent leaders have been in short supply throughout their history.

"I have to keep reminding Franklin that it was because of his deal with Hitler to divide Poland, Great Britain went to war in the first place."

"And I have to keep reminding you, Winston, that an enemy of my enemy is my friend."

Alicia stepped in. "I don't mean to interrupt you gentlemen, but I only need a few more minutes of your time."

The President flashed his smile once again. "I apologize, please continue."

"Thank you.

"From 1948 through 1989, the world was under the cloud of nuclear annihilation. This fostered a political climate that sacrificed morality in the name of the survival of humanity. Wielding the atomic bomb and its threat of Armageddon, Stalin was able to keep Eastern Europe under Soviet occupation and the rest of the world destabilized. The United States and Great Britain did their part and in some cases worse in Central and South America. This was our version of the Iron Curtain, a phrase you coined Mr. Prime Minister when Russia swallowed up Eastern Europe."

"When the Soviet Union collapsed in 1989 from the weight of fifty years of building ever increasingly expensive weapons systems, the world was supposed to breathe a breath of fresh air. Instead, regional conflicts exploded, with the United States the only superpower left in the game to broker peace.

"Unfortunately, our nation proceeded to elect a series of political leaders whose only concern became their own bottom line. Because of this, the arms producers ramped up their killing machines, which meant of course the weapons had to be used. *Blessed be the peacemakers* became kill everyone that doesn't share your vision of Capitalism. Seventy plus years of military adventures not only bankrupted the economy, but also removed any sense of the moral high ground.

"None of these mistakes justified what happened on 11 September 2001, when Islamic terrorists from Saudi Arabia hijacked and crashed two passenger liners into two of the tallest buildings in New York City."

Alicia paused as the lights dimmed again to show the two airliners flying into the Twin Towers, followed by collapse of both buildings and the people in the streets fleeing the dust clouds.

When the video ended, and the lights came back up, Alicia continued her history lesson. "They also flew one aircraft into a complex you have just broken ground on Mr. President, the Pentagon. Over three thousand civilians and military personnel perished in the attacks. This led to draconian measures taken under executive order by President George W. Bush that was the end of civil liberties as we knew them under the Constitution."

President Roosevelt was confused. "You definitely have painted quite a depressing picture of our future. What is your point in showing this to us?"

"Because what is happening right now, leads directly to this future I speak of. The world population is over 7 billion, of which over 1 billion are starving. Sixty percent of the world's population lives in war torn countries on four continents. The world's economy crashed in 2008 and never recovered. With all the military expenditures, financial system disruptions, and political corruption, the world's economy remained mired in a deep recession that ninety-nine percent of the world's population will never see the end of."

Alicia knew both men were going to hate what she would say next even more. "The days of one nation holding the reins of power over another will have to come to an end. Mr. Prime Minister, you need to end imperialism in all its oppressive forms, and then invest capital into those freed nations to allow them the resources to build their own stable governments. This will pay off in the long run as they become peaceful trading partners with you, instead of the failed states they will become if you don't."

Churchill lit up again. "You sit here and presume to dictate to the leaders of the most powerful countries in the world as if we were school children to be scolded."

Not surprised by his anger, Alicia was ready with her response. "Mr. Prime Minister, the window of opportunity is a small one, and once it closes, the turmoil that follows will be disastrous. We don't have the time for political niceties, so you'll have to excuse my rather harsh assessment. You are here because only your two governments have both the political and economic models in place to lead the world away from the horrors we showed you."

Roosevelt, unlike Churchill, was not prone to emotional outbursts and was by nature the more practical of the leaders. "Whenever a nation rises economically, this has historically threatened those nations already on top. Inevitably, if this economy proves profitable, this will come at the expense of others and lead to a backlash which is usually armed conflict. Do you profess to have the answer to this basic flaw in human nature?

"Furthermore, the most basic of issues you've left out of your argument, Secretary Calhoun, is who will reign in your own basic impulses? Once we cede our authority to you, what restraints are there to keep you from becoming the next Caesar, Napoleon, or another Hitler?"

Again, Alicia was ready for this argument. "We can only believe providence has brought us here because no one on these ships wants to follow this example, Mr. President. Try to think of us as crossing guards who only wish to see its charges safely across the street.

"For instance, I'd like to begin with United States racist policies toward its ethnic groups that included the continued enslavement of millions of those you label as Negroes. With the billions of capital saved by ending this war prematurely, you will have the means to free up funding to elevate this disenfranchised segment of our country's population. This will act as a starting point toward true equality under the Constitution. Furthermore, this will serve as an example to the rest of the world that you can give up your country's hypocritical stance of civil rights for some, but not others."

"Sounds to me if I agree to your demands, Miss Calhoun, what I'll have instead is a second civil war. Not much of a choice I'm afraid, though you'd make a great friend of my wife in trying."

Eleanor Roosevelt's greatest disappointment in her husband's Presidency was how he had caved in to the Southern Democrats on race relations. She thought he made a deal with the Devil to ensure their votes for the New Deal.

"What you fail to understand Mr. President," Alicia challenged, "is the issue of civil rights won't go away. It will continue to plague the country over the next century at a great cost for all concerned. We are offering a chance to create the opportunity to resolve these hypocrisies by choice, instead of by force."

Alicia placed on the table two sets of documents, one for Churchill, and the other for President Roosevelt. "Take some time to read through these documents for they contain the history you are reluctant to change. After you read them, let us know if you still think our ideas unreasonable. We'll leave you alone with your staff to discuss your response. If you need anything, there will be a Yeoman waiting outside the door to serve you. You can use the phone on the table to contact us, or your ship. When you reach a decision, just pick it up and you'll be connected."

With a nod from Sean, a Marine in full dress blues opened the door and three white male stewards entered the room to remove the computers and offer their guests refreshments. Sean doubted if Roosevelt had seen anyone other than a black man serving in this role.

Afterward, Sean and Alicia met Tony in his cabin for a much-needed drink.

"Well that went about as well as could be expected."

Tony wasn't sure if Sean was being sarcastic. "I don't know about you guys, but that had to be the weirdest experience I have ever lived through. We were in a room with two of the most famous men in history, and I felt like I was back in my eighth grade history class with Mrs. Fletcher."

"You were brilliant Alicia," Sean praised. "Even better than I could have hoped for. You treated them like any other politician." Sean took a sip of his Jack Daniels Single Barrel. "And I'm with Tony, the whole thing felt queer."

Alicia shook off the compliment. "You'd know, if you had spent most of your waking hours dealing with politicians and their handlers, regardless of their image, one is pretty much the same as the other. We also have the advantage of their historical records. In Churchill's case, I read most of the books he authored when I was at the Naval Academy. While Roosevelt fought for revolutionary changes in American society, Churchill's goal was to continue Great Britain's dominance over world events.

"When you think of the sacrifices this generation made, between surviving the depression, and then jumping right into fighting World War II, it isn't any wonder history holds them in such high esteem. In the space of four years of war, they helped elevate our isolationist nation from a third world military into the greatest force the world has ever known."

Alicia thought for a moment about what she said and shook her head. "God, doesn't that sound like a lead in to a cartoon."

"I was always kind of partial to Captain America myself," Tony quipped. "Speaking of which, he fought the Red Skull in the Captain America movie in 2011. You ask, 'What is the relevance of this arcane knowledge?' The Red Skull fought for Hitler."

Alicia chose to ignore Tony. "I can't fault Roosevelt's motivation to turn things around, what with poverty rates among senior citizens exceeding fifty percent. However, I do wonder if he gave any thought about the level of corruption putting so much money into the hands of Beltway politicians would create. Social Security became the world's biggest piggy bank for Washington insiders to plunder."

Tony quickly disavowed Alicia of any notion the President was a babe in the woods. "My guess would be yes, he would know. How could he not know after swimming with these sharks his entire political career? Give me a break, his sole goal was his legacy as a man of the people. Easy enough to do, if in fact you were raised with wealth as he was and had no idea of what being a man of the people meant."

"And this coming from a man raised with wealth. How ironic."

"It takes one to know one, Alicia."

Sean sat comfortably on the couch quietly sipping his JD. "It's safer over here," he thought as he watched his compatriots spar.

Tony continued to rile Alicia up. "So no, I don't trust the President. However, you do have to give him credit for his actions throughout the war. He was, after all, a great wartime president."

Alicia acquiesced on the point. "That's true. However, I'm optimistic Churchill has the power of personality to show Roosevelt the value of what we offered. Although I do believe that once we defeat Hitler, the Prime Minister will find a way to break every promise as soon as it is convenient. I am sure they are discussing this option right now. He will convince Roosevelt that for now, they haven't anything to lose.

"Keep in mind, these leaders will not accept the social ideas we presented. All we wanted to do was plant the seed and be able to receive the necessary supplies to take our next step."

In the Admirals Ready Room, it was quiet as Roosevelt, Churchill, and their staffs looked over the documents Alicia left for them. The first image Roosevelt viewed was of a black man hanging grotesquely from a tree. The caption underneath, dated March 15, 1950 stated, "Racial Tensions Rise in Louisiana. Fifth hanging in a month."

What followed this was a chronology of violence that led to the inner city riots of the 1960s, and included the assassinations of the

Reverend Martin Luther King and presidential candidate Robert Kennedy. The following pictures showed how affirmative action laws led to the election of the country's first black president in 2008 and ended with this short statement from Alicia. "If you act now, you have the chance to shorten the suffering of millions by decades, even if doing so lowers the national economic status white people now so unfairly enjoy."

Tucked into these pages were also pictures of Eleanor Roosevelt handing out food to impoverished black children in Mississippi. An article written in the 1990s told of the work she performed while her husband ignored their plight because of the political risk.

"Here we are sitting in the middle of the Pacific," Churchill raged, "being given orders by a woman who shouldn't exist. How dare she presume England has lost its ability to maintain its empire?"

True to his character, Churchill began to work his own agenda. "Though I am loath to agree to any of her demands, based on how quickly they dispatched the Japanese, maybe it would be worthwhile to support their plan against Hitler. Besides, it wouldn't hurt your country to change how you treat your Negroes."

"Be careful where you cast stones Winston. Our hypocrisies pale next to what the British Government has sanctioned over the last two hundred years to maintain its empire."

"It's irrelevant Franklin. If we refuse to agree to their agenda, whom could they turn to? Besides, I have an idea." Reducing his voice to a whisper the Prime Minister spelled out the seeds of a devious plan. When he finished, everyone in the room agreed it would make Alicia's demands irrelevant.

An hour later, Roosevelt picked up the phone and requested their return.

"Madam Secretary, I've decided the risk is worth the reward. The perfect person to introduce your civil rights bill is Representative Lee Geyer, a Democrat from California. Using him will not seem out of place. He has been trying without success since 1939 to push through an anti-poll tax amendment.

"Further, this would be a natural extension of an action I already took last June. I issued Executive Order 8802 which prohibited racial discrimination in all federal departments, and with all federal defense contractors and their unions."

The President stopped for a moment and shook his head. "I have to admit the groundswell has been growing in the country to change the way we treat our Negroes. Especially when we as a country started to question how Hitler could be so evil while right here at home we allowed such atrocities of our own. I will have a bill ready thirty days after the end of war with Germany. However, I don't see how I can garner the votes for passage of such a bill. Will this satisfy your demand?"

"I can only ask that you make a serious attempt, Mr. President."

Churchill looked at the President as if he was pushing him for something more.

"Relax Winston, I haven't forgotten."

He then flashed another smile and asked Alicia, "Will you transfer authority of your forces to United States civilian authority after you return from Europe?"

Prepared for this question since they left Japanese home waters, Alicia was quick with her response. "Once hostilities end, we'll begin the process of integrating our forces back under civilian control, contingent on the political fallout the end of the war creates. In the interim, you should avoid any public acknowledgment of our existence while working out the details. Once we are successful in Europe, we request the use of the base at Guantanamo Bay, Cuba to service our ships and sailors. This will give us the necessary seclusion away from the public.

"At this point, I'd like to leave our tactical planner Captain Knox with Admiral Kimmel to discuss the resupply of our ships for our operations in the Atlantic. He also needs to give you the dimensions of the Enterprise so the engineers at the Panama Canal can prepare for its transit through it. This ship was designed to pass through the canal when she was built, but because the flight deck overhangs so far off the ship's hull, they had to remove buildings close to the canal and set the light posts further away from the canal."

President Roosevelt nodded in the affirmative to Admiral Kimmel, as Tony handed him the information.

Churchill added. "We would also like to add members of our Navy to your expedition in the role of observers to help facilitate a level of trust and achieve a better understanding between one another."

Tony thought to himself, "You mean, get some people onboard to spy on our capabilities."

Alicia noticed the concern on Tony's face, but figured it would be easy enough to limit the guests movements while aboard the Enterprise. "I think it's a great idea Mr. Churchill." She also figured the complexity of their technology was beyond their understanding and would only help to drive home they were the only ones capable of making use of it.

"I must add it has been a revelation to see a woman handle authority with such alacrity as you have, Madam Calhoun." President Roosevelt finished by flashing his famous charm her way.

"Thank you for the compliment, Sir." Alicia had to admit the man oozed charisma from every pour of his body.

Sean wanted to make it clear whom he would allow onboard. "You may send Admiral Chester Nimitz to represent American interests, and Admiral James Somerville from the Royal Navy, but not their staffs."

Churchill was curious. "If you don't mind my asking, though Admiral Somerville is an excellent choice, how did you come to select him for the honor?"

Sean realized they would have to be more careful about whose names they threw out. He decided to play it safe in answering

Churchill's question. "Considering the difficulty of his orders, his actions against the French fleet at Mers-el-Kébir in North Africa after the French had agreed to an armistice with Germany was handled with as much restraint as could be expected."

The real reason Sean picked Admiral Somerville occurred a year later in the Indian Ocean. With foresight, he had moved the British Eastern Fleet from the Maldives to East Africa before the Japanese advanced through Burma and captured the Andaman Islands.

Churchill was getting restless, feeling he hadn't come any closer to understanding the limits of their capabilities. "I understand your need to keep your secrets, but while we're waiting, can you give us an idea how you were able to destroy the Japanese Government?"

"I suppose it wouldn't hurt to tell you our overall operational objective," Sean answered. "We knew it would be easy to disrupt the Japanese Government by simply removing a few key people. Based on historical records we were able to figure out who they were and where they would be."

Sean paused for a few seconds and changed to a more serious tone. "In regard to the precision of our attacks on Tokyo, we are capable of hitting *any* target, *anywhere* we choose, *all* of the time. One of our attack planes can do more than the combined efforts of every bomber based in the British Isles. Just how we can do this, I'm not at liberty to say."

A clearly agitated Churchill went off again. "How can you be so cavalier about your capabilities when men and woman are dying every day because of the brutality of the Axis powers? I don't see how you can wear your United States Navy uniform and not give us every one of your technologies to use."

This time President Roosevelt did not intercede and everyone in the room became uncomfortable in the silence that followed.

Once again, Alicia bridged the divide. "If I were sitting in either one of your chairs, Mr. President and Mr. Prime Minister, I would feel the same way. How in God's name, in the middle of a world conflagration, can we refuse direct orders from our Commander In Chief to join forces with our fellow citizens? The simple answer is it would take at least three decades for either one of your countries to build the necessary infrastructure to reproduce fifty percent of what we carry on our ships. This does not account for the scientific expertise needed to understand it. In other words, if we listen to what you want us to do, the probability of hundreds of thousands of more casualties is extremely higher."

"Whether we agree with her or not Winston, the lady makes a good point. However Admiral Phillips, I will hold you to your promise that this will change when we prove our goals are one in the same."

"You can count on it, Mr. President. I'd like nothing more than to step aside and let my Commander In Chief assume control of this battle group." As Sean finished he acknowledged Alicia's efforts with a wink.

They took up the next hour to finalize an informal agreement, with most of the time spent handling Churchill's many objections. Eventually he caved and was the last one to add his signature.

Sean had decided to keep the existence of the two nuclear attack submarines and the Enterprise's propulsion a secret for now. They had dealt the first hand, and the next three weeks would determine if it was a winner.

It was 2030 hours when the leaders left the Enterprise for their return to Pearl.

Early the next morning brought three steamers to where the Enterprise Task Force had anchored, fifty miles northwest of Oahu. They transferred fuel and supplies to the Laramie and the Amelia Earhart after refueling the destroyers and cruisers. By mid-afternoon, the Enterprise Task Force raised anchor and steered southeast for the six-day cruise to Panama where Admiral Nimitz would be waiting to come aboard.

Meeting History

Looking out on the peaceful expanse of ocean the first day out of Hawaiian waters, Sean reflected on the thousands of unresolved problems the crew of the fleet represented. How long could he keep the lid on their seven thousand different personalities? The number of sailors on report for failure to follow orders had tripled from the normal average. Some of the charges involved severe cases of assault. The usual scenario to deal with major infractions would have been to fly the offenders stateside for courts-martial, but this was no longer an option.

He tried to think ahead. The minute any one of them returned to the general population, they could use their knowledge to manipulate this era for personnel gain. He laughed at the thought of four sailors recreating their own versions of Beatle songs while they donned their signature mop tops.

Another issue that bothered both Sean and Tony was the fleet would be vulnerable in the restricted spaces of the Panama Canal locks.

Admiral Kimmel assured them before they left Oahu the military command in the region would clear all shipping and unnecessary personnel from the area of the locks in preparation for their arrival.

The next morning, now well clear of the Hawaiian Islands, Sean was on the bridge of the Enterprise staring out at the ocean. Tony came up behind him unnoticed. "So—, which one of our many problems has you staring at nothing?"

Sean continued to stare at nothing while he answered. "What kind of life will our sailors have after we return from Europe? We can't force seven thousand sailors to spend their lives isolated in limbo while we run around trying to save the world. Besides, I can't see either Churchill or Roosevelt accepting the shellacking Alicia gave them. Now that we let them see who we are, and what we want to do, do you really expect their full cooperation?"

"On the bright side, we do know they are dying to find out our capabilities, and as long as you and Alicia don't throw away our advantage, we should be okay for now.

"Concerning the crew, I don't mean to sound like I have a problem with the way you and Alicia have handled our situation so far, but you're right we haven't paid enough attention to securing the crew's future. With everything you have on your plate, I figured I'd give the problem some thought."

From the delicacy of his introduction, Sean knew Tony had done quite a bit of thinking. "We've got some time, so what wicked plot is developing in young Captain Jack Sparrow's mind, and what will it cost man?"

Tony laughed at the combination of Disney and Mel Brooks humor. "It's simple when you think about it. We can become a corporation, with all of the crew holding shares. Instead of giving our technology to the government, we license its use to companies who agree with us about how they will use the individual technologies. This should ensure enough capital to support a comfortable lifestyle for all concerned. Hell, this corporation will become powerful enough we can become the next American cartel to rule the..." Tony froze.

"What's the matter? You look like you've just been told your girlfriend is late."

Then Tony stunned Sean. "They're going to take the ships while we're in the locks. That's the perfect time to try."

Sean pictured the massive Enterprise towering over the Miraflores Locks, elevated and isolated, with a small crew controlling the gates. "What could they possibly hope to gain?"

"You said it yourself a minute ago. Churchill is pissed off and known for making emotional decisions. The man has been under a lot of stress for the last two years fighting alone against Hitler, and then we show up and take over."

Sean still wasn't convinced, but knew the safety of the task force was his first priority. Sean took a moment to consider just how easy it might be. "We could be successfully attacked a number of ways while trapped in the canal. Better safe than sorry," he thought.

"The estimated time to move through the forty-eight miles of locks and lakes is normally between eight to ten hours. However, whether they try to take our ships or they don't, we know they will clear sea traffic ahead of us, which means we can transit the canal faster.

"Give me a plan to control the Canal's forty-eight miles for the six hours it will take us to go through."

Tony closed his eyes to picture what he remembered from his own transits through the canal. "They'll expect us, so we'll need to increase our speed to show up early to see how they've arranged the defenses. We would have to send SEAL squads to secure both the Miraflores and Gatun Locks before we enter the bay." He stopped to consider another problem. "If they did take our ships, what do you think their plans for us would be?"

"Probably keep us in a secret prison somewhere like, oh I don't know, maybe Cuba. Ironic I should pick Guantanamo as our choice to home port." Sean then went into high gear. "Notify the fleet to alert their Special Operations teams and Marines to prepare for action and bring the squad leaders over to the Enterprise in three hours for a briefing. Get Commander Thornton here now and give the order to increase speed to twenty five knots."

Tony looked at the navigation chart and began to calculate the distances. "The Amelia Earhart and Laramie won't be able to sustain more than twenty knots. The increase in speed will put them a half day behind us by the time we reach the Canal."

Sean had decided before they left Hawaii to keep knowledge of the submarines existence hidden, so he ordered the Seawolf and the Hampton to take the Arctic route to New York. He was irritated he didn't consider they might have to fight their way through the canal, and now that decision would leave the supply ships exposed.

"It can't be helped," Sean replied.

Tony's face lit up with a bright idea. "If they did lay a trap for us, I know how to get Roosevelt to agree to let them transit the canal after we force our way through."

"Hold that thought," Sean interrupted. "I think it would be wise if we added Alicia to the conversation. We need to bring her up to date."

Fifteen minutes later in the Admirals Ready Room, they had finished laying out Tony's fears to her when Commander Thornton arrived. Sean exchanged salutes and shook his hand. "I need you to work with Tony to plan a series of diversionary attacks that will allow us to force passage through the Panama Canal, possibly against hostile American troops. Oh, and I probably don't need to tell you, but I'd prefer to accomplish this without casualties."

For the first time Tony could remember, Thornton smiled.

"And I thought it would take longer for you boys to need us to pull your asses out of this cosmic fire. We're going to need a hell of a lot of flash bangs and rubber bullets."

Over the next hour, the rest of the Marine and SEAL Special Ops squad leaders arrived and began to discuss possible scenarios with Tony. Sean and Alicia mostly watched while they pulled together a rough picture of what they would be up against transiting the canal. They found grainy pictures that showed gun emplacements, with their locations around the surrounding areas of the Canal, and compared the pictures with maps of the region. Written alongside the different colored tags that marked the locations of artillery pieces was the estimated number of soldiers necessary to operate them.

Thorny formed tactical squads to capture the Miraflores and Gatun control stations, and Marines would suppress any approaching defenders. Tony decided their best chance to rush the canal would be 2200 hours, three days from now, on the 30th. This would leave seven hours of darkness for the transit and utilizing

Specter's stealth while on Gatun Lake.

After the commandos left, Alicia looked humbled and confessed to Sean. "Of all people, I should have been able to see betrayal was a possibility. Hell, I've been around Washington doublespeak for most of my life and I know better than to take anything at face value."

"I think we were all taken in by their larger than life personalities." Sean felt equal responsibility. "Thank God, for Tony's cynicism. We assumed they would want to see us remove Hitler before they tried to enforce their will on us. Who are we to them?"

"An unknown, that's who, with the power to decapitate their governments at will. Tony couldn't resist. "I *can't* understand why they would feel obligated to make a move against us. Or maybe we'll arrive in Panama Bay and there will be a PBY waiting with Admiral Nimitz, and we'll all sip Margarita's while we peacefully cruise through the canal."

Alicia ignored Tony's sarcasm. "What do we do if there isn't any visible confirmation of the betrayal? Do we still take the locks?"

"Good question. We'll know on the 30th when we're close enough to send the F-35s in for a look-see." Sean then switched gears. "Tony, you said you have an idea about how we can get the supply ships through the canal."

Tony smiled sadistically. "What do you suppose their reaction would be if we threatened to destroy the locks?"

"Obviously, I think they would do anything to ensure that doesn't happen," Sean answered.

Tony brought up another issue. "If Roosevelt wants our ships, we should also expect he sent a powerful naval task force to take control when we're captured. Imagine their surprise when they find out we've cleared the locks a day earlier than planned."

"And this helps us, how?" Alicia asked.

"We go John Wayne on their ass." With the glee of a boy with a new popgun, Tony explained his idea.

Over the next two days, they researched the defenses arrayed around the canal and discovered more effort had gone into the protection of the Canal Zone than Pearl Harbor.

It was the night before they were to reach Pacific Bay, the entrance to the Pacific side of the canal. Regardless of how many times Sean looked at the final plan, there were too many moving parts and assumptions to suit him. "There are still too many things that can go wrong."

Tony shook his head in exasperation. "All I know is that if the President decides to make a play for our ships, he obviously didn't understand the significance of our taking out the entire Japanese war machine in two weeks. What chance does he think he has with a force a thousandth the size of them against us?"

Alicia was with Tony. "Add the fact the Japanese were already battle tested, where the American Army at this time ranked thirty-sixth in the world."

Sean seemed unusually timid. "You're right."

Sean downed the last of his coffee and sat down heavily on the couch in his Ready Room. "We can't spend all of our time worried that everyone we come into contact with doesn't have ulterior motives that are contrary to our best interests. I just want to make sure we don't make it impossible to interact diplomatically with the entire world."

"So what are our options if we are forced to fight our way through the canal? Turn around and go back? Back to where?" It was not as if Tony had not run all of the scenarios through his mind. "Turn off that big old brain of yours and let's focus on what we know works. Besides it's still 50/50 whether there is a problem anyway."

Tony put his coffee down and stood up. "All I know is I am hitting the rack and will sleep like a baby who hasn't a care in the world. Tomorrow will only be one more page in this little adventure that probably doesn't even exist. Maybe dragons will show up before it's over. Now that would be something."

Both Alicia and Sean laughed at the idea.

Before Alicia say goodnight to Tony, Sean tried to add one last thing. "Too be sure, check in with Thorny before…"

"Sean!" Alicia grabbed his arm and steered him out of the room. "Goodnight Tony."

The next morning a cloaked F-35 launched off the Enterprise flight deck and headed to the Canal. It flew the entire length of the canal system and the surrounding environment videoing the locks and the artillery emplacements. The pilot then focused the cameras on the approaches to the canal from Quarry Heights, where the Army quartered the largest concentration of its soldiers.

This base was five miles to the northwest of the canal entry on the Pacific side. Fort Amador lay below the Bridge of the Americas at the canal's Pacific entrance. Further analysis of the reconnaissance video determined the requested preparations to make way for the Enterprise had taken place along Miraflores Locks, but not the Gatun Locks.

Later that afternoon Sean, Alicia, and Commander Thornton were in the CIC with Tony watching the surveillance videos.

"What you found out about the Army's deployment in 1941 was a big help Alicia. I had no idea there were over 20,000 troops stationed in the zone at the time."

"You're welcome, Tony."

Tony sat down in front of a large vertical display that showed the entire length of the Canal. "Because the work to clear the way for the Enterprise is done only along the Miraflores Locks, we can assume they want to trap us on Gatun Lake. Pretty much what I expected and planned for by the way. We will have to force our way through the locks."

Sean tried to remain optimistic. "It could be because we are a day early they haven't gotten to making the alterations to Gatun yet."

"So why aren't there any signs of construction?" Tony countered.

"Good point. Everything our surveillance has exposed lines up with what Alicia and Renée dug up." Sean looked at Tony to continue.

"Okay once again." Tony moved the mouse to show where they would drop the SEAL squads into isolated choke points to block the troops sent from Fort Sherman from reaching the canal. "Diversionary attacks will create enough confusion in the darkness to have their GIs chasing after ghosts. Once this is confirmed, Commander Thornton will have two squads in position to seize the Miraflores and Gatun control rooms while a strike force of F-35s will take out the communications towers.

"Immediately after we get confirmation the towers are down, an EA-18G Prowler will be overhead to jam any other radio signals they use to coordinate their ground forces. There will be a complete blanket over their ability to communicate with their troops on the ground.

"If all goes according to plan, the Missouri will be in position at the first lock when the towers blow. She'll pass through first because those around the canal will be able to identify her as a battleship of the US Navy. The Missouri's unexpected arrival will most likely confuse them, but they shouldn't be hostile immediately. The destroyers and cruisers would enter next, with the Enterprise the last through."

Tony then looked up with concern on his face. "That is if we're able to take full advantage of our night-vision goggles. A full moon is only three days away. Our meteorologists have assured me the cloud cover we are in now will continue throughout the night. If it doesn't, I'm afraid the odds go up we will have to inflict some casualties along the way.

"Once we are through the final locks, we will be able to form up the task force and engage Specter before we are under the guns of

Fort Sherman on Toro Point. They built this installation to defend from the sea, not forces coming through the locks.

"The code name for the operation is Hoodwink."

Commander Thornton surprised Tony with his reaction. "The plan is simple enough to work. It's nice to see that unlike most of the senior officers I've had to endure, you haven't forgotten *everything* I've taught you about covert operations." This was as close to a compliment Tony would ever get from the gruff SEAL Commander.

Sean looked closely at the access roads around the canal shown on the graphic display. "It looks like their forces will have difficulty reaching the Gatun Locks with only one access road available to them. It shouldn't be too difficult for us to disrupt their movement.

"Commander Thornton, everything is contingent on the speed of your assault squads to keep the GIs from blocking the canal in front of us. We won't have to worry once we make it through the Miraflores Locks, because we will engage Specter while on Gatun Lake."

"My men will be ready Admiral."

"Our success depends on it, Commander."

Sean took a minute to understand how Tony dispersed their forces and nodded his head. "Your plan is big on deception and speed. If our people execute their orders, chances for direct combat should be minimal. Let's get the Commanders of the units together at 1800 to brief them."

"As far as the soldiers guarding the locks are concerned, to them it will be as if the devil himself crashed the party."

"Let's hope so Tony."

Throughout the rest of the day and well into the evening, everyone from the aircrews and the SEAL squads to the lowest rated personnel learned what role they were to play in the likelihood the US Army would attempt to board and seize their ships.

At 2100, while the fleet was still twenty miles outside Panama Bay klaxons sounded throughout the Enterprise sending the sailors to their battle stations in a ballet of organized chaos. Throughout the task force, sailors readied for the transit through the canal. Some positioned fire hoses to repel boarders, while Navy SEAL squads loaded into Seahawks.

From high up on the bridge, Tony watched the launch of the helicopters from the Enterprise and cruisers. They would insert the SEAL squads under the cover of darkness into the jungles behind the Army bases and near the control rooms for the locks. At the same time, launches began to ferry Marines to Panama Bay on their mission to commandeer the tugboats. Thankfully, a layer of clouds blocked most of the moon's illumination, but the fact he could still see the launches a mile ahead made it still too bright for Tony.

While he worried about that, an EA-18G Growler launched off the deck of the Enterprise on its way to jam any radar signals from the canal. Not long after the pilot gained altitude, her backseater located the search radar and began to jam it.

With the likelihood of a threat from a night air attack in 1941 considered zero, the radar operator on duty chalked up the interference to just another problem with the fledgling technology. He spent fifteen minutes trying to clear up the signal before he gave up. The last thing he would do is wake up his Commander with news the radar was on the fritz again, especially after he had witnessed the abuse the last person received who had made that mistake.

In the CIC on the Enterprise, Sean and Alicia monitored Operation Hoodwink, keeping in contact with the two F-35s he had ordered to patrol the Atlantic side of the canal to make sure the ocean was clear of warships.

Twenty minutes later the extent of Roosevelt's deception became clear when the pilot of one of the F-35s reported in. "Three carriers and two battleships confirmed, escorted by fifteen to twenty ships one hundred fifty miles northeast of the entrance to the canal at an estimated speed of 15 knots."

Tony had entered the room as the news came in and Sean braced for his sarcasm.

"You think they sent them to help take the lampposts down at the Gatun Locks?"

"Thank you Tony. Let's get on with it."

"Aye Aye Admiral. I feel sorry for those ground pounders. They're never going to know what hit 'em."

Sean, more out of anxiety than necessity, went over the initial phase of the plan. "Once we cut off communications, we will be able to isolate their forces on the ground. After we pass through Culebra Cut onto Gatun Lake, the danger to our ships from Quarry Heights and Fort Amador will be behind us. Considering the confined spaces we will be stuck in, I'm not comfortable that we can pull this off without inflicting friendly casualties."

"Relax Sean. We have the best-trained sailors from 2014. Moreover, we have SEALs going into an environment they spend their days dreaming about. Compared to how they train, this is going to feel like a game of paintball."

"Thanks Alicia, but it will be live rounds the GIs will be firing. A million things can go wrong."

She didn't have any response, knowing Sean was right.

Ten minutes later, the coastline their radar had displayed for the last hour came into view through the darkness.

At exactly 2200, explosions that took down the communication towers rocked the jungle both north and south of Quarry Heights and Fort Amador. Out in the Harbor, Marines had taken control of the tugboats that pulled up on both sides of the Missouri to guide her into the first lock. The appearance of the Missouri only elicited confusion among the soldiers on duty. It was as Tony predicted, no one saw the Missouri as a threat. That is until they heard explosions. Before the GIs could react, Marines on both sides of the locks appeared out of nowhere and disarmed them.

The sound of explosions put the staff in the control room of the Miraflores Locks on edge. The tension turned into terror when six heavily armed masked soldiers dressed in black rushed through the door. The Lieutenant then ordered in his finest southern accent, "If y'all would please follow normal operating procedures until I say otherwise, that would be just dandy. I'm sorry we forgot to bring something other than our weapons to the party. You'll have to excuse us; we were in a bit of a hurry."

A series of head nods confirmed their compliance, as they went to work activating the pumps and hydraulics to move the ship through the locks.

On both the port and starboard sides of the Missouri, the crew set bumpers to protect the ship. The sailors who manned the hoses watched as additional Marines repelled onto the docks. It wasn't long before they had complete control.

After the locomotives had pulled the Missouri, the cruisers, and the destroyers through the locks, troops started to show up ad hoc. What greeted their sight was the massive shape of the Enterprise materializing out of the darkness as it approached. The Marines from the Missouri directed diversionary fire in front of the soldiers that forced them into a hasty retreat to find cover.

In a little less than two hours, the six ships slipped through the locks, though to everybody in the Enterprise CIC, it seemed like forever.

Once all of the ships were on the lake, they increased speed to fifteen knots to shorten the time of their transit.

On the bridge, Captain Folger took a moment to admire the choreography of the Seahawks that flew back and forth from their missions. Some returned units of the diversionary forces who had fulfilled their mission, while others returned the strike squad sent to the Miraflores control room.

Meanwhile, the CIC Officer provided a mission update. "Admiral, we have received reports of minor casualties to our forces. So far, we haven't heard any news about casualties to the forces attacking the locks. Although without their ability to communicate, we can't be sure there haven't been any."

"If none of our forces have reported inflicting casualties, let's hope this is true." Tony didn't have any illusions their luck would hold through the Gatun Locks.

At that moment, one of the cloaked F-35s on patrol over the canal reported troops from Fort Sherman headed to the Gatun Locks.

With explosions out in front, alongside their flanks, and in their rear, the Colonel in command of the soldiers trying to close on the locks realized for all of the explosions rocking the jungle, none killed any of his men or came close enough to endanger them. It seemed like whoever was attacking them was making an obvious attempt to avoid casualties.

This brought to mind the bizarre set of orders he received from Washington. His troops were to intercept a fleet of ships that would try to enter from the Pacific side of the canal. Adding to this cryptic order was the lack of an identity attached to whom it was they would be fighting. Capture the ships and hold their crews until further orders. "Hell, for all I know this was an exercise to test our readiness," the Colonel thought. The mere idea that a belligerent force would try to force its way through the canal system was sheer madness.

Even with that improbability, the overall Commander of the Caribbean Defense Command, General Frank Andrews, had not given him enough specifics on the threat. With Japan out of the picture, the Colonel could not think of any scenario that played out logically to explain who was attacking them.

The Colonel's original orders were to send eighty percent of his forces to aid Quarry Heights, and to wait for the carrier to be in the locks before they took control of it. The problem was they were supposed to arrive tomorrow night, after the relief force arrived from Norfolk and was on station to reinforce his troops.

The source of the Colonel's current frustration came from three, five-member SEAL squads armed with either the M-14 Sniper rifle or the M4A1 assault rifle and aided by their night vision goggles. Their task was to keep any troops from reaching the locks.

Earlier an F-35 completely tore up the roadbed, so the SEALs had taken position in an area of dense forest impossible for tanks to penetrate. It was a perfect location for a few men to hold off a large force. One squad had taken up positions to control the southern side of the road one hundred meters into the forest. Another SEAL squad controlled the northern access.

Lt. Franklin Morris, the Commander of the squad directly in the path of the oncoming soldiers, sent two members forward to reconnoiter and make contact with the Fort Sherman forces. Two hundred meters ahead of the SEAL's position, they reached a bend in the road.

One them reported, "I've got an armored column stopped a little less than five hundred meters from your position. It looks like they can't go any further with their tanks and are trying to decide what to do. Wait a minute. It looks like they're sending their own reconnaissance party forward."

Lt. Morris had to decide quickly whether to let the infantry come to him, or move his squad to his scout's position. He calculated the range of the Sherman tanks 75 mm main gun, and ordered his scouts to return to his current location. They returned five minutes later, and took up position as the Fort Sherman reconnaissance force appeared around the bend.

"Let them have it," Lt. Morris ordered.

The roadside on both sides exploded with gunfire, highlighted by the extra tracer rounds the SEALs had added for effect. The sniper on point chuckled at the sight his night vision goggles supplied of the soldiers diving for cover.

"Cease fire," Lt. Morris called out.

The firing stopped and the forest returned to silence for the next ten minutes. During the interlude, Morris contacted the SEAL squad leader on the other side of the road and they sent their marksmen to guard against flanking maneuvers. Morris then called in for diversionary strikes from an F-35 circling the area. He also ordered his men to change their positions to guard against possible mortar attacks.

"I've got movement. It looks like they've set up a skirmish line to probe our flank. I estimate 20-25 hostiles two hundred meters from our position."

Lt. Morris called in the coordinates and one minute later the forest one hundred meters ahead of them erupted in explosions.

It took a few moments to recover, but the soldiers continued their advance, albeit at a more cautious pace.

"Let's make some noise," Lt. Morris ordered.

With this command, every SEAL took a deep breath and let out the loudest scream they could and began to pour fire over the heads of the advancing troops, driving them to cover. Every time one of them would try to advance, tracers came whizzing close enough to their head that they would wisely fall back.

This went on for the next half hour, driving one of the SEALs to yell across the gulf between the forces, "Get a clue. We can see you, but you can't see us. Do us all a favor and stay put for a little while longer. And by the way, who the hell is Kilroy?"

From the Colonel's perspective, the world had turned upside down. This unknown force was obviously able to bottle up his company in the middle of the night as if it was nothing. They also had the ability to disrupt communications and were able to know exactly where to position their attacks to stop him and his men cold, without casualties. Some of his men had earlier reported strange loud chopping sounds coming from the sky.

So far, the Colonel felt helpless against the tactics used against him, and he had no alternative route to get closer to the locks. It was also obvious to the Colonel they could take him and his men anytime they wanted to, but they didn't. He decided to wait it out to see what daylight brought and ordered a ceasefire.

He went forward and yelled across the divide. "This is Colonel Jack Stewart, commanding the US Army forces out of Fort Sherman. I have ordered my men to hold their positions. What is your intent?"

Lt. Morris answered. "Thank you, Colonel. Our orders are to hold you here until daybreak. Your cooperation will insure there are no casualties."

With that, the jungle fell quiet until about 0400 when the Colonel and his men heard those strange loud chopping noises again.

✦

The Missouri was now only twenty minutes from the Gatun Locks when they received word the SEAL squad was in command of the control room. Continuing their good luck, there was little sign of additional defenders arriving to contest their passage.

A cloaked F-35 flying in a racetrack pattern over the canal, confirmed the threat from Fort Sherman neutralized. The fort's soldiers were still closer to their base than they were the locks. With the fort's gun emplacements pointed out to a threat from the sea, the task force cruised through without drama, except for the destruction of the lampposts and buildings that the canal construction crews had not removed.

While the Enterprise was in the last lock, crewmembers helped bring aboard the Marines who controlled the docks through the hangar opening. The trip finished in less than six hours without the loss of a single sailor or soldier to either side.

Unknown to anyone at the time, five sailors had decided they were through with life under the constraints of the United States Navy. With their world turned upside down, they figured their commitment to the Navy would not begin for another seventy years, so they used this as their justification to jump ship. They slipped off the Enterprise unseen with their laptops and any other personal items they thought would make them rich men when sold to the highest bidder.

When the aircraft carrier USS Enterprise cleared the locks, the task force reformed around her. Seahawk helicopters landed on the flight deck with the last of the SEAL squads who had kept the United States Army units from trapping the ships in the locks. With Specter engaged, they passed invisible under the silent gun emplacements at Fort Sherman on Point Toro. Contact with the supply ships still on the Pacific side of the canal established they would arrive at Panama Bay in six hours.

Lt. Daniel Osaka handed Sean a transcript.

After reading it, Sean chuckled and turned to Tony with a sly grin. "Osaka intercepted communications between General Andrews and the Admiral in command of the task force headed our way."

"Who'd they send?"

Excerpt • Book II

From the Judgement In Time Series
Imagine A New World

While Captain Folger dealt with the deserters, at the White House President Roosevelt was on the phone with Churchill. "It is obvious by their early arrival in the locks they saw through your plan. I had no choice but to let them proceed when I received the news Admiral Phillips was with Admiral Halsey aboard the Wasp. Based on the reports I received from General Andrews, they blew through his forces like butter in the middle of the night without inflicting casualties. According to his Commanders on the ground, not only are their ships and weapons years beyond ours, but their night fighting abilities are incredible as well."

Always quick to recover from miscalculations, Churchill reached his own conclusion. "That they went out of their way to avoid casualties showed great restraint."